LOOKOUT

LOOKOUT

CHRISTINE BYL

DEEP VELLUM
Dallas, Texas

A STRANGE OBJECT
Austin, Texas

Published by A Strange Object, an imprint of Deep Vellum

Deep Vellum is a 501(c)(3) nonprofit literary arts organization founded in 2013 with the mission to bring the world into conversation through literature.

The chapter titled "Cody Kinzler" was first published in a slightly different form as a short story, "Hey Jess Mc Cafferty," in *So To Speak: A Feminist Journal of Language & Art* (Spring 2008); *Sudden Flash Youth* (New York: Persea Books, 2011); and *Brevity: A Flash Fiction Handbook* (New York: Columbia University Press, 2016).

Library of Congress Cataloging-in-Publication Data
Names: Byl, Christine, 1973– author.
Title: Lookout / Christine Byl.
Description: Dallas, Texas : Deep Vellum ; Austin, Texas : A Strange Object, [2023]
Identifiers: LCCN 2022046454 | ISBN 9781646052295 (hardcover) |
ISBN 9781646052554 (ebook)
Subjects: LCGFT: Bildungsromans. | Domestic fiction. | Novels.
Classification: LCC PS3602.Y45 L66 2023 | DDC 813/.6—dc23/eng/20220926
LC record available at https://lccn.loc.gov/2022046454

ISBN 978-1-646-05229-5
ISBN 978-1-646-05255-4 (ebook)

Cover design by Kelly Winton
Interior design and layout by Amber Morena

Dedicated in memory of Uncle Lloyd
(Lester Lloyd Norwood Jr., 1942–1991)

and to all selves, seen and unseen

Why not now go toward the things I love?

—NATALIE DIAZ, "GRIEF WORK"

LOOKOUT

PART ONE

\\

One response to loss is the remaking of things.

—LIA PURPURA

START SMALL (1985)

THE SUMMER OF THE FIRES started cool and damp. A heavy snow in early May buried pasqueflowers and daffodils and the barely rising shoots that would become the season's crops, but by the end of the month, the sun lit up like a match. Standing water dried faster than it had in years, and by June the once-puddled ground was hard and hot as a steel skillet. No one remembered the cold.

Midsummer, Cody Kinzler woke to light. Bedtime and morning looked alike, crickets and stars hidden by sun, the only thing visible the strut of day. By the time Cody stirred, dark was hours gone. She lifted her arm against the light between the slatted shades, the back of her hand tanned above her moon-white palm.

In the mornings, Cody's father was outside. Always. She often ate breakfast alone—Louisa sleeping late and their mother with the hens or in the garden—and Cody looked out the window to see the weather unchanged. Hot. Blue. Bright.

Cody was nine. Old enough to pour her own cereal or make toast, dark and hard, topped with a soft-boiled egg cooling from the stove. Her mother said too much salt, but Cody liked it between her teeth like sand. She practiced wolfing her eggs like her father did, fast so she could help him with the stock before he left for work. Josiah bent around the stall gates and horses' necks like wire, his hand laid firm on withers or ruffing a satiny neck against its grain. The animals' morning noises hushed as they fell on their food and the sun shouldered into the dim barn between cracks in the warped boards. When Josiah left for the hardware store, Cody returned to the house to see who had appeared—her mother from outside, her sister from their bedroom, wordless and sticky-eyed. Louisa slept like it was her job.

All morning, Cody roamed. Pasture to aspen grove, riverbank to gravel pit, she ranged like a prospector. The dogs followed close, disappearing in brush after squirrel or scent to emerge again later so reliably that Cody hardly noticed they were gone. She sat on the paddock fence and scratched the horses' flanks when they pressed her legs. She trapped mice with a baited tin can, held their noses up to hers and let them go. She bounced pebbles at the chickens, which ruffled them into great squawking piles, and then chased them until she could lift one in her arms, light as a loaf of store-bought bread.

Margaret glimpsed her daughter when she thought to look, but mostly Cody's day slid past in unwatched hours. Louisa darted in and out of her games, less often than she used to, as phone calls and girlfriends and moody hours in her room supplanted their sisterish rhythms. Alone, Cody dug holes, sorted dirt and stones into piles. She rarely threw rocks anymore, not even small ones, since Clint Lindsay put out the eye of a crow by accident. The bird had staggered the schoolyard in circles, its eye a bloody pit, wings spread, croaking angry protest. Cody loved the chickens and would rather have put out her own eye, or Clint's. She liked to cause a ruckus, not to harm, but sometimes it was hard to tell the difference.

Cody lay on her back in the grass looking at the sky and the mountains pushed against it, flat as paper shapes in the harsh sun. By noon, the air shimmered. The Kalispell daily on the kitchen table said *'85 Western Montana's Hottest Summer in Years.* The dogs panted even in the shade.

"Cody," Margaret said, "she's our dreamer." Cody didn't call it dreaming. She called it pretending. Or thinking. When she saw a red-tailed hawk, she practiced her call. She could imitate a barred owl, a handful of songbirds—robin, meadowlark, chickadee—and a great horned pair calling back and forth. Raptors were her recent interest. Cody preferred fierce to pretty.

ON THE FIRST MORNING when smoke hazed the eastern horizon, Cody went out to the barn and Josiah wasn't there. The wide doors loomed shut, the iron bar slotted into its groove. She entered the side door to vaulted dark. The horses and mules shifted in the stalls with soft and windy noise. Even in the building, she could taste faint smoke. She patted her horse's nose.

"Where's Pop, Daisy girl?"

The door at the back of the stalls stood ajar but the rear shop was empty, too. In the dark, the logs and boards and Josiah's half-built projects looked asleep. The table saw was covered with a tarp and Cody lifted an edge and crouched to peek beneath. As a littler girl she constructed forts under the table saw—an ominous, noisy roof—until her father told her he didn't want her too comfortable near a dangerous tool. Now she counted the rough planks stacked against the wall: four shelves, she knew, for the wardrobe he was building.

Cody found her mother on the side of the house pulling snap peas from the snaked vines. Her hair was tied back with a knotted navy kerchief.

"Where's Pop? He's not in the barn or the shop."

"Upstairs," Margaret said. She bit an end and spit it out before chewing the rest of the pea. "Sleeping."

"He'll be late for work. The horses aren't fed."

Margaret trimmed another pea with her teeth and handed it to Cody. "He isn't feeling well. Let him rest. Can you tend the stock?"

Yes, she could. Cody swung the barn doors wide and, with the cement block, propped them open to give the horses light. Pulled apart a bale and loaded fresh hay in troughs. Filled each water bucket with the hose and rewound it properly on its metal wheel. She fed Daisy by hand, first the pea and then a clump of hay, the horse's warm muzzle peeled back to blocky teeth and shining gums. A bee drifted in and buzzed like a low plane.

Upstairs, her parents' bedroom door was shut but not latched. Cody pushed it open with her finger, a crack to peer through. The room was as dark as the barn. Josiah lay in bed, a lump beneath the quilt, curled to face the wall. Too hot for covers, she thought.

"Pop," she whispered. The quilt moved up and down while he breathed.

"Pop," a little louder. He didn't answer. Cody had never seen her father sleep during the day. Not once. She closed the door and twisted the handle so it latched without a sound. The hallway was roasting and she escaped down the stairs and outside in such a hurry that the back door slammed behind her and bounced.

All day, he was quiet and she was loud.

THE NEXT MORNING Cody went out to the barn and was relieved to see the doors standing open. From outside she could hear boot heels clacking against the planked floor. She leaned in to look before she gave herself away. Josiah wore clean Wranglers and his summer straw hat—store clothes.

"Are you all better, Pop?"

He turned toward her. "I'll be fine."

AFTER LUNCH Bobby Watson stood outside the back door with his freckled runny nose pushed up against the screen like a tiny pig.

"Can you come out?" Bobby asked. He lived across the road not quite to the T. The Kinzlers' nearest neighbors were the Lindsays, who shared the fence line and were more like family than friends. The Lindsay boys, Clint and Nate, teased Cody for playing with Bobby, who was grubby and unkempt in a different way than regular ranch kids. Not dusty jeans and hat hair, but a pallor to his yellowish skin even in summer, a smell like cooked onions hanging on his clothes, from living in a one-room cabin where the bed was next to the stove. The kids at school said Bobby was dirt-poor. Not one of them was rich, not even the Lindsays, certainly not like TV or the kids from Whitefish High with their fancy uniforms for sports. But Bobby was something else. Cody knew his father had lost his job when the sawmill all but closed, but really, Bobby had never had more than he did now. His shoe soles flapped at the toe and he brought a sack lunch that you could tell was almost empty even from across the room. Other kids ribbed him. But Cody's mother always said play with anyone unless they're mean. In that case, leave them alone.

At the river, the wind stirred up the air and the smell of smoke drifted in and out while Cody and Bobby threw bits from their pockets into the water. String, lint, paper, chicken feed—the current pulled it all under and down, skidding in and out of the eddies that cupped the rocks. The river was fast here even for the dry season. Cody wore her bathing suit under her shirt, but knew better than to swim without a grown-up. A girl from the high school had drowned the year before, a half friend of Louisa's, that tall red-haired girl with a braying laugh who could ride bareback. The river came into Cody's mind sometimes—the kicking white surf on the rocks, how it made her feet so cold they disappeared. Another hot day she saw a grizzly standing out in the river up to its shoulders, its big neck and scoop face sticking out, the way a dog's does when it swims. As she watched, the bear shrugged out of the water and toward the opposite bank where it stood on the rocks and shook so hard she could hear it over the river's rush. It surprised her how skinny the bear looked, dressed in wet fur that hung from its belly like a fringe.

Bare-legged now, shorts held high, Bobby was up to his shins in the river where an eddy stilled the current enough to stand in. Cody watched from the bank as Bobby pissed in front of his feet.

"Gross," she said. Bobby waded in front of her, peeing. "Get away! I don't want to see your stupid little wiener."

Cody's disgust pleased her. She pinched her eyes shut and put a finger in each ear to block out the sound of urine pouring on water, but peeked when Bobby turned away. She thought of peeing in the bathtub, so yellow coming out, and then invisible.

"My wiener is not little. And you should see my dad's."

"No way," Cody said. "G-R-O-S-S." To her it looked like a tiny plastic toy, a rubbery finger puppet left over from a birthday party. Bobby zipped his pants and splashed out. His gaze roamed behind her and settled. Cody turned. There was Clint. Thirteen and half-tall, always looming bigger than he was, Clint was part neighbor part cousin part wild, and Cody drew toward him one day, and shrugged away the next.

"Look what I got." His smile a dare. A large box of matches came out of his pocket and lay in the palm of his hand, balanced to show.

"The wood kind. They don't bend when you light 'em." Clint struck one match against the box edge and let it burn. Cody stomped a foot as the flame got close to his fingers. He flicked it into the brush. She watched the arc, ready to spit on the ash, but the air extinguished any spark.

"The fires—" she said, then stopped. They'd heard for weeks about the Glacier Park burn, spreading to Forest Service land, how many acres. But the wind constantly shifted and this hour, the sky sat blue and harmless, no smoke in sight, the only scent faint as a far-off campfire.

Clint ignored her protest. "They light on stone." Against a rock big enough to sit on, he struck another match. It hissed and flamed in a quick snap. Clint handed the box to Bobby, who lit two more and thrust the box at Cody's chest. She pushed his arm back. Matches were a risky game, forbidden in any weather.

"Bobby, I know where a weasel lives, in our shed, where we can watch." Her voice was bright as she could make it. She didn't address Clint but he answered her without looking.

"What baby cares about a shit-fucker weasel." Clint stood up on the balls of his feet and rocked back, grinning at the sky. He cursed enviably, as easy as talking. Bobby watched them with his hands by his sides. Cody lit the first match with stiff arms, blowing it out fast, the tip barely blackened. It was hard to breathe.

"Don't waste them." Clint snatched the box from her. "Use them all the way."

Cody tore the box back and held it behind her. Clint could change the day like a switch flipped on, a bright zing. She hated to be bossed but it made her brave.

At home she was allowed to light matches to start a morning fire in the woodstove or touch the candlewicks to flame. Out here in the sun, the matches were dimmer, but the heat felt near.

They passed the box back and forth and the rest of the matches—fifty?—went quick as they lit sticks and grass seed-heads, letting them burn, then dropping them in the river where they hissed out and shot downstream. Clint mouthed the sound of dropped bombs and Cody's insides went night quiet. She lit one purple match tip from another, the blended flame an instant brighter surge. Clint licked his fingers and put out a little torch between his pointer and his thumb, so Bobby did it, too. Show-offs.

The last match caught Cody's sleeve. She watched the loose cotton threads curl and go ashy, mesmerized, and so she let it go too long. When she mashed the cuff against the dirt it left a blackened smudge at the wrist. Her favorite shirt, a blue summer-weight chambray like her father's, with pearl snaps and red stitched pockets. Too hot for that, Cody, her mother said. But Josiah never wore short sleeves.

Cody smelled her cuff. It stunk. She imagined burnt skin instead of cloth and looked up to see Clint squinting. He could turn his baby face into a threat.

"Cody, you tell our dads, I'll—" Clint motioned, his hands a blend of wring and punch. It looked ridiculous but scared Cody anyway. Clint was smart enough to hunt down his own trouble and turn it into someone else's.

CODY INVITED BOBBY IN for a snack—cornflakes and milk—though she hated to watch him chew, his mouth wet and loud as a cow and his head hung down, shoving, shoving. He ate like this at school too, and Cody wanted to tell him that letting your hunger show so much was dangerous, like a window in your bedroom with no curtain.

"Dis-*gus*-ting!" sang Louisa when she flitted through the kitchen in her swimsuit. Bobby watched her with his mouth full and his eyes gaped. Iced tea sloshed in Louisa's glass and her painted toes knocked against the pale wood floor like a red sound. Cody's own feet were coated with sap on the bottoms, thick enough on the heels to stick a pin through. She called them her summer shoes. Cody sat next to Bobby at the table and ate with one hand, her shirt sleeve pinched in the other palm. Out the window, Louisa spread her towel in the grass and lay on her belly with her Walkman's headphones over her ears. She sipped her tea through a straw and the sun hit her skin and made it shine.

BY DINNER CODY HAD FORGOTTEN about the matches. After they'd cleaned up the kitchen she draped on the arm of her father's chair and her hands combed his beard, tickling, when Josiah grabbed her wrist and pulled it toward him. Her burnt cuff sat black in his lap.

"What's this?" Josiah's voice was stern, and Cody's giggle halted in her throat.

"Oh, Pop, that was—I did that . . ." She couldn't think of words. "I . . . got dirty."

"This is not dirt. Where did you get a burn?"

Cody tucked her bottom lip under her teeth. She backed off Josiah's lap, but he wouldn't let go of her hand. She stood before him with her arm out as if she were reined.

"Cody, where did you get matches?" Josiah leaned forward in his chair and held her by the shoulders.

"Was it from Clint? Answer me." His face moved with the deliberate words. His voice was deep and angry as he ever got, and Cody knew better than to persist.

"BobbyWatsonhadmatches." It came out fast. Her father never ran into Bobby's parents. No one would know what she told.

"And you lit them?"

Cody nodded.

"What have I told you about matches?" he asked. His loud voice drew Louisa trolling by the open door to investigate this rare shout, but she didn't enter the room.

"There are fires burning in the park, Cody. Twenty miles from us. What have I told you about matches!"

He'd said it so often, she knew the exact words.

"You only light a match to start a flame," Cody whispered. Josiah took hold and led her upstairs to her room. He strode with his arm wrenched behind him, dragging her along. At the doorway, he pushed her forward.

"Sit," he said, pointing to the beds.

Josiah left the room and yanked the door shut past the warped doorjamb so it would be hard to open. Cody sat on Louisa's bed weaving her fingers through the holes in the afghan, still for what felt like an hour. She touched the soft spots under her eyes, pressed until she saw black and green. Her skin felt sticky. She could hear Louisa in the bathroom talking on the phone, the cord stretched under the door from the hallway cubby, tight enough to trip on. It was boldly light out. The sun would not set for hours more and the after-supper birds were still silent, even the referee bird that always sang first. Then her father returned.

"Cody, come." Josiah was calm. He took her hand back into his palm, a glove now instead of a leash, and walked her down the stairs, past her mother laying out bills in stacks on the wiped table.

"We'll be half an hour," said Josiah to Margaret, who looked up from her calculator and nodded. Cody dropped her eyes so as not to plead, ashamed of her badness. In the yard Josiah picked up a Pulaski leaning against the shed and kept Cody by the other hand. They walked away from the house, away from the river, toward the south corner of the property where an old logging road shambled into the woods. The late evening air hung low and still and Cody smelled the sugary scent of ponderosa bark, thickest after the day's heat. Before she was old enough to know them by name, she called them Pancake Trees. Their smell reminded her of Saturday breakfasts when Josiah made thin crepes in the shape of her initials, drizzled with maple syrup from the glass bottle with the tiny handle, much too small for a finger. C.M.K.: Cody Madeleine Kinzler. Crispy where the edges bubbled against the buttered iron skillet.

The trees opened up into a small meadow. Josiah dropped her hand and moved so quickly ahead of her it was as if they'd arrived separately. Cody knew this clearing well; she played here, piling seed cones into heaps, hucking them at the giant pine at the edge of the clearing. Her father said it was a grandfather tree, old and tall with rough, thick bark that glowed orange as a robin's chest. Her aim was good and she hit it squarely every other time. She'd had two real grandfathers, one she'd known and one she hadn't.

Her father stopped and Cody spotted the dirt strips right off, four shallow trenches around him in the grass that formed a square as big as her bedroom, and inside the lines, low brush, grass, a few needled branches. Josiah's matches came out of his pocket, wooden, the same blue and red brand as Clint's, though his box was full when Clint's was nearly empty. He looked at Cody and struck one match, then bent and lit a stalk of grass near the square's edge.

"Stay there," he said. Josiah crossed the plot and struck several more matches, planting them into brush. At the far corner of the plot, he picked up a blue cube water jug and walked the dirt perimeter back to her, leaking water onto the exposed soil trenches.

"Pop?"

By the time Josiah reached her, the patch flamed in front of them. Smoke rose. The individual fires grew hotter as they ate the dried white grass, the reddish needles, downed branches and mounds of cones. The small fires reached each other so their edges joined until, with a sudden burst of air like breath forced out tight lips, the center of the square surged into one flame, high as Cody's waist. Josiah pushed her forward toward the dirt line, too close, and she backed away.

"Pop?" Cody said it again. Josiah stepped behind her and did not answer. The fire spread outward. She felt warmth on her face and legs. The air twisted and she realized that heat was something you could see. Cody looked back at her father. The fire advanced towards them and she heard the pop and hiss of seedpods and the squeak of sappy limbs drying fast. Cody cried out again, but her father made no motion and the fire burned so hot that her face felt tight and the liquid dried in her eyes: erased tears. Cody saw the ponderosa in the corner of the field and all she could think was that the fire would burn up the grandfather. She didn't back away from the fire as it approached the line only a few feet in front of her. When it nearly reached her shoes, Josiah stepped forward and swung the jug, spraying the rest of the water out over the flames. The smoke turned in an instant from white to gray and the smell of doused ashes blanketed the plot. Cody put her face in her hands and cried.

When her father approached, Cody stiffened as if he were a stranger but as Josiah crouched low, her own knees folded. She sobbed with her face burrowed in his shirt. It smelled like chainsaw gas and the animals. Josiah squatted in the grass holding her against him and as her crying lessened, Cody peeked over his shoulder at the plot. Inside the dirt lines the grass was gone, the square flat and smoldering. A few tiny flames quivered but under her gaze they paused longer, then disappeared, as if the dirt were a swallowing mouth. No pinecone left. The muggy char hung thick but outside the dug lines, now dry, the world began again as green and live as usual. Josiah lifted her up in his arms. His hands joined under the pockets of her jeans and her legs swung, toes pointed downwards.

"Cody. Every fire starts small."

"Okay," she whispered.

Their chests moved together. Cody rested her face on her father's shoulder and her feet dangled near his kneecaps. She'd be ten years old come fall, and in his arms, too large and awkward, she felt older. She was parched and tired and the corner of her mouth wetted his shirt. After a few minutes, he set her down. Her legs tingled as she straightened herself.

"Run home," Josiah said. "I'll be a few."

He picked up the Pulaski and walked into the ashes with his back to her and kicked apart the piles of debris. With the adze end of the tool he turned up the dirt and dragged the last cinders with his feet.

Josiah half turned. "Go, Cody." She ran.

"MATCHES, DUH," Louisa said to Cody, scolded and sad. "If you're going be dangerous, dummy, at least you better do it with me," and Cody knew then that her sister was old. Twelve was grown enough not to be bossed, old enough to offer what she'd already learned. It had been ages since Cody asked, but that night in bed she begged for a story, the one Louisa first made up when Cody was too young for school, a gift she offered her little sister upon her return: *Once upon a time if you were a horse*, the first story began, and for years, other versions, always the same rhythm. *Once upon a time if you were a horse you wouldn't go to school, but you could run anywhere you wanted. You could go to the school and the kids would see past the chalkboard out the windows and there would be the horse, and the children would point and say to the teacher, okay, can we go outside, a horse on the playground is looking in the window!*

In bed, the smell of fire hanging on Cody even in clean pajamas after a bath, Louisa said, okay fine, and offered up a story, slow at first, like a gift she'd rather keep: *once upon a time if you were a fish, you could swim in the cold river and not be cold, you could swim through the tunnels below the earth that no one but fish can see. When you live in the water, nothing can burn. Some fish swim together in a gang and this is called a school, and some fish swim alone, flickering above the stones.* Cody drifted asleep to Louisa's voice, her mind a minnow darting in flames.

By late summer, the whole state was on fire, smoke on every horizon in plumes or clouds or a thick quilt depending on the wind, the sun a red glow you could look at straight on. On clear days, the Washburn fire lookout was visible atop the ridge to the east. It hadn't been manned in a decade, but Josiah said this season a firefighter lived up there with binoculars and maps, never sleeping more than an hour without waking to scan. Even in September's darker nights, the stars remained invisible, the moon ghosted beneath a gray sheet.

When Cody saw the black sky and heard the neighbors breathless, *closest I ever seen flames to that boundary,* when the campgrounds got shut down and no one ran saws for fear of sparks and she watched the smokejumpers up from Missoula at the diner lunch counter with their grimy faces and bloodshot eyes, then she wondered—was her father frightened, too?

DOYLE LINDSAY

JOSIAH IS AN OLD FRIEND of mine so I do not claim to be the best source for an objective take. The way I see it, he's the kind of man you admire or you hate, depending on what kind of man you are yourself. The easiest piece to say first is that Josiah is good at things. He is handy, quick, his face pleasant. He can build whatever, from a cabin to a cradle. His wife loves him and is worth loving. Same with his girls. What else is of any value?

Josiah is a crack shot, better than me by a long margin—rifle, shotgun, pistol, which any patient man can be decent at, but also with a bow. Once, when we were in high school, I watched him open the pasture gate with an arrow, from thirty yards. He hit the metal tab that freed the latch from the clasp and the gate swung open. We walked through from his land onto mine.

"Stupid," he said when he picked up the arrow and found that the metal had blunted the tip. He took aim at himself.

Josiah learned to shoot from his father, Hank, who was a friend of my father's. This is where we balance the books, because my father was well loved, and Hank was a drunk and difficult even when he was dry. When I say our fathers were friends, I stretch the truth a little. They were neighbors. Hank had few friends. He was a good hand if sober, which wasn't often, but even then, you couldn't trust him. After a while, no one gave him what they valued. That mistrust has given Josiah something to prove. For better or for worse, around here the kind of man your father was matters long after he's gone.

In these parts, you're a ranch man, a farm man, or a woods man. Josiah's father trained horses and Josiah packs mules and rides, but he is a woods man to the core. He's worked in forests most of his life, first peeling logs for a timber builder, then as a traildog in Glacier, a sawyer on a hotshot crew, even one season working for Boise Cascade on a clear-cut operation in the Swan Valley but he quit that before it became a habit. Now he runs his father-in-law's hardware store. He works in the woods on the side. He makes furniture, from trees he says, not from lumber, and when you see his work, you know what he means. It belongs in the forest somehow, not in a room. A table puts a clearing in your mind. A dresser makes you look around for a stream.

At Thanksgiving or auctions or picnics when our families gather, Josiah stays on the edges, never at rest. I cannot picture him in church. Even at the store, his territory, he seems uneasy, his hands busy at useless tasks, wiping an already clean counter, opening and closing the blade of his pocketknife. But put him outside—say he's felling trees, or packing mules—and the awkwardness dries up. It's as if there are edges to him that he doesn't know himself, or can't explain. Perhaps they matter less outside.

Josiah speaks in as soft a voice as he can get by with. Noisy people quiet to hear him. He puts in a hand when one is needed. He prefers to be alone, I think, but even so, he is good company. He listens when others talk. Because of his father he is not a drinker and when men get loud or mean he eases them down, levels them out, unless they're past the point where anybody can. Then he knows to walk away. He can laugh at himself without looking a fool. You can see why he holds my esteem. Except for his father, he has everything. A sadness too, though. That, I suppose, I do not envy.

When Josiah was fifteen, his mother, Lucy Kinzler, who laughed like birdsong and rescued spiders when she swept, laid down in front of the ten o'clock Great Northern on the far side of the Flathead. That train has stopped running now, and the bridge that used to span the river where it flows through the canyon has long rotted. Summers when we were boys, Josiah and I fished from the flat-topped rocks that sloped towards the water's edge under the tracks, and when the train passed overhead, we'd feel the trestle vibrate. Trout skirted under its shadow. It could be ten degrees cooler on those rocks. Hot days, we'd lie flat, our backs bare against the slabs, lines slack in the water.

True secrets are rare and someone may know why Mrs. Kinzler killed herself, but I do not. The talk around town has never provided an answer that sticks. Josiah didn't speak about it then, or since. How would that maim a boy, your mother choosing such a gory fate over the one with you in it? I would not want to talk about it either. Josiah's older brother Henry was seventeen when Mrs. Kinzler died. He joined the service a few months later in the usual muddle of heroics and escape. Henry died two years after his mother when he was stationed in Southern California. He died a peacetime death, fell off a pier too drunk to swim with friends too drunk to save him. Josiah never said a word about that either. His past is a heavy load, but he has not drawn attention to it.

Before we were twenty, Hank died of liver cancer, no surprise, as by then he was mostly bed-bound. After Hank was buried, Josiah was thoroughly alone, barely a man, with nothing but thirty acres of dry land, a ramshackle house, and the place so deep in him he couldn't leave. I was at Ag school in Bozeman when he met Margaret Blanchard, a girl from Columbia Falls I had known in high school, an alluring person, one year older, who I always thought would go somewhere interesting. Over the years, she has come in and out of my house freely and I have depended on her. My own wife, Iva, has suffered our whole life together with monstrous headaches. Some weeks she is fine and others incapacitated, and then Margaret has so often stepped in, stayed in my family's wings, steady and helpful. I love having her near, but Margaret was not the girl I guessed would stay.

When Josiah had kids, his first a year after mine, it surprised me. I can't say why, exactly, except Josiah didn't seem to need completing the way I felt I did. If you had asked me would Josiah have children, I'd have said no. Early on, even a wife was a stretch. It was easier to picture him alone.

But Margaret claimed him, or, I suppose, they claimed each other. They had no children at first, and by the time Ida and I had Clint on the way, it appeared they might not. But then came Louisa, and a bit after, Cody, named not for Buffalo Bill, as she likes to state, but for her mother's aunt, Great Cordelia, and for Lake Coeur d'Alene, where Josiah had taken a happy vacation—with my own family—when we were children. He loves those girls, and I can see his ease with them that I have not found with my own sons. The way I see it, you get a family you were born to and a family you make. If you're lucky, one of them suits you.

STATE FAIR (1969)

WHAT MARGARET FIRST LOVED about Josiah was his hands. Give me those, she wanted to say. She watched them from a distance, how they lay still against the thighs of his worn jeans or, when ill at ease, he pulled at his fingers till the knuckles cracked. Margaret was used to working hands. Her father, rancher turned shop keeper, had a grip like a dog's jaw and her mother was keeper of a spotless homestead, her hands red from canning and bruised from chores. But Josiah's hands were his own. Not any laborer's hands, meaty and calloused, but also long-fingered, freckled tan and covered in fine hair so the backs of them reminded her of animals more than people. A fawn's dappled skin or the roany hide of a good horse.

Margaret had not known Josiah in high school. She was one grade older, and when they'd both graduated and she met him in a friend's backyard mid-summer, she did not recognize him. After, she knew about him only what she'd heard from the undependable source of others: Josiah was a fine carpenter for a boy barely grown, his father had been a notorious drunk, he was alone in the world. But that was later. At the barbecue, Margaret stood by the grill waiting for a hotdog and Josiah prodded the coals with a stick between the grates. He knew her. Doyle's crush from sophomore year, though had either of them ever spoken to her? He stuck out his hand and took hers, enfolded it like she was welcome news. She wasn't delicate, but right then she felt so.

A movie, they decided. Start there. Margaret had been on her share of awful dates arranged by friends worried she was too picky (a girl like her should be, but at some point, Margaret, you have to try). Josiah arrived in front of her parents' house in his white Ford pickup. He met her on the porch—she waited at the window to save him ringing the bell—and they walked down the steps together, Margaret careful, more wobbly than usual in sandals with a wooden wedged heel. She could feel her sister watching. At the hood of the truck, in the middle of her sentence, Josiah stopped, waiting for her to finish before he opened her door. His head cocked toward her while he listened. Margaret let her hand rest on the window, noticing that the truck was hard used but clean. The mud flaps were dusty and streaked where water had recently dried. The door swung wide and squeaky on its hinge.

The inside of the cab was clean, too, and tidied. Margaret could see the lines left by the vacuum hose in the plush red seat cover. A car wash? The vacuum plugged into an extension cord on the side of his house? The thought of him doing that for their date made her smile. The cab smelled like gear oil and summer, a machined odor mixed in with the alchemy of leaf and sun and dust and sweat that, to a person from a certain part of the west, was nothing to note. It was what you'd say a place smelled like.

The first time they kissed behind the hog barn at the Montana State Fair in Great Falls, Margaret felt as if she'd known Josiah a long time and they'd already been apart—a war, a migration, something big. It was a strange feeling, as if, alongside a vast understanding, there was a space between them. She couldn't tell if it came from him or from her.

By the time he kissed her, Margaret thought Josiah was shyer than any boy she'd ever known. Weeks in, he'd reach for her hand, press his shoulder to hers. When he finally clasped her to him, tipping her head back with the force of it, she realized it was just a sureness he took. Not shy at all.

They'd driven to the State Fair together, hours east, with consent from her folks to be overnight on a date because her aunt Abigail offered to put them up in Great Falls, where she lived alone in a house like a museum. Abigail had never married and she ran an antique store, pirating treasures before they sold.

Aunt Abigail was sweet on Josiah right away. Her eagerness to please embarrassed Margaret. She wished they'd eaten supper at placemats around the kitchen table, but Aunt Abigail set up the formal dining room, china and candlesticks laid out on a linen cloth with napkins to match. Like a Sunday dinner with strangers.

"Aren't you *handsome*," said Aunt Abigail, tucking her folded-together hands beneath her chin so they pressed her throat and chapped her voice.

Aunt Abigail's doting focus was like a microscope and at the dinner table, Josiah seemed too large to Margaret, the china dishes fragile in his hands.

"More ham?" Aunt Abigail said. And Josiah would take another slice. "More potatoes?" More. "More applesauce?" More, more. If they took two hours to eat, it would not have surprised Margaret at all, and when they left the next day for the fair, she told Aunt Abigail not to expect them until late. Neither had money to spend on fair food for an entire day, but the thought of another evening like the previous one was a sentence.

Margaret won a pie in a target contest and that saved them buying lunch. They ate the whole thing straight out of the tin pan. The apples were soft and basted with cinnamon and vanilla, the crust perfect, the slotted top crisp, not burnt, but suggesting it. Josiah slipped his fingers along the edges of the aluminum grooves, coating them with the last of the sugared apple sludge, and Margaret teased and lunged as if to lick his fingers. She imagined them in her mouth for hours.

The following spring Josiah told Margaret, if you'll marry me, we'll have to make each other happy in our own way. We won't be rich, but we won't starve. I have my own place. She knew that, though she'd never been there. She wanted to say yes, but she worried about the house, the sadness in it he'd told her about: father's drink, mother's dread, brother gone.

When Josiah finally invited her to the house at the end of July—after they'd lived with her parents for two months while he worked on the place and she balanced the books for her father's store in town and stayed purposefully away—she was relieved that he'd made it their own. He'd scrubbed the house snout to tail, a wall of Pine-Sol when you opened the door, all trace of his father's cigarettes aired out or covered. Margaret stepped over a bucket and a stiff bristled brush on the front porch steps where he'd been bleaching the water-stained planks when she arrived.

Josiah swung the door wide. A blank slate, he said. He had painted the walls cloudy white and she felt like she was beneath a turned-over china bowl. At the windows hung new curtains. I found the material in the attic, he said, and this fact—that he could sew—hinted at all she didn't know. His mother's antique sewing machine was one of the first electric models, too small for his legs to fit easily beneath, and many years later Margaret still felt those curtains to be the best gift he had ever given her. A different fabric in each room, and his knees, stiff from the effort of it, the way he'd made himself uncomfortable to welcome her.

It was the land that sold her—dry open meadows unfit for heavy grazing, a small creek at the property line, and the huge old trees scattered amidst the second-growth groves butting up to Forest Service land. Wind, wood, water, space. Later she understood that the land was an oasis, a place they could both be at home, larger than the rooms.

To her that home was a gift, absent the ghosts of drunk and struggle. But Josiah had never been clean of the house's heavy history and it was a weight to live there his whole life. To him the gift was the hardest kind of offering: a sacrifice. She wished she had noticed the cost of it sooner.

The night before the wedding there was a picnic at the Blanchards' house. Aunts and uncles, cousins and friends, toasts and talk and teasing. Josiah was polite and serious. He was unused to the attention of a boisterous group. After the guests had cleared out and he and Margaret sat in the backyard under August dark, listening to the clang of dishes from the kitchen and her parents' voices filtered through the screen, Josiah spoke.

"I have a worry," he said. Margaret leaned against him and lifted her hand to his face. She felt the edge of his lips with her nails, cut blunt, his shaved skin catching at the tips.

"You're sure I can give you what you need?"

"I need you," she told him. She thought of her words at the picnic table that night as her vows. What came later mattered less.

Early in a marriage, who could know what you needed, anyway? At that time, the first order of business was children, but a miscarriage threw them off, that what others made look easy could be difficult, and then a few years later, when Margaret had stopped thinking there was only one thing to want, the girls came. The first months were blurred with joyfulness at the usual things—tiny fingers and the smell of their scalps—and also a clutching panic that no one had mentioned.

When Margaret was nursing Cody, who fed constantly, the family cow got mastitis. Margaret felt as if all she did were nurse, or wash her shirts, always wet or damp or encrusted or drying. Josiah usually milked in the mornings before he left for the store—he'd grown up with cows, Margaret had not—but for whatever reason, that morning she did it, setting Cody in her cradle and Louisa in her high chair with the kitchen door open even though the fall air was cool. From outside the barn Margaret could hear the cow shifting and moaning, and when she got close she could see in the dim light the bright red udder swelled up like a rubber glove blown to bursting. When Margaret entered the stall, shifting the cow's bulk and reaching to touch a teat, the cow bucked back and a vile smell rose up, like old bandages and past-turned cheese. She leaned on the planked wall and threw up into the next stall. The cow died a few days later, which even the vet said was fast, and they'd never had another cow since. Margaret couldn't get out of her head that they'd nursed something to death. They bought milk from the Lindsays after that. When the girls were old enough, they walked across the fields and brought it home in sweating glass bottles.

MARGARET DID NOT KNOW WHAT Josiah loved in her first. Where other men said it outright—*Your mother got me with her banana bread* or *The minute I laid eyes on your sister in that yellow dress, I knew I'd marry her*—Margaret could only guess what Josiah had noticed.

At the fair, he'd said words she held on to, a murmur, maybe not even meant for her to hear, though Josiah took enough care with speech that she snatched it for herself. *When you kiss me, I feel like you're telling the truth.* It was something for a boy to say who had been so often lied to. In a way, it was more valuable than one story—a hat, a certain laugh, a favorite meal. It was a tenor, instead, a much larger gift. Still, Margaret wished for the comfort of knowing Josiah's exact desire. Wished she could point and say, *this*. This is what he loves.

DORIE BLANCHARD

MY SISTER WAS THE PRETTY ONE, I always thought. In junior high she grew her short hair long—twice as glossy as any old Pert commercial—and me and Michael argued over it, who could braid it, who could comb it out after her showers that smelled like steaming fruit. She spun in a slow circle with her hairbrush outstretched and whoever she pointed at when she stopped got to brush. She'd saved up babysitting money for an expensive one with a brown wooden handle and special bristles—I wasn't allowed to use it—but even plastic would have been a trophy. You felt proud for the rest of the night. Michael liked to brush Margaret's hair even after he got older and began to keep to himself. Our father said it wasn't right for a growing boy to be concerned with his sister's grooming, so Michael only did it in our room with the door closed, which our father also forbade. Doors unlocked, open unless you were sleeping. Our father did not like secrets, which meant anything he did not know.

Margaret was not very vain, not like she could have been. Lord knows I am vain, and I am half the looker she is. The first time Margaret brought Josiah home it was almost funny. Michael was gone by then and I was so excited to meet him—a boy! A boy!—and I danced around and bugged her like a little brat, I'll admit it. We weren't used to her bringing boyfriends home. She held herself a little apart from other kids her age. On weekends, she read in our room until her face had lines from her pillow or the wicker chair. Margaret hardly went to the proms or school dances. Later I discovered all the stuff you could do that Margaret had never cared about, never told. An after-school choir! Parties on weekends! Who knew?

It surprised me when she married Josiah. When I first saw him, that day he drove up to the house and got out of his truck, I thought, well, he won't last. Too much cowboy. Margaret read "lit-rature," pronouncing it like our grandmother, and she went moony over dashing British gents from PBS and "New York City boys" she told me were all poets. But they were imaginary, and Josiah, he was real.

That first date she ran out to meet him so he wouldn't have to come in and be subject to us—she didn't say that, but I knew. With another boy who picked Margaret up at home, I'd whispered to Mama, loud, so they could both hear, *I thought she said he was cute.* Ha! He *was* cute, though—I wanted to shame, to hold that tiny power. Josiah was more handsome than cute—a grown man, to me, with his own truck and his tightly tucked shirt. When Margaret walked toward him, I watched Josiah sneak a look over at her, but mostly he stared at the ground. He seemed shy, and she did right, protecting him.

Cowboy or not, he stayed. Later that summer Margaret brought Josiah in, first only for a few minutes while she got ready in her bedroom, kicking off one pair of shoes for another, fiddling with the clasp of a necklace, and I lingered close so that when she got frustrated, I could step in to help. She twisted her hair up off her neck and I handed her bobby pins to fix the last strands. Eventually, Josiah stayed for dinner and our parents leaned toward him, our father jesting, punching him on the shoulder, like he was playing a part. "The son I should have had," he told our mother one night after Josiah and Margaret stepped out onto the porch and I spied on them from the upstairs window. "He'll grow into the kind of man I can see eye to eye with." I knew he was really talking about Michael, and what kind of man he never was. From the bedroom window, it was too high to see if they kissed.

Josiah got used to us. His seriousness cracked a little—how could anyone stay straight in the face of my silliness? I learned his sense of humor, and how far to push before he'd arch an eye. I teased Margaret that Josiah was sexy and then put my hands around my neck and gagged at the word. I thought Margaret picked Josiah because he was so different than us. Our family was a jumble of puppies with a stern barking father and a harried mother who licked our scruffs. Josiah was no dog at all. Maybe an elk, watching from the side of the road, or the kind of bird that perches on a branch and scans. You don't notice it at first, but once you do, you can't look away. I told my theory to Margaret once, in hopes she'd tell me which animal she'd be, but she only smiled.

I always thought Margaret would leave. When Michael went away his last year of high school, that opened the door. There was a whole world out there. Not that he told us much about it, but after Michael disappeared from our house, his letters still came, a note every so often, a postcard from Eugene, a Christmas letter from Berkeley, far off places we'd never heard of. When a certain type of envelope dropped through the mail slot I'd race to grab it, and Margaret would come close if she knew mail from Michael had arrived.

We scrutinized the postmarks and huddled to look for the cities in the atlas folded open on the dining room table between us, the pages stiff and musty as a basement. When we put our fingers on the black dots (or red stars, the capitals), then we could trace how you'd get from one place to the next. Everything connected: here was a river, there was a highway. A mountain range to get across, an ocean where you had to stop. Michael wasn't dead, like our mother worried, or damned, like our father said. He'd just gone off to another place and made a life there. Anyone could. Imagine that.

PAY ATTENTION (1987)

ONE SATURDAY IN SEPTEMBER, Cody saddled Daisy right after breakfast. She used to ride with her sister but Louisa had turned fourteen in July and didn't want to go anymore, especially not on weekends. Now there were boys: the new kid, Jess McCafferty, and a senior named Brandon with his own truck. Even Nate Lindsay was interesting again. Fourteen was much different than almost twelve. So, Cody was on her own. Fine. Daisy was good company. A young shapely brown mare with a black mane and tail, Daisy had a smooth trot and walked like she was in a parade. Cody loved cantering: Daisy the water, herself a small boat. The dogs stayed home; Brisket, the cattle dog, was too old to keep up in the heat, and Jade, the husky, gave horses wide berth. She didn't deign to follow.

Cody spurred Daisy down the dirt road to burn off the barn steam, then west cross country to the top of the butte. It was an odd formation, the only one around, rising out of the meadow grass like a high stage made of dirt. Daisy was a natural at switchbacks, traversing up the steep side slopes and then pivoting direction on instinct. Cody hardly guided her. The loose gravel poured away from Daisy's hooves and left dark streaks of moist soil. On top of the butte it was breezy and warm, not so high as the mountains but above most of the trees, and you could see in all directions. Cody dismounted and let Daisy graze in the rocky grass while she poked around, looking for arrowheads and scat.

To the north lay fenced grazing lands, cows dotting the grass, their calves old enough to wander off and young enough to bleat and bray when they realized they were alone. To the south was Forest Service land, eventually turning into the Bob Marshall Wilderness, where the Kinzlers took horse trips and Josiah had worked as a packer at Big Prairie before he married Margaret. To the west, ranches and eventually town; to the east, a finger of Forest land again. Cody knew every direction, including home, the Lindsays' place one further east, across the old split rail fence that needed repairs each spring. Mr. Doyle and her father did it, but now she was old enough to help.

Cody's father said to pay attention, and she did. She was beginning to think she knew quite a lot. She could tell what time it was without a watch, within a few hours anyway, if she could see the sun. The ordinary birds—violet-green swallow, bluebird, golden eagle—she knew those, male and female, juvenile and grown. Ponderosas' reddest bark faced south or west (not always), though her father wouldn't verify this and so it was still under investigation. Part of knowing meant being able to tell the difference between a fact and a hunch. Juniper berries were actually tiny cones. Cottonwoods grew on river bottoms—rottenwoods, her father called them, since whether they fell by wind or saw or snow load, the punky heartwood gave way beneath a finger like a sponge—and aspens higher up than birch, following drier soil. Poplars had the only yellow leaves, and the rest of the trees were evergreens, except the larch, whose needles changed late in fall. A river always told its origins, her father said—walk upstream long enough and you'd find where it started. If you were lost, you could follow water downstream to a ranch or a road, but it might take days.

Cody found no arrowheads, which were next-to-never rare, and the only scat a greasy squirt from a startled grouse. She climbed onto Daisy's back and rode down the far side of the butte into its shadow.

A woodpecker flashed above and she tailed it, trying to identify which kind. Hairy was huge, downy was dainty. Pileated was rare, but hard to mistake. Flickers, in the same family, like a cousin, with a candle of a name. Thinking about woodpeckers is how Cody rode into the herd of cows. She came up over a rise into dozens of them clumped up in the trees, grazing, some of them asleep standing. She didn't recognize the brand—2AA. Despite all the years she'd spent on horseback and helping with the mules and milking the Lindsays' kitchen cows before they became meat, Cody was not a ranch kid. Big groups of cattle, all fat and pressing, made her uneasy. When the first cow noticed her, it bellowed and the sound passed among them like a wave. Cody heard them telling each other what to do. When one cow made a sudden move, another followed and soon the mass of them, thirty or forty head, ran in front of her, the calves mewling so pitifully Cody worried they could be hurt, except it seemed unlikely they all had the same trouble. Stop whining, she thought.

The commotion flushed birds out of the canopy and the air crescendoed as the cows trampled past her from all directions in the forest. *Stampede, stampede!* she shouted, a word she loved bucking off her tongue. Daisy snorted at the rustle and the usually placid horse's excitement gave Cody the idea to play cowgirl. She kicked Daisy's belly lightly and they burst into a canter. As she approached the cows behind from the left, they turned right. When she cut back to the right, they veered left. It was magic. Cody didn't quite dare ride up the middle of the herd, but she steered them from the side. She was surprised at how easily they moved under her direction, this way and back, down the hill she'd climbed when she first discovered them, and then through meadows and stands until they emerged into the open and there was a larger herd.

Cody came up short, yanked Daisy's reins back too hard and the horse nickered and stood with her chest heaving. The cows slowed too, seeing the new group, and then joined up, poured into the herd like a stream of water into a pool—instantly blended. The large herd didn't appear to register anything, not the new cows, not Cody and her horse. The cows settled and Cody could not tell which ones she had herded at all. None paid her any attention. She imagined if the cattle were hers and no one was around for a hundred miles and she was in charge of bringing them home. She rode up the side of a small clump but they didn't budge. The game was over. Cody looked up and she didn't know where she was. She scanned for the butte on the skyline but saw only mountains high and trees below. Daisy's flanks were dry and her thick ribs barely moved.

At first, Cody backtracked, no panic, but when she entered the woods where she thought she'd come from, it wasn't right. Too much lodgepole, all jack-pined, the trees close together, when she'd passed through open groves. She rode all the way around the clearing looking for a fence or a road with a cattle guard, any sign to place herself. It was just a field. Trees on all sides. She hadn't crossed a fence line, but if she was on Forest land, the cows could be free grazing, no house or ranch nearby. Maybe no road for miles. The air was cooling and by the light, it was after four. Daisy stamped her hoof and craned her neck as if shaking off flies, but there were none. If the sun was in the west by now, their shadow would be like a compass needle. She had to go east to the butte, Cody was sure. She walked the meadow's edge until she saw a good break in the trees, rechecked the sun, and turned Daisy toward home.

When she came to a lake, Cody felt frightened for the first time. It was a small lake, easy to swim across. But it was not familiar. She gave Daisy reins to wander to the edge and drink. After she finished, Cody pulled the horse's head up and rode around the shoreline, scanning for a clue. The water level was low and the sandy edge marked by rounded cow hooves, churned up where the herd came to drink. Did a trail arrive here, a worn strip she could follow back to a hitch rail or a parking lot? She only saw evidence of animals, the cows, plus elk hooves and bird feet. No beer bottles or spent shotgun shells. No dog prints, indicating people nearby, teenagers or hunters. No horseshoes, no boot prints. Nothing.

They circled the lake. Cody looked for the outlet stream that she could follow, but Daisy kept twitching, fidgeting her neck, and Cody rubbed constantly to calm her. It was getting dusky, too dark to follow anything. Beneath her legs the saddle felt loose but she didn't want to get off to tighten it. Cody entered the woods again, keeping her eastern tack as well as she could, and gave Daisy reins, letting her find the best way through the tight trees. She thought she heard a chainsaw rev in the distance but when she froze and listened, it was only a stupid cow with a bleat like a far-off engine. The sandwich and apple she'd eaten on the butte seemed ages ago. It was probably dinnertime. Her mother would be worried. Set the table, Cody. She wished she could.

AT 7:30 MARGARET PULLED four elk steaks off the grill and asked Louisa, where's your sister, but Louisa didn't know. She had been out since lunch with friends from school—don't ask who, she thought, older boys, etc. Margaret knew Cody's routines. She'd be unaccounted for all day, off in the woods or reading in the cool barn, but she didn't miss dinner. Cody ate like a young wolf, lifting scraps from others' plates to gnaw at the tiniest piece of gristle or pushing the marrow out of the center of simmered stock bones. Neither Margaret nor Josiah was prone to worry. It's light so late, she probably lost track of time, they agreed. If she isn't back by eight, we'll call around.

"She might be at the Lindsays'," said Louisa, but Nate had been with her, and Cody didn't usually go looking for Clint.

"I'll ride up and see. I need to talk to Doyle anyway," said Margaret. They finished dinner and left the bones on the porch for the dogs.

CODY KNEW, FROM TIMES OUT with her father at night, that when you were traveling, dark could sneak up. You paid attention to your path, thinking about where to go, or following your father, and then you're squinting as it gets too dark to see. In the forest, it made sense that trees blocked light, but when she rode out into the open, it was dim there, too. The sun slipped behind the ridge to the west and in front of her was another small lake. Two lakes—a chain of small lakes? Where *was* she? She rode to the edge of the water and Daisy drank again. A feeling was rising up in her that she had never had. She couldn't say more.

Minutes away from the lake, it was too dark to see far, the saddle so loose as to feel vaguely dangerous. Cody dismounted, swinging off the stirrup. The saddle slid to Daisy's opposite side so when she unbuckled the cinch beneath Daisy's belly, the saddle fell to the ground. The horse stepped sideways, and tossed her head and Cody grabbed for the reins but Daisy dropped her neck and nosed aside a bush to find grass. Cody tried to lift the saddle onto the horse's back but every time Daisy felt the weight of it against her flank, she took two steps to the side and the saddle fell to the ground.

It was a small saddle—she'd almost outgrown it—but still heavy, and Cody coached herself with her mother's advice about positive thinking: *you can do it*. She tried until her arms tired from lifting and catching, and then she looked around for a mounting stump like the one she stood on in the paddock, but there was no sign of cut ends, only big trees and brush. No split rail fences. No fallen logs. No boulders. In this open grove, old trees shed their low branches so that forest fires couldn't travel from the ground up the trunks. Cody scanned for a place to get higher, a little hill, anything. If only she were taller. Finally, she set the saddle down. She couldn't think of a way.

Damnit all, she tried, first in her mind then out loud, but it only made her think of Louisa, who was tall, and far away.

Leading the horse by the reins to the closest tree, Cody noticed a sore spot at the base of Daisy's neck where the blanket must have slipped and the saddle rubbed her skin. She laid one finger on the sore; it was wet as a mouth, and Daisy flinched. No wonder the horse had been antsy. Cody looped Daisy's reins around a sapling. She went back to the saddle and dragged it beside the horse. She folded up the pad and blanket and laid them across the saddle in a neat pile in the dark.

Cody knew to stay put. Otherwise she'd be wandering. She had only a little water in her canteen. Crying would make her thirsty, but tears came anyway. She sat atop the saddle like a seat, her knees cocked near her shoulders. She rubbed the blanket between her fingers, using an edge to polish the dusty saddle horn.

The blanket, from Josiah's childhood, was larger and thinner than the ones you could buy at Ranch Supply. It had come from Javier, a cowboy who'd worked Josiah's father's horses when Josiah was a teenager. Javier had come north from ranch country in Mexico to find work and Josiah still knew a few Spanish words that Javier had taught him, which he in turn taught Cody: *adios, buenos días, lo siento, hola*. She'd learned more words from Westerns—*compadre, cuidado, vaquero*—and also that Mexico was a hot and sunny place, maybe like Montana summer all year long. September was the edge of fall, and the air cooled fast with the sun gone.

Cody pushed at her eyes with her fists. She felt that being a baby might kill her. She had to act grown, as if she were brave. Pretending helped. She thought of the desert island kids and orphans from books and that's what she pretended. She was lost, left behind, shipwrecked. She'd have to make do until morning. If she had a match, she could make a small fire. Clint would have matches. Her father would. Even Louisa, for smoking stolen cigarettes. Cody felt young and ill prepared.

She used a stick and dug a little hollow in the dirt to curl up in. She pulled her socks as high as they would go, buttoned her sleeves and the neck of her shirt. She laid herself on the ground, her hip in the swale, and rested her head on the saddle like a pillow. Cody spread the blanket over herself and though she wasn't warm, she was warmer. She listened for Daisy's breath and listening was something to do. She smelled her saddle, the leather and the oil she'd rubbed in. Smelling was something to do.

CODY'S SADDLE HAD BELONGED to Uncle Michael. He gave it to her the only time she met him, on a visit when she was eight years old. Winter was brightening, ready to turn toward spring, when Grandpa Blanchard died. Aunt Dorie came from Spokane and Great-Aunt Abigail from Great Falls, and Uncle Michael was coming, too, an event in itself. Michael hadn't been back since he moved away, their mother said.

"Why not?" Cody asked.

"Sometimes children have trouble with their parents, with the place they grew up, and they go look for their own place. Uncle Michael did. And when he found it, he didn't need to come back. Until now."

Louisa gave Cody a meaningful look, the raised eyebrows and tight mouth that told Cody she wasn't quite old enough to understand.

"What kind of trouble?" Louisa asked.

"Never mind the trouble. He hasn't met your father, can you believe that?"

It was hard for the girls to imagine knowing their mother without knowing their father. Like knowing winter but not knowing snow.

"It's because you eloped, right, Mama?" said Louisa. "That means you didn't have a wedding. So Uncle Michael couldn't come?"

"We did have a wedding," Margaret said. "But a personal one. Not a big event."

"That's a bummer of a wedding," said Louisa. She was very interested in weddings then. She drew pictures of brides and grooms and the cake and people dressed up in clothes the girls never saw in town, not even at sometimes-church—Easter, Christmas—with their grandparents. Only on television.

"Why do you like weddings so much anyway?" Cody mostly

drew pictures of horses and birds and trains and dogs and different kinds of plants.

"I just like fancy things," Louisa said. Cody didn't care for fancy things at all.

Grandpa Blanchard's was the girls' first funeral. Cody remembered few details except for touching his stiff hand, and Uncle Michael surrounded by people who had known him since he was a child and hadn't seen him in so many years. It seemed more like a party for Uncle Michael than a funeral for his father. Cody couldn't talk to him because of the crowds, although she stood nearby. Michael put his hand down to hold her shoulder or her arm as if to say, I feel you there, stay near me. So, she did.

Uncle Michael gave her the saddle on the day before he left, at breakfast in the nook that overlooked the backyard. The garden was under melting snow, still several feet deep, and songbirds perched on the wire tops of the buried tomato cages with their feet only a few inches off the snow.

"Let's play Christmas grapefruit," said Cody, pulling her bowl close as soon as her mother set it down. She and Louisa played the game with oranges, too, although the sectioned grapefruits and the small-toothed spoon made it her favorite version.

"What's that?" said Uncle Michael. He was interested, not just pretending.

"Louisa, you tell," said Cody, already slurping sections into her mouth.

"Well, it's based on Laura Ingalls," said Louisa. She took a serious tone when explaining to adults. "They always got an orange for Christmas in their stocking and Cody's favorite parts in Little House are about the food. Mine are about going to town, or birthday parties, like Nellie Olsen's, even though she's quite mean."

"I like when they have the pig roast, and making maple syrup," said Cody.

"So how do you play Christmas grapefruit?" asked Uncle Michael. He took an interest in what most grown-ups did not.

"Well, we pretend that we got these for Christmas, in our stocking, and maybe they are the only fruit we'll get this winter, and we eat them so slow, and we say *mmmmm*, and pretend that they're really, really special."

Louisa and Cody spoke the Little House lines because Louisa liked to act—*aren't we the luckiest children, Laura*, and *I don't believe I've ever had such a tasty fruit, Mary*—but Cody's favorite part was the delicious coolness, the part sweet and part sour tongue. She liked to imagine she lived in tiny rooms roofed with sod. No lamps, no plugs. In place of the shower, a tin pan.

When they were finished, squeezing the halves so the last juices poured into their bowls and down their wrists, Uncle Michael said that was the best way to eat a grapefruit he'd ever tried—*delightful*, he'd said, good at the Little House voice the first time, *what a treat!*—and Cody smiled.

"Speaking of Christmas," he said. "You two stay here. I'll be back in a flash." He disappeared into the guest room. Clear the table, girls, said their mother, but before they could rise, Uncle Michael returned with a black rectangular case and laid it on the table.

"For you, Louisa," he said, snapping open the metal latches. Inside, a guitar nested in a purple velvet impression exactly its shape, which Cody admired almost more than the instrument itself. How it fit, just so. She touched the velvet with gentle fingertips, as if it were the coat of a shy horse. The guitar itself was reddish brown with black markings on the body, and a bright embroidered floral strap. Louisa did not know how to play the guitar, but she had studied the 1960s in history that month and told Cody all about the hippies. Based on what they knew of Uncle Michael and the look of that strap, it was a hippie's guitar. They could both tell.

Michael disappeared and returned again, this time with a small saddle draped over his arms. "And for you, Cody. Since you are the rider."

The saddle was shiny as a new penny, dark as an old one, and small, the seat of it covered in fancy scrolling, with a string of leaves and lines that looked like cursive in another language. The stirrups were cinched up so they hung close to the edges, the brass details still golden and unscratched.

"That was my guitar from high school, Louisa. And this was my saddle when I was a kid." Uncle Michael laid his palm across the seat, rubbing the rivets with his pointer finger. "I found them when I was cleaning out my folks' place. I tuned the guitar, Lou, and the saddle's just the right size for you, Cody. I oiled it all up. You'll be able to ride that for years, I bet. Small as you are."

Laura Ingalls would have known what to say but Cody did not. She felt the saddle horn nestle perfectly under her palm and couldn't find a single word.

THE DARK THICKENED and Cody guessed it was nine o'clock. She was sleepy. A half moon was rising and she wasn't sure if it was waxing or waning, another misstep in her quest to pay attention. A full round moon would have been handy, its light bright enough to travel by. Her favorite, the fingernail moon, sleek and curved, might have consoled her a little. This half moon was nothing special, but better than dark.

Cody heard a sudden sound, like a car pulling into a gravel driveway, and she sat up and listened, holding her breath. Lowing honks and the slap of water—it was only a flock of ducks landing on the lake.

Cody pushed the blanket off and stood. She caped it over her shoulders, scanning for a faraway light. Nothing. She laid back down and twisted herself in her hollow. She wrapped the blanket around her fists to pull it tight to her chest. Her hipbones felt sharp and sore. The saddle was a poor pillow. Cody tried not to think about her bed at home with the heavy quilt folded at the foot. Her saddle blanket was still damp from sweaty horse flanks and smelled like the barn. From her stakeout a few yards away, Daisy nickered. Even Louisa would worry by now. Her mother would be frantic, a state she did not reach easily. Her father would be out on his horse or the four-wheeler looking for her. She listened for an engine but could only hear a little wind. Cody thought of hollering, but felt sure she was not close to the house. The ground within shouting distance of home she definitely knew.

Cody must have fallen asleep, because she woke with such a snap of fear she almost thought she was dead. Something licked her face. She put up her arm to her face and tried to be sensible. A coyote would not lick you. A wolf would not. A bear would not. As her vision adjusted to the dark Cody saw the Lindsays' dog, her white-bibbed chest glowing. *Brindle,* she whispered. *Where did you come from?* The moon had risen higher while she slept, and the angle cast light into the trees like the lamp on a post outside the barn. The world was brighter. Brindle circled and nosed under her palm. When she slipped out of sight into a shadow, Cody felt almost desperate. She stood and called and Brindle came back to her. Daisy bent and tamped the ground with her hooves and blew out her nose. Brindle ran ahead of Cody ten feet and barked. Looked back. Cody followed. The dog knew where it was going.

"Brindle, wait." She spoke roughly, like she'd heard the boys do. Brindle waited.

Cody ran back to the tree, folded up her blanket and laid it carefully over the saddle, the fringe out of the dirt. She felt better leaving a tidy pile. She unlooped Daisy's lead from the tree and, with no saddle to hitch it on, held it coiled in one hand. With Daisy by the reins she followed darting Brindle, watching her close as a lit flame. They wound through trees and into a boulder field that looked familiar, but she couldn't place why. Maybe she was wrong.

Brindle trotted ahead, tail up and wagging. Cody hurried to keep her in sight, worried that she'd be left again, only now without her blanket for warmth. She should have thrown it over Daisy's back. Stupid. Once, Brindle disappeared and Cody went rigid, listening, Daisy's neck bumping against her back, her wet breath on Cody's unraveling braid. She looked up at the moon with the clouds passing over it so the sky appeared to be moving as if she were on a ship, and then Cody had the feeling that almost everyone does at some point in a childhood. She realized the world was bigger than she had guessed. With only the slightest shift, she could disappear, she could cease to matter at all. A moment of terror passed, and she went on.

Brindle emerged from the trees into brightness again, and a few minutes later when they reached a fallen log high enough that Daisy had to stop, Cody scrambled up on the leaned trunk and hauled herself onto Daisy's back. For a while the spell of moving kept her awake, but following Brindle through trees and field and trees, she felt sleepy again. In a saddle, she'd snoozed before, awakening if the horse changed gait, but bareback, she worried she'd fall.

So, Cody did what came easy: imagined Uncle Michael in front of her, like her mother had said they'd ride when she was young. His back straight and his cotton shirt cool against her palms. If she relaxed, she'd slump against him and he wouldn't let her fall. With her eyes closed, Cody could feel Uncle Michael's warmth in front of her. She opened her eyes and yes, there he was—his shirt white. His long hair dipped past his collar.

After five, ten minutes they came to a fence line, an old split rail, not the barbed wire that separated their land from the Forest Service. A bit after that, Cody saw light in the distance and by the time she figured out she was coming at the Lindsays' place from the south, the house dogs had begun to bark. Mr. Doyle was out to meet them before they reached the dirt driveway. This was the back way, a route you never went unless you were coming from up the hill cutting wood. Cody could not wrap her mind around it. How could she have been twenty minutes from the Lindsays' and not known where she was?

Entering the kitchen's warmth, she shivered. Cody could tell things were serious with Mrs. Lindsay up, in the kitchen in her nightgown. She was sickly, people said, with terrible headaches and a tiredness that moved in and lasted for months. A few weeks before, she'd been in the hospital again, and Margaret went over some nights to make dinner for the family, or sent the girls over with a casserole. Cody hadn't seen Mrs. Lindsay in a month or more, but there she was at the stove, her calves visible between the hem of her robe and her slippers, as small as a bird's legs. Her hair was puffy in back, but neat around her face.

Clint and Nate were in bed, Cody hoped. She couldn't bear any teasing. Mrs. Lindsay made her a cup of hot cocoa and rubbed her shoulders. Cody tried to explain but being lost was hard to put into words. She couldn't even remember the cattle brand, a clue to where she might have been. But Mrs. Lindsay hushed her and pulled Cody's head to her thin chest. "You must have been so frightened, child," she said. "But now you're safe." Her fingers were dry on Cody's cheek and thin as bones.

Mr. Doyle called her parents. "She's here," he said. "I'll run her home." When she emptied her mug, Cody thought of Daisy and rushed outside but Mr. Doyle had already put the horse in a stall and given her water and hay. Even though it was after midnight, Daisy ate. She kissed Daisy's nose and beneath Cody's lips, the horse's big jaws moved her muzzle while she chewed.

Mr. Doyle drove Cody home in his new truck, which she was almost too tired to notice, though the dashboard lights were different than his ranch truck, all kinds of symbols and flashes and dings. The moon cast a milky light over the road beyond the headlights.

"Half moon," said Mr. Doyle. "When the light's on her right, she's increasing in might, when the light's on her left, she's growing bereft."

"What's 'bereft'?" asked Cody.

"Sad," said Mr. Doyle. "Though in this case, it means waning."

Cody filed the rhyme away.

She was so exhausted, her head felt detached from her body. Mr. Doyle drove slowly and the needles of the pines against the dark looked so sharp that Cody thought they could puncture the sky, send it rocketing around like a popped balloon, shedding all its stars. The heater hummed its hot breath into the cab and her eyes narrowed and narrowed until they closed.

The next morning when Cody awoke in her own bed in her clothes, she knew she had fallen asleep on the way home, even though the drive was less than ten minutes and Mr. Doyle would have gotten in and out of the cab several times to open and shut the gates.

"Who carried me in?" Cody asked when she came into the kitchen. Being asleep in Mr. Doyle's arms seemed excruciatingly babyish.

"I carried you," said Josiah. He'd have been waiting outside in the driveway. "You were a sack of potatoes," he said, and roughed her hair with both hands.

Her mother hugged her so hard it hurt her neck.

"Don't you ever do that again." Margaret held her away at arm's length and lifted Cody's chin with her hand. "What happened to you?"

Cody decided to keep the stampede to herself. "I got lost, but I don't know how." She didn't mention Uncle Michael either, or the feeling she'd had, like the world was a hole you could fall down.

"If you knew, you wouldn't be lost," said her mother.

Josiah went to get Daisy. "When I come back, we'll go look for that saddle," he said. Cody had forgotten about the saddle, an oversight almost as sickening as losing it in the first place. A saddle was expensive, and hers was extra special, an heirloom, not to mention the blanket, which her father had had since he was a little boy and had never lost. Mr. Doyle must have told him the saddle was gone.

"Pop, I didn't, I—Daisy had a sore and when I unbuckled it to check, the saddle slid off and I couldn't get it back on without the stump. It was really cold." She finally cried. Josiah hugged her then, a quick squeeze. He walked to the Lindsays' to ride Daisy home.

Margaret cradled Cody's face between her palms. "Listen to me. You're a brave, brave kid. We'll find the saddle." Cody wasn't sure.

Later that morning they went out to look, Cody on Louisa's horse, Charlie, so Daisy could rest. Louisa had play practice and was gone before Cody woke, but she sent "good vibes," Margaret said, using her fingers to quote Louisa's words. Cody led her parents up the back road and told about the route she had followed Brindle home. The fence line, the boulder field, the two lakes. It took hours, and they made a circle twenty minutes wide in every direction. Margaret spotted the saddle first and kicked her horse toward it in a trot. Cody followed and when she glimpsed the shine of leather nestled in the brush, she was so relieved she almost cried again. So much crying. The saddle looked misplaced, and Cody tried to explain how, in the dark, it had seemed like an edge, the safest place to leave something behind. The blanket was gone. They looked all over on foot but it was nowhere. Bad things were adding up. The blanket lost, Daisy's sore, not knowing where she was. All of them were bad, but the last one was worst.

"You weren't too far from home," Josiah said. "A mile, maybe."

"I know," said Cody. She started to say how at night, coming from a different way, everything was backwards, but even to her own ears it was an excuse. She knew the blame was in the half an hour with the cows. Even in your own place, you had to pay attention.

AFTER GRANDPA BLANCHARD'S FUNERAL, Uncle Michael meant to stay a week, but he decided to leave early. Raised voices from the living room drew the girls to lie on their bellies at the heating grate, where they sometimes listened to their parents argue about money, or, after school conferences, discuss what their teachers had said. Now Margaret tried to convince her brother to stay. "Michael," she said, "please. No one—" It was quiet. "I think they're hugging," whispered Louisa. The heat kicked on and blew dust up, which made Louisa run to her pillow and muffle her sneeze.

The last afternoon before Uncle Michael left, Louisa brought up a handful of grapefruits from the box in the root cellar. 4-H sold them every winter for a fundraiser, and Louisa had won a prize for the second-highest sales. Louisa said, "For you to play Little House at home." Uncle Michael laughed and tucked them into his pockets. "My, what a generous gift!" He got the voice just right.

The girls were out front in the yard throwing snowballs at the fenceposts when Mr. Lindsay dropped in to say goodbye on his way into town with Clint, who waited in the truck. He hardly talked to them lately. Nate said he was a rotten jerk. A brother could say that easier and mean it less, but not how Nate said it. You knew it was true.

Once Mr. Doyle was inside the house, Clint leaned out the window and said in his hoarse, almost-changing voice, "Your uncle is a fairy."

"He is *not*," said Louisa.

"Yeah he is," said Clint. He was such a know-it-all. Louisa stamped her foot.

"Well, you're an asshole," she said. Cody palmed a tight, wet snowball and chucked it at the windshield but Clint didn't flinch.

"What a potty mouth, Miss Louisa." Clint's tone taunted, mean as mean could be. If Mr. Doyle heard, Clint would be in trouble, but the adults were inside, and tattling was awful. Cody knew that's exactly why bullies picked times when no one was watching. Bullies were smart. When Mr. Doyle left, Clint said goodbye to Louisa and Cody with his hand out the window, twiddling the fingers in a stupid little wave.

"What's a fairy?" Cody asked Louisa in bed that night, whispering, in case Uncle Michael was still downstairs. He slept at Grandma's house but stayed late talking.

"I think it's because he lives in a city. It means he can't ride, I think. He can't shoot. It's not good."

"Who cares what Clint Lindsay says. Mama said they always used to ride. I like Uncle Michael."

"He gave you his saddle, of course you would."

"Before that, I mean. I liked him before. He tells good stories. I like his voice."

"Girls," Louisa said, "I can't believe how big you are, girls, how lovely you both are, so like my sisters, prettiest girls in town!" She imitated his speech, breathy with a flourish as if he were in a play, but it sounded fake, almost mocking, while Uncle Michael's tone was kind. Louisa sighed. "That's not quite it."

"Don't do that, Louisa," Cody said.

"I won't," said Louisa.

UNCLE MICHAEL SENT A POSTCARD from California every Christmas, but they never saw him again before he died. For years after his visit, Cody thought of him when she rode on the shiny saddle that had once been his. He was never closer than the night she was lost, though, before the moon came up and Brindle appeared, when she knew just what it meant to feel strange in your own home.

CODY KINZLER

HEY, JESS MCCAFFERTY, what are you doing here? I've never seen you in our store before. I bet you're looking for my sister, but she isn't here, and even if she was, I'd say, "Louisa isn't here right now," because she doesn't love you anyway, Jess. I know you know who I am, but you walk by without a word—what's so interesting about the floor? Do you know I'm by myself? Pop trusts me, even though I'm younger than Louisa, and besides, she has better things to do than hang around in a hardware store all summer. She says, "You'll get it when you're fifteen." But I like the smell of the linseed oil Pop rubs into the countertop, and the light in the glass above the front door. I can read when the store's empty. Louisa, she likes things faster. "You can sleep when you're dead" is what she says.

You think my sister's in love with you, don't you, Jess? I know she's made you think so, sneaking out the window at night, dropping onto the flowers, into your hands. But sisters get each other, and that's how I know, she's making a fool out of you, Jess. She likes you okay, how your eyes make her feel, like it's hot under her skin. But like and love are two different things. "Louisa, you better look out," I tell her, but she already knows.

You only smile at me because I'm her little sister, otherwise you'd never even see a girl like me, would you? Well, you know what, Jess, Louisa lets me borrow her clothes—I'm wearing her jeans right now, the ones she embroidered at the hem. We wear the same size, but she likes them tight and I like them baggy. "You're so lucky, Cody, you're so skinny," my sister says, and she won't eat at dinner sometimes and she stands in front of the mirror at night and sucks in her cheeks and holds the skin around her middle with both hands. Hey, Jess, did you know that me and Louisa have shared a room since I was born? I could tell my sister from a hundred strangers lying down in the dark, just by the way she breathes.

I know how far she let you go, Jess. Does that shock you? She tells me stuff she doesn't even tell her friends. Never mind what she tells you. I heard her say, "Oh Pop, don't worry, he's definitely not my boyfriend." She rolls her eyes and twists her necklaces around her hand. If I told you that right now, Jess, you'd drop your eyes and smile and you'd act like you didn't care, but if my sister didn't love you and you knew it, you'd care.

Sometimes Louisa lies on the bed on her back and she traces the outline of herself. She presses her finger into the top of her head, runs it along her hair, down over her ear, under her chin where it meets her neck and all the way down until she can't reach without bending and then she starts up the other side. Let me tell you, Jess, Louisa knows where she starts and where she ends.

What are you up to, Jess, running those hands over everything? Don't you know what you're looking for? I bet it's not sandpaper. I'm not going to ask you if you need any help. If you need it, you can ask me. Do you even know my name? I think you do, even though I know Louisa doesn't talk about me when you two park in your junky pickup. I've watched you, Jess, the way you jog alongside her in the dark as she tilts her head away. In the morning, I can see the places where your feet pressed down the wet grass, and she tells me where you went and what you did anyway, so you've got no secrets from me, Jess McCafferty.

Are you still watching to see if she's going to come out from the curtain behind the register? Are you looking at me? You think I don't see you because I'm reading, but it's only a catalog for lawn tools. You're used to eyes on you, anyway, aren't you, Jess, all the girls in three grades crazy about you, something about your tan arms and faded shirts and the way your bones fit under the skin of your face.

But come on, Jess, you can see she isn't here so you might as well leave because you are starting to look aimless, and I don't think that's how you want to look. My father will be back any minute, and he'll notice you, you can bet. Is this how you first looked at Louisa, quick meeting her eyes, then smiling after you look away? You can't love her like she needs to be loved, Jess McCafferty. She's too much for you, and deep down, you already know. You need a different kind of girl and I'm not saying she's me, but just think twice about Louisa.

You guess I can't see you over there? I saw you slip that knife in your pocket, looking at me between the shelves. Who do you think you are? It doesn't matter what I say, does it, Jess. I can't change how you feel about Louisa. But I could get you in such trouble, I could tell my father like that, you know. I'd do it, too, watch me. Hey Pop, I'd say, Jess McCafferty was around here today, looking for Louisa, taking what isn't his.

THE CABIN (1989)

WHEN JOSIAH MOVED OUT, Margaret was not surprised. Beneath his steady patience a restlessness yawned, and the past nine months, far worse than that—ordinary melancholy turned to an anxious torpor that settled in the house like a skiff of dust. First, they chalked it up to winter—the lessening light had affected his moods for years—but come spring, the returning sun didn't lift him.

In the barn one morning, the girls at school, Josiah pitched clean hay into troughs—Louisa's job, undone—and Margaret rummaged among the handled tools for a hoe.

His voice stopped her, her name spoken serious, one word with silence all around it. Yes? Margaret said, and Josiah explained what he was thinking with his back to her and he did not see the way she paused, one hand on the wall. Javier's cabin down below the house, he said. He'd fix it up. Walking distance. He'd be out, but not gone.

"Can we try?" Josiah said, turning toward her, finally still. He looked at the floor as he spoke. "I've been . . . unhappy. I know it hasn't been easy."

Margaret waited.

"Maybe this can change something," he said.

Margaret looked at him straight. "It's hard not to feel you're leaving, Josiah. A step at a time. If that's what this is, I'd rather you just go."

She paused, then spoke again, braver than she felt. "If you need to, you can go."

But Josiah took her by the shoulders and shook his head. He pulled her forehead in so it pressed his and whispered. *Please.*

Margaret tamped the urge to cling and instead let him go after what he was always looking for: some room of his own to move around in. Between the house and the woodshop at the property corner stood a small cabin, built by Javier, the ranch manager from back when Josiah's father trained horses for a few years. Josiah had admired him urgently. Javi, he called himself, or *gaucho,* for a joke. Quick and easy with animals, he could fix or rig anything and was kinder to Josiah than any grown man had yet been. All summer, Josiah helped Javi lift the cabin logs into place and mend tools, eager for any task, and Javi helped Josiah build sawhorses, the boy's first complete project, from drawn plans to the last driven nail. Those sawhorses still stood in the barn, faded and rickety where the nail holes had widened in the aging wood. The girls' saddles sat on top.

The cabin was ordinary: 14 × 14, three-sided logs chinked along the lengths. A narrow bed under a paned window, a countertop made of slabbed log. Attached to the built-in pantry wall, a hinged table: up, the legs swung flat and it covered the shelves, and folded down, it fit four leggy stools. There was a wood-burning cook stove with a pancake griddle built in and an old icebox. No interior walls, all open. Whatever was in a certain corner made it that room. Couch—living room. Food—kitchen.

Once Josiah got the idea to move to the cabin, it was hard to believe he hadn't thought of it before. When he was in the woodshop, he could look out the window above the tool bench and see the cabin's chimney stack, to gauge if the woodstove needed tending. If the cabin was plain, the shop was a proud accomplishment. Open and light, every local tree represented. A project a man would want his father to see, but when Josiah finished it soon after Cody was born, he imagined it through Javi's eyes instead: a square room under a steep-pitched roof, high enough for lumber laid across the rafters under the peak, long lengths sorted and shelved like library books: sawn boards, peeled poles, trim. Javier had left after only one season—he had a young family in Mexico, and anyway, no one lasted, working for Hank, a hard and stingy boss who ranted more than he paid. One morning in the fall Javier wasn't there when Josiah went out to the barn, and when Josiah asked his father where Javi had gone, Hank only said, "They can't be relied on." Josiah knew about Javi's daughters—one Josiah's own age—and how he missed his wife, who he'd known since they were children, and whose photo he'd kept, creased near to ripping, in the back pocket of his faded jeans. Josiah had seen the picture so many times he could remember the woman's face, but Hank didn't even know about Javi's daughters. When he was much older, Josiah knew reasons Javi might have had to leave without a goodbye, but even as a child, Josiah knew a "him" from a "them." His father never did.

Neither the cabin nor the shop had ever been plumbed, but water flowed from a wellhead put in by an earlier owner who meant to build a house there. A deep, stainless-steel sink stood out back, with a water barrel filled by gutter runoff, and there, Josiah brushed his teeth, ran wash water, cleaned trout. At the kitchen sink in the cabin, a metal canister water jug with a tiny spigot, which Josiah kept filled from the wellhead with five-gallon buckets, one hanging from each hand. When it was too cold to shower with a watering can hung from the eave, Josiah planned his baths for evenings at the big house, dinner with the girls and Margaret. Several meals per week, one bath.

"I'll be back and forth. I want you to come to me anytime," Josiah said when he told the girls about the new arrangement. "I don't mean to disappear from you."

I need to see myself, he did not say. The girls were quizzical, and he let Margaret explain: "Your father has had a hard winter." They'd known that all along.

"A big fat grouchy bummer of a winter, actually," Louisa said. They laughed, all of them, relief shouldering in, at least for a moment.

"Thank you," Josiah told them. Cody sidled up and nudged her head under his arm the way a horse would, looking for sugar or an open palm on its mane. Watching them, Margaret's optimism poked up like a green shoot beneath a load of dirt and sadness.

The furniture stayed at the main house, all the pieces Josiah had built in the way he'd become known for. His reputation was growing. People talked about the objects, but also, how he made them. Josiah found his wood in the forest, where he chose fallen trees that came down in storms, some green and splintered, some dry winterkill, wind-stacked in tangled piles. He cut standing live trees, too, a few truckloads per season, for projects where pliable green wood was better than dead. The trees were largely softwoods, conifers, and Josiah was partial to ponderosa pine, Doug fir, some larch. Hardwoods meant diamond willow for intricate detail, or paper birch, its bent lines pale and intimate, even the bark a treasure. Aside from the materials to frame his shop, Josiah rarely bought lumber. The point was working with wood he could see standing out the back door. When he had to purchase a two-by, he'd look for a waned edge, knots in the face grain, or whorls the mill couldn't plane out. He craved the unwieldy, what others passed over. Dead or split or gnarled.

Finding the wood could take as long as hauling it out. Josiah walked the forest for days. Shopping, he called it. When he found a good tree he felled it, or, if already down by winter or wind, he bucked it into moveable sections and dragged it to his truck, with a tow strap looped through the eye if he was alone, which he often was, and sometimes with the Swede hook, his arms awkward behind him and a taut pain in his shoulders. The log tong was really a tool meant for two. When Cody grew old enough to help, she would grab the other end of the hook's handle, but she was small and Josiah tried not to lift too hard and pinch her hands against the ground, or push her backwards as he leaned into the weight. Teaching her how to move and carry slowed him down some, but he was glad to do it. Cody furrowed her nose, trying to lift like he did, and bit her lip with her tiny teeth, white as a young dog's.

Josiah piled the hauled logs on the side of the nearest logging road until he carted them home on his old F-350 flatbed with stake sides and humped front wheel wells. In the yard he straddled the log and peeled off the bark in long strands, his forearms pumping. A green log shot pockets of sap, which could make an eye run worse than onions. When a log was stripped to its white slippery core, Josiah left it to bake through the hot months, covered by a tarp in rainy June, and then, before the wet fall set in, he stored it to cure in the shed for a year. As he bucked the chosen logs into measured sections, he began to see clearly the pieces he had imagined when first he scouted the trees: long logs for a tabletop, small rounds for the seat of a stool. Some logs he milled into boards pinned with bricks and rocks to prevent warp and cupping as they dried. Cody collected flat stones and trundled them up the gravel driveway to Josiah's shop in her yellow metal wagon. A wheelbarrow when she was old enough to balance it on its single tire.

Josiah learned to plan ahead. The small mills had closed and Boise Cascade wouldn't do an odd job anymore, so there was little room for a last-minute order, or a clean slate if he botched a piece. He meant to buy a portable sawmill and prep other people's wood, but money was tight and he could not justify the expense until his own pieces had begun to earn. He had a Stihl 066 chainsaw with an Alaskan mill, a simple metal frame attached to a bar thirty inches long, and with it he'd rip rough boards and plane them flat enough that on top of a finished table, you could balance a coin on its edge. He left his pieces unstained, only a clear oil coat to show the grain, unless he was asked to do otherwise. He wouldn't use paint.

Josiah had begun making furniture for the house when he and Margaret were first married, before Louisa was born. He'd sold nothing for years, and the house grew full as a showroom. Inside, the furniture forgot him. In a hallway, a kitchen, he rammed his limbs against corners of tables and found it hard to sit comfortably on the kitchen bench. He knocked over glasses, broke towel racks and knick-knacks, banged his shins. The legs of chairs tripped him up. All the grace he could manage went into the making. Once finished, they became household objects like any others and he fumbled around them, off-kilter, apologizing.

Cody's bed he made of ash a year before she used it, unwilling as she was to move out of her crib, where she stayed until her toes pressed the foot board and she slept at an angle to straighten her legs. She felt safe there, Josiah knew it, and when she said she didn't want a big girl bed, they let her stay. I'm a small girl, she told them. And she was, tiny for so long, they almost worried. Small-boned, a little bird of a kid who Louisa could pick up and sling around like a backpack, strapping Cody's thin arms over her shoulders, their hands buckled. The bed stayed in the shed where Josiah made it, taking up too much room. When Cody finally allowed it into her bedroom, Josiah unpegged the slats and the frame and hauled it up the stairs in pieces. Cody watched from the corner of the room as silent and watchful as a spy.

It's not so bad, kiddo, he told her the first night he tucked her into the bed. You'll be used to this one in a week, you'll forget about the crib. As he told her this he wondered if she would. Cody had a way of holding on to things—persistence, you'd call it one time, stubbornness another—much longer than you'd think a child could. It was daunting.

Eventually, Cody grew. She got strong enough to grab the lowest branch of the elm in the front yard, jumping to catch it in her palms and chin-up like a tiny Marine before swinging her legs and pulling herself up with her clasped bare feet. Cody was tall by high school, though she remained delicate, offset against a steely manner, as if to make up for her little bones.

JOSIAH HELD INSIDE HIMSELF an inventory of projects gone wrong. A perfect slab wasted, a cracked mortise, the half-built pieces he'd racked apart with a crowbar, or thrown onto the burn pile, lit before anyone could see. Also, a list of his favorites, never mentioned, unwilling to let himself rest in what felt too much like pride. From a chunk of mahogany Margaret found at a ranch auction, he'd fashioned the breadbox that sat on the countertop. A Doug fir rocking horse he'd made for the girls with a saddle seat long enough to ride double. A piece of ash became a box with a wooden latch that he kept on the dresser, locked. And Margaret's mirror, the full-length glass rimmed by redwood that pivoted on a dowel, the ends, outside the frame, carved to mimic cones. A friend had brought him the old beams salvaged from a building in Butte that was torn down after a fire. When he first worked the redwood, carving arcs from charred angles, his hands smelled like smoke for days.

Josiah gave Margaret the mirror for Christmas one year when the girls were small. After Margaret put them to bed, Cody still in her cramped crib, they opened their gifts together. For Margaret, a wrapped note under the tree: *go upstairs in our room*. Josiah followed her, nervous as a boy who had chosen jewelry for the first time. When he looked into the room, he wished he had tied a ribbon around the mirror, to indicate it was the gift. He was relieved when Margaret walked straight to it and laid her hand flat on the glass. She rocked it gently back and forth on its fulcrum and smiled, meeting his eye in the reflection.

A few years later, during the first dark time after they'd married, Josiah walked in on Margaret brushing her hair at the mirror, seated in the wicker chair that had come from her great-aunt

Binnie, and smoothing the hair from her part down over her shoulders as if she were petting a mane. He had never seen this gesture from her before, taking such focused care with herself. He backed out of the room quietly so as not to disturb her but she heard him and stopped. Josiah froze in the doorway; he knew how little she liked to be watched.

She dropped her hand from hair to lap. Am I beautiful, Margaret said, as uninflected as if asking what time a person would be home. He nodded, maybe he said *mm-hmm*, though later he could only recall silence. She got up and they both left the room. The question surprised him, as he'd thought her beauty so clear as to never need mention. If it was sunny and anyone could see it, you wouldn't ask about the weather. Of course, what Margaret meant was "Am I beautiful to you?" and that was quite different. She was. He wished he'd told her so.

MARGARET AND JOSIAH STAYED MARRIED. What people thought, what the arrangement looked like from afar, that made a story of sorts, but no one else's take was quite right. Margaret and Josiah worked it out, devised a life some others might have longed for, if they had thought to try. When Josiah came up to the house for dinner he walked across the field in six minutes, not via the road, out and around two miles the way you'd come by car. He slept at Margaret's place once a week, maybe more. The girls went back and forth between like the land was one big house, half of its rooms outside.

It was not how Margaret thought she would live with her husband. Sometimes it was not the way she wanted. But, she would say this—it was honest. There was nothing between them measly and dark, a resentment that grew by eating itself. After they'd kissed that time at the State Fair, Margaret thought but did not say to Josiah, when you kiss me, you're opening a door. Over years of their marriage—any marriage, she guessed—doors had opened and closed, sometimes slammed. Now the room itself had changed.

The first week after Josiah moved down to the cabin, Margaret went out to feed the hens and check for eggs, and there was a difference. A new space around her. It took a few days to set in, but that morning, outside in the early sun with the girls off to school, she felt newly attuned. The barbed wire at the top of the garden plot to keep out the deer—twisted and rusty, dew globes glinting on the spikes—reminded her of Christmas lights strung around a tiny, roofless house. The last patch of nearby snow hunkered on the north side of the chicken shed, iced at the edges, the top strewn with melted indents of needles. Up in the hills, more snow, but thawing fast, and the sun not quite above the ridge yet, though soon it would be. The world roomy, as if she could grow to fit it.

The chicken hutch was quiet when she entered. She moved through the roosts to lift eggs out of the straw in the empty boxes, rousing the resting chickens into noise. They shook their bodies and loose feathers shed from stretched wings. The friendly birds approached her as always in a rushing pile, like kids pushing for a treat, Lady Red walking figure eights around Margaret's slightly spaced feet. The white ones had come from Doyle as older birds, not raised from chicks, and they were always aloof. White chickens, Snow and Lacy and Mashed Potatoes—Mashy, for short. The girls were good at names.

What did it mean that the world felt roomy? Nothing she'd anticipated, or thought to express. Margaret had let Josiah go because he asked her to. Set them free and they will return, she knew that. But now that he was gone—not far—she couldn't deny her gain. Josiah's ups and downs, a bit removed, did not press so heavily on her. She could wake with her own plans, her own moods. Margaret had always shifted herself too easily, she knew, even with her sister, her mother: their anger made her timid. Josiah's sadness, it tired her. Now, without him nearby to rest on, her mind wandered in its own way. She liked it. There was a lot to think about.

Josiah took little with him to the cabin. His favorite mug, an afghan, the goods that made a home: a door mat, a coffee pot, candles. At the house he left most of the books (Margaret read five to his one), and all of the furniture, even his bureau of clothes. He wore the same pants and shirts for days in a row until they were dirty, and he traded them in for a nearly identical set. Margaret washed his clothes with the family's—removing foam earplugs from pockets and shaking his pants to loosen the woodchips from cuffs and creases—and returned them, folded, to his drawers.

The animals sorted themselves. Brisket followed Josiah everywhere, and Margaret kept the rest, the chickens, the ducks, the barn cats, and Jade, who rarely left the girls' sides. The horses and mules lived in the barn near the house and Josiah came up to ride from there. The animals didn't belong to buildings, not even to people. They answered to the land more than anything.

JADE

I TAUGHT BOTH GIRLS how to walk on ice and when they were small their father did not allow them on lakes or rivers no matter how frozen without me. They never knew this rule, but I did: if they wandered in winter, I followed them close. My feet can tell hard ice from thin. I can sense water beneath snow and weave around open leads and find a path that keeps my paws dry. No one in boots can detect this.

Often the ice nearest shore is thinnest, and other times, out in the middle where the ice has been solid for long paces, a hole will open and the water there is deep. Ice can feel many ways. Cracking is easy to sense and so is ice as firm as ground, but other forms are hard to know. If you step out onto ice and hear a boom or a crack like a shotgun, be cautious, but not afraid. Deep sound means a hard freeze. Shallow ice will crack but not resound. Snow on top of ice looks solid but can be dangerous because you cannot see a thinning.

When the winters were strong, I wore a harness and pulled the girls on their small sled and as far as snow covered the ground, they could ride. They dragged the sled to the top of the low hills and slid down and shouted. The faster they flew, the more I barked and ran. I could not help myself.

In summer, the children went without their boots and their feet looked pale and worrisome. They never licked their soles or cleaned between their toes. Sometimes I do it for them still, though skin without fur feels foreign to my tongue and I can taste their socks much stronger than their skin. My own feet taste of every place I've walked, and the creatures who walked there before me.

I eat the dry biscuits the girls hide in their pockets because they smile and pat my head but best is the taste of their fingers when the biscuit is gone. I sleep curled in the woodshed where the chips from split firewood cover the ground. They have made houses for Brisket and me and painted our names on the top and on cold nights I am invited to sleep inside with the cats, but I prefer the shed to all. I can see and smell the night. I can rise any time and mark the fence and watch for owls and listen to the dark. I keep them safe. The mother sleeps in the house with the girls. She has always known the best ways to stroke my fur and arrange my bones. She pulls my legs and kneads the web of skin between the pads of my toes and I can close my eyes. Her hands will never hurt me. I rest. My legs run and twitch in my sleep. I think that is what they call happiness.

The girls are older now and I do not have to keep watch so close. They come and go, the bigger girl with boys, the younger one more frequently alone. Lately a new man comes to visit the father in his workshop. He is taller and his voice is bright. He helps carry one end of a log or move the noisy tools. Sometimes I rest on the cabin porch during the day and keep watch over them instead. The new man smells of his clothes and his soap. It is hard to smell his body, though if I lean on his legs I can find it. His hands are clean. He scratches between my ears without looking at me but his fingers are firm. When the younger girl comes down to the shop he pulls back from the father and his task and goes to greet her. Freddy, she calls him. She has never seen the way his hands seek each side of the father's face, and rest there. It is summer now. I have never seen him walk on ice.

MARKET DAY (1990)

NEXT TO THE TRAIN DEPOT in West Glacier, a weekly summer market had sprung up, a small cluster of ten to fifteen artisans, Josiah and Cody among them the last two weeks. Margaret talked him into it. New customers, she said. He needed those. Business was steady, but still not quite enough to justify quitting the hardware store, which he badly wanted to do. Margaret's father had started that store from a one-room hobby—a junk drawer too big for its britches, he used to say—and Josiah and Margaret had managed it for Mr. Blanchard since he retired only a few years before he died. Now, Josiah worked one long day a week, most operations left to Margaret. Mrs. Blanchard had moved to Great Falls to live with her sister Abigail and rescinded all care about the store. "I have no interest," she said. They'd have to decide—sell it, hire it out, pass it on to the girls. Mrs. Blanchard kept her thoughts to herself. She didn't trouble with what others might or might not do.

If Josiah thought about his father-in-law he could become anxious, projecting Mr. Blanchard's disappointment, were he still alive. Josiah could not explain it to convince a businessman, his reasons transcending profit or loss, but he wanted to give the wood a whole try. He hoped jobs might come in steady enough to bank on. It was a way to stay alive, that was another of Josiah's thoughts, which he never said out loud. To Mr. Blanchard, staying alive was a given. What else would a man do? Any words sounded more dream than plan, most real when Josiah didn't think about it directly or try to explain. His father-in-law was dead, so he didn't have to. Josiah's work had begun to draw attention, clients approaching each month, but it remained to be seen if people passing through the area would pay for his pieces at a market. Locals knew to find him at home.

The booth—a lumber and plywood frame tarped with an army green oilcloth—held two or three pieces of furniture, luminous showstoppers that would catch anyone's eye (though who would buy a vanity, passing through on a train?) and then a few folding tables spread with smaller pieces. A handheld mirror, stones inlaid among the wooden slats. Boxes of all sizes, small for matches or cigars, one large enough to store a rifle. At the cash table, Josiah worked on a jewelry box, attaching the metal clasp and gouging out a spot where the tiny hinges could imbed, their shape mimicking whorls in the grain. Cody was fourteen and wandered in and out of the stall helping Josiah, then roving away after some kid her age, or a loose dog.

The artisans around Josiah's booth varied. One woman sold home-canned fruit preserves and her booth glimmered like a jewelry shop as sunlight refracted off peaches and cherries and huckleberries in glass. Another man sold elk jerky and preserved meat of all kinds—buffalo, venison, strips of dried rabbit. His orange vinyl banners lined the highway: BEST MEAT IN WEST. Despite an aversion to sitting on a stool in front of his wares, Josiah thought himself a good addition. You could stock a pantry, then buy shelves for it. He wasn't too proud to try.

Josiah had been sitting alone, Cody off to buy hotdogs, when he became aware of a man at the front of his booth, tall, a little stooped, opening the doors to a cabinet and closing them again. The latch caught with a satisfying click. It was the first item a passer-by could see, no glass yet, but shelves inside doors with empty windows framed. Putting glass in a piece of furniture that still had to be moved several times seemed imprudent, at best. Unlike most browsers who stopped at the stand, this man was neither someone Josiah knew, nor a tourist. The latter were obvious, easy to recognize by their Glacier Park T-shirts and tiny bear bells strapped to purses and belt loops, their talk among each other either loose and unburdened, or with the stressed undertones particular to people on vacation, worried about their budget, the train departure, or whether it would rain. This man moved through the tables and along the edges looking at the pieces, with no gesture indicating awareness of anyone else, so Josiah worked at the hinges. Tighten, open, shut, sand, a little oil. Give a man some space. Josiah never exactly forgot him, but when the man spoke it was a surprise.

"You can't possibly make a living from this."

It was barely the polite side of a sneer. The man hedged closer in, running his hands over the furniture, not carefully, not as if to inspect, but greedy and distant at once like a hungry man at a buffet finding nothing he liked to eat. Defense rose in Josiah. His fists clenched, and he released them.

"It's nice enough stuff, but really." The man chuckled, a nasal rattle. "I'm not talking hand-to-mouth—an actual living, enough to feed your family?"

"How do you know I have a family?" Josiah said. He pictured himself alone in the woodshop in the evenings, speaking to no one for days except Freddy who'd come a few times a week, and sometimes stay. His lips, his narrow waist belted in his jeans.

The man stopped and looked at Josiah, his mouth pursed. "I guess I don't know the first thing about you, do I." With his half smile, one eye narrowed, as if his face could not commit to an expression.

Josiah shook his head. "No, you don't." He moved around the tables, gathering his scattered supplies. He brushed a pile of finish nails into his hand and his fist closed around it, a sharp metal stash against his palm. He circled his space tight, the way an animal would if it sensed a threat.

"I've heard a bit about you, though," said the man. "My brother knows you."

"Who's your brother," said Josiah.

"Freddy Coughlin."

Freddy already in his mind—he often was—Josiah started, as if he'd conjured up this man to police his thoughts.

"Ah. Mr. Coughlin. I wish you had introduced yourself right away." Josiah did not like to be kept in the dark. He did not care for a man saying one thing and meaning a hundred others. It set him on guard.

"Freddy has been a big help to me," said Josiah. "My wife encouraged me to take an apprentice, for the jobs I can delegate. My girls do some too."

"Ah," said the brother. "Wife, girls. There is a family, then."

"You knew that," said Josiah. The man gave one nod and nothing further.

Josiah knew that he wouldn't do this again. Margaret would be disappointed; it was simple for her, chatting with strangers and moving from one task to the next. She put others at ease. But he didn't see the point in displaying himself like this. Anyone at all could come and talk, when perhaps their reasons for stopping had little to do with the furniture. They might be trying to find things out, wanting to convince, or convict.

Earlier that day one disheveled man with untied bootlaces dragging beneath his feet had stopped at each vendor's stall, seeking a new audience for his ranting: who was in bed with whom, how they were all fucked. On his way from Josiah's stall to the next one, the man stepped on a shoelace and nearly tripped himself, as if he were drunk. His eyes were loose and baggy and his voice too loud, but it wasn't alcohol that made him unkempt.

Later, a missionary couple wandered in, Mormons, perhaps, but it wasn't clear, even after Josiah looked over the pamphlet they left when he said he didn't want to talk about God or his son, sending them off, polite, but firm. "He died for you," they said on their way out, but since they'd never mentioned Jesus by name, it sounded sinister. Strange, that you'd go through the trouble of printing up a pamphlet meant to convert people to or from something—eternal salvation, the error of their ways—and not make it clear who you were. What were your stakes? It was the God part that mattered, he supposed, if it mattered at all, which to him, it did not. People were so convinced of their beliefs, but zeal troubled Josiah. He wondered how it arose, if such clarity was a habit you tended toward, or grew into. Was there anything he'd die for? He couldn't be sure.

The man spoke loud enough to startle Josiah again. "I wanted to check you out." He threaded his fingers and bent them back until they gave an ominous crack. "Freddy's been spending so much time, I'd like to know who with."

"With me. With my wife, with my girls."

Freddy's first days at the ranch came to his mind, how Cody had turned toward him like arnica to sun and even Louisa, focused on her impending move to college in Oregon and barely home, basked in the light he brought.

"See, Pop, Freddy left home," Louisa told him the first night they all had dinner together up at the house. "Tell him, Freddy. It isn't just me."

Josiah picked at the hinges and waited for the man to speak again.

"I wanted to meet you. To make your acquaintance," said the man.

"Well, we haven't," said Josiah. "Met."

The man forced a slight smile. His lips were chapped, the skin under his nose and at the edges of his mouth raw, as if from wind, or rough kissing. Josiah guessed wind.

"You haven't said your name, asked mine, shaken my hand," said Josiah. "That's making an acquaintance." He stuck out his hand then, against his leanings—Josiah Kinzler, he said—and the man took it as if accepting a snake. His firm grip was a surprise and though usually Josiah clasped hard, he flinched at the man's clammy palm and forced himself to press it, a second too late. The man raised his eyebrows again, the air of superiority he had exuded since arriving thick enough to touch. Josiah wished he could pick up a mood in a hand and toss it behind him, beneath the table with the wood shavings and dust. Start this encounter over, or end it before it began.

He lifted his eyes to see Cody elbowing through tourists with the hotdogs she'd gone for. The Assembly of God ran a grill stand near the depot. Nice enough folks, not too pushy. A doughy youth pastor and a rotating cadre of dads, some he knew from the sidelines of school sports, their cheering vigorous. Josiah and Cody had called that church "The Ass of God" for years, a joke that arose between them as they drove past the sign when Cody was learning to read and sounded out the words slow. They never made the joke in front of Margaret. She'd say, "You two are terrible," and shake her head.

Cody had reinvented the joke at their first market, the week before: "I smell the Ass of God," she'd said when the men in their clean pressed jeans and football sweatshirts fired up the barbecue. Josiah laughed hard the first time she said it, her face so straight you'd hardly guess she understood her own humor. Now she opened the steamy bag and handed him two hotdogs in damp waxed paper, overflowing with relish, the ketchup coagulating. It reminded Josiah of blood at the edges of an open wound. Did the church folks think of Christ's sacrifice when they squirted lines from the big plastic bottles? All the Christians he'd known craved symbolism. He set the food on the table. Cody met Josiah's eye and looked at the man, sidelong, a quiet question.

"Cody, this is Freddy Coughlin's brother. I haven't gotten his name yet. Sir, this is Cody, my younger girl." Cody smiled and looked at the ground the way she was prone to when meeting someone new. Josiah hadn't observed her beyond his own eyes in a while, out in the world like this, and it stunned him, how grown she was.

Her brows were Margaret's, high arches over greenish eyes, and she stood with a poised ease, ready to move should the need arise, but relaxed until it did. Sometimes Cody seemed more deer than girl, and she was hardly girl anymore. "My younger daughter," he corrected.

"The *daughter*, I see. I'm Scott," said the man, finally. The name made little impression, for how long he'd kept it back.

"You're Freddy's brother?" said Cody. "Freddy's my favorite. We love him."

"Do we."

"Yeah, oh yeah, he really helps. He's a fast learner. Well, my dad is a good teacher, I guess." Cody's openness was disarming to Josiah, who knew how much less than this she usually offered, but the man shrugged.

"What does he teach, is the question," Scott said.

"Wood stuff. Furniture." Cody swung her hand around. "You can see. Making this. No one is better than my dad." Josiah couldn't recall when he'd ever been more thankful for her voice.

Scott Coughlin nodded but didn't speak. Cody shifted her weight back and forth on her feet as if she were preparing to leap.

"I'm sure I'll see you again," the man said. "I've got my eyes open." He raised two fingers in a V and tapped the pouched skin beneath his eyes. He turned abruptly to leave and caught his hip on the edge of a table, jostling the pieces. "Look out," he said, under his breath, and steadied the table with a flat hand. Then he left. From behind he was a soft-bodied lump, absent the scalping edge he'd flashed in conversation.

"That's Freddy's brother?" said Cody. "The one who wants to buy a ranch?"

Josiah felt his pulse in his arms, the tendons taut from his shoulders to his palms. His mouth dry as paste. "I guess so. You know what I do."

"What a shithead. Freddy's way better. "

"I'll say," said Josiah. "Hard to believe they're even related."

"But they do look a little alike. The nose?"

"Hmm."

"Do you think people say that about Louisa and me?"

"What?"

"Hard to believe we're related."

"Nah. You're peas in a pod."

Cody's eyes on him made him pause. He rarely said what he thought about anyone out loud and he saw her note it.

"You're both good girls. That's the difference. It's harder to see a resemblance when one is good and one is awful."

"Kind of like Clint and Nate."

"Clint isn't awful," said Josiah. His voice halted further disagreement, and Cody felt the surge of confusion that Clint so often provoked. He was easy to hate sometimes, lately more and more so, but he had been in Cody's life for so long, even she knew it wasn't simple. Once when she was maybe twelve, she'd gone up to the Lindsays for milk, letting herself into the barn behind the house where the bottles were kept in a chest refrigerator with a glass lid, like you'd find in a store. You helped yourself and made a mark on the sheet of paper taped to the top. Kinzler was its own column, and every ten hash marks, it was time to pay.

The house looked empty but as Cody turned to go, she heard Clint's voice, a half shout, half cry—*Mama*. Cody approached the house and set the milk on the porch. They'd changed to plastic jugs recently with a handle on the side, much easier to carry home across the fields than the glass bottles, which got slippery with condensation in heat and were hard to hold by the neck and Cody remembered setting the jugs on the step and entering the screen door into the kitchen. Mrs. Lindsay lay on the floor in front of the stove, slumped on her side, vomit on the linoleum, and Clint bent over her, holding her shoulder, and calling out, *Mama, mama, come on, sit up.*

"Clint?" Cody said. He looked up and she watched as shame and fury got pushed off his face by fear and relief, as sure as a cloud front moving across the sky. It's her head, he said, help me, and together they eased Mrs. Lindsay to seated, her head lolling weirdly, eyes glazed. Her dress dragged in the vomit and Cody fought the urge to gag. She and Clint joined hands behind his mother's back and under her thighs and half lifted her, half dragged. She was lightweight, but flopping. Clint's big boyishness dwarfed his mother and Cody both, and though perhaps he could almost have carried her alone, Cody saw herself a help. When they got to the couch, Mrs. Lindsay fell into the cushions like a dropped load. Their clasped hands had been tools, but now felt strange and Cody stepped away.

Clint brought his mother some water and sat next to her on the couch while color came back into her face from forehead to chin, as if it were poured. Cody slipped out the front door and was halfway home before she remembered the milk. It was on the back porch where she'd left it, moisture beaded on the sides. She tucked her fingers into the plastic handles and through the window she could hear Clint, singing: *How I wonder what you are, up above the world so high*. She knew that twinkling song. Had she ever comforted her mother? She couldn't say.

JOSIAH REARRANGED THE ITEMS on the table in front of him and Cody noted the hotdogs, damp and cooling in her hands, and set them down. "Take these, Pop, I got you two, they looked kinda small. And two for me. Three bucks, no change. They're getting cold." She raised one to her mouth and took a soft bite, half the bun disappearing down her throat. It still surprised Josiah, how much she could eat, far more than he did at any given meal. She'd been that way since she was little, out-eating boys twice her size at class pizza parties. Eleven slices, Louisa would report, and Cody would smile into her sleeve. Josiah had never been ravenous.

"Have you ever talked to Scott before?" asked Cody with her mouth full.

"No." He had hardly even thought of Scott Coughlin, though Freddy had mentioned when he first arrived a brother who might follow shortly, a troubled relationship he wanted free of.

"Why was he so nasty?" She swallowed and took another bite.

Josiah knew exactly why. Two men, a certain kind of friendship—it could catch someone's notice. Someone like Scott. Someone who'd seen his younger brother leave their home with rumors around him. Who couldn't imagine any needs different than his own.

"Who knows," said Josiah. "People can be small." Josiah could not see how to explain more than that to Cody and he pivoted toward safer terrain as surely as if he'd twisted on the ball of his foot to evade a hole in the ground.

"What did he say to you?"

"He asked how I could feed my family, if we lived hand-to-mouth."

"What does hand-to-mouth even mean?"

"A farmer, you grew food to live. You picked it and ate it. If you're hungry, and someone handed you an apple, you'd eat it. No saving, no selling, no buying. Hand, mouth."

"Isn't growing food to live *good*?" said Cody. "Like the garden." She wiped the edges of her mouth with her finger, leaving a smear of ketchup.

"People want to buy and sell. It's how they feel big." He gestured at the tables.

"Well, we're not hand-to-mouth."

"More like hand to pocket to mouth," said Josiah. "Not exactly poor, but there isn't much need for a bank."

"I love pockets." Cody stuck a hand in hers and pulled out rubble—a tube of lip balm with a pink cap, a small round stone. She unfolded a scrap of paper and looked it over, then crumpled it and tossed it at the trashcan.

"I also love Freddy," she said, eyeing Josiah to gauge his agreement. "Never mind his douchebag of a brother."

"Easy," Josiah said.

WHEN THE MARKET CLOSED LATE-AFTERNOON, Josiah had sold a handful of small pieces and one of the bookshelves and given away all of his business cards. He had to write his number on the back of those, having printed them with his address but forgotten the house phone, so seldom did he use it.

Josiah dumped his two cold hotdogs into the trash and Cody helped him load the largest remaining piece, the cabinet, sliding the feet onto cardboard and shimmying it into the back of the truck where Josiah padded it with blankets and strapped it down so it wouldn't rock or scratch. He wrapped up his small tools in their soft leather pouch and set it in the jump seat of the cab. Cody held the money box on her lap.

"This is quite a bit," she said.

"Nothing to complain about," said Josiah.

Cody hadn't handled much cash of her own, besides bills that came folded in birthday cards from Aunt Dorie or Great-Aunt Abigail. Grandma Blanchard sent checks, and most of Cody's hardware store pay went straight into the bank and an allowance came sporadically in quarters when Josiah or Margaret remembered. "The tooth fairy called and told me she's short on cash," Margaret explained on those mornings when the girls' bloody molars still lay under their pillows.

Cody smoothed and sorted the bills and bundled them with rubber bands while Josiah drove. They often kept an easy silence in the truck together—when she was young Cody asked to go for "quiet drives." Not everyone could think and watch without speaking. But now Josiah's mind kept returning to Scott Coughlin, and more than that, his dishonesty with Cody, hiding from her what she didn't know to look for. It wasn't the same as easy quiet and he was glad when she spoke.

"I was talking to the church guys for a bit when I got the hotdogs," she said. "They wanted to save me, big surprise."

Josiah gave no response because all he could think to say was uncharitable, and he knew his reaction was not for the Christians, but for judgments wherever they came from.

"You don't believe in God, right, Pop?"

"Not like that."

"Like what, then?"

"I'm not sure. I think if I could say it right out, it wouldn't be any kind of god."

Even to Josiah, it was an unsatisfying answer, but Cody didn't ask more and he didn't clarify. She looked out the window, her forehead pressed against the glass and the cash clutched in her hand. They passed the McKintry place at the turn off the highway and old man Bud stood bowlegged out front tending his burn barrel. He prodded down into the drum with a shovel handle, his hand around its skinny neck below the upright metal head. Bud noted the truck and lifted his other arm in a wave. Trash smoke blew acrid in the windows as they slowed to corner, gravel shifting beneath the tires.

A few minutes later, Cody again. "How old do you suppose you have to be to have peace of mind?" He could hear in her words the pastor's syntax. The search for that goal had hung heavy on him his whole life, a weight which he had hoped she would not inherit.

"Another thing I do not know, Cody."

A pressure rose in his lungs. Peace of mind, Josiah thought. I'd die for that.

FREDDY COUGHLIN

I NEVER GUESSED there were so many kinds of nails. The first weeks I worked for Josiah, it seemed like I'd never known anything. I was young—twenty-five, and from the east, a city no less, out to Montana on a lark—and I hadn't done much in my life yet besides school, which in certain parts of the west, I found, hardly counted for anything. Still, when I turned up at his workshop and Josiah showed me around, the scope of what I did not know confounded me. Tiny nails for assembling the seats of chairs, nails as long as my hand for framing walls, and 12-inch spikes for tacking together logs. Common nails and box nails, brads, roofers, finish nails, tacks. Masonry nails. Ring drive and duplex. Dipped nails and brights. It was another language. Just when I thought I was starting to know—not all of it, not by a long shot, but more than I had come with—after I quizzed myself standing in front of the jars and boxes, matching the pieces to their labels, then Josiah would use another name. A pound of galvies, he'd say. Or, grab me the sinkers. How many times did he redo a task without drawing attention to my mistake? At that point, he was one of the only men I'd known who passed up chances to make me feel foolish.

I came out west because my brother wanted to buy a ranch. He'd heard about Montana, how there was big, rough land there and he imagined himself a Western icon, a big, rough man. I offered to go first and look around. I had lost a job, a love went bad, and I was ready to leave, kind of ashamed, I'll admit it. He sent me out with a list of properties to visit, and I did.

One of the first ranches I went to look at was up the Kinzlers' way, and that's how I met Josiah, a wrong turn up a long gravel drive, and in that country, the houses so far apart, you don't know you're off base until you've gotten out and made yourself a nuisance. Such an impression, the sight of the porch, shaded in the early summer heat, and how Margaret greeted me, like any friend she might have been expecting, though I'd soon find that no one besides Doyle dropped in, as Margaret told me when she served me coffee in his mug. Cody sat on the front swing in cutoffs and a T-shirt, shucking corn, the silk clinging to her arms and hands, and the dog—this is Jade, said Cody—laid in the shadow of a wicker bench, a furry mass, her eyes shut and paws trembling as she chased rodents in her sleep. I never did visit the ranch farther up the road that day, but on the Kinzlers I was sold.

Josiah invited me to come and work with him and that summer Cody was fourteen, watchful. Josiah told me she was shy and not to take her silences as judgment, but from the start I talked to her as a friend. I think that's why we became close; she liked to listen first, more than she liked to talk. Louisa was reaching outward, often going or gone, so I'm sure that was part of it, too, Cody hungry for a companion to take her sister's place. When you are a younger child—I know this, I'm one too—it can be hard to make your own way. You're used to following, watching for an invitation into the older world. Cody was more self-possessed than I ever felt at that age. Still, something in her needed to look up. I was there when her sister left, just as she was looking.

The ranch is not my place, of course, though a part of me takes ownership. I keep a tiny apartment in town, but I spend much of my time up there. First, I did it to help Josiah, and later, because it became a home to me. I always offered to watch the place so Josiah could go away with his family. After I had been there a short while he certainly could have trusted me. The animals knew me, and for all I didn't know about nails, I found I had a way with stock. I could curry a horse better than you'd guess. I would have been useful if my brother had bought a place, but that fell apart, no surprise. Scott didn't have the patience it takes to root in a small town. He wanted what he could buy, and when what he wanted was not for sale, he left. Good riddance, to be honest.

But Josiah never leaves. I'm glad for that. I get up every day wondering what I will learn from him. Some days, nothing. But the place feels most like home when he is there and I can sense him. See his neck bent over his work, his thick hair eddied at the nape below his hat. Make out the shape of him—narrow slope of shoulders, strong thighs—beneath his clothes. The boards of the shop floor flex under his weight as he approaches me. Many times I've stayed with my back to him longer than needed, to savor his footsteps closing the distance between us.

FOREST WORK (1992)

SINCE CODY WAS OLD ENOUGH to follow her father, she had been learning to work. As a little girl she swept the sawdust out of the shop with a broom twice the length of her and lined up jars of hardware in rows. While Josiah notched logs or milled boards in the noisy cloud of the saw, Cody straddled the shaving horse and pretended to ride, or piled the scraps and cut ends from under his workbench, making ships and towers with too much wood glue that dried in scales on her hands. By five she knew a nail (point) from a bolt (threads) from a screw (threads and point). When she turned eleven, he guided her with power tools, let her run the sander to grind logs to a fine white finish, or feed boards through the planer so they came out square. Cody learned not just *on* and *off*, *green* and *dry*, but also *mortise* and *tenon*, *in-process* and *finished*. *Perfect* and *ruined*.

More dangerous than the shop was the woods, with variables of weather and wind, but there, too, Josiah invited her. At nine she tagged along watching at a distance while he felled trees, until he let her pound wedges and clear brush at the base. At twelve she helped him limb a downed spruce—he with the chainsaw at the heavy limbs near the stump, and she on the slim branches she could whack with a hatchet, the axe handle still a bit too long. At thirteen she ran a chainsaw to cut cookies from firewood logs. Josiah stood behind her at first, his bare hands beside her gloved ones on the handlebar. Before her first solo felling, at fourteen, he had her practice face cuts for months, on low stumps, then one atop another on short snags with broken-off tops. For five years, she'd spent weeks of the summers working with him.

Now sixteen, Cody was quieter than the little talker she'd once been, the tag-along, tugging on arms, Pop-how-come-can-I-try-which-way-look-at-this. She did not want to cut up logs into firewood on the bucking stand in the yard, and did not especially want to help Josiah haul logs with the swiveling steel Swede hooks when he needed a hand, or peel bark with a draw knife, yanking through the cambium, sap coating her arms and hardening the seat of her jeans to pitchy stone. With Freddy around, her father needed her less for odds and ends. But Freddy was stiff and nervous on the saw, so when Josiah went into the woods to cut, it was still with Cody or, increasingly, alone.

Today they drove down Fielder's Road in the newish Ford, the old flatbed finally consigned to the property, fine for hauling logs at home but too old to trust in the woods. Doyle's wrecker was down and a tow out here would be a hundred bucks, or more.

"You cut today," Josiah said.

"Don't want to."

"Want doesn't matter."

"I've hardly cut in a year. I'll fuck it up."

"Save it," Josiah said. He'd told her for years, only cuss when you need to, and she felt a short flare of shame at her unwise use.

"I fuck up everything." Her voice dared him to correct her again.

The cab was quiet but for the rattle of a periodic cattle guard beneath the tires and the chug of the diesel engine. It was a tenser quiet than their old driving rhythm. Louisa had left in August for college and lately Cody was shadowy and remote, as if a role had been left empty, and someone in the house had to take it on. Teenaged, Josiah supposed, though Louisa's testing had been buoyant, and his own memory of those years was no darker or lighter than any other time. Sometimes he saw in the way Cody carried herself a certain rigid spine, a bubble around her that you could poke at but not penetrate. He wanted to warn her, but how do you say to someone, even your child, open yourself, before you make a habit of not-needing. He still had to remind himself.

Josiah pulled the wheel hard to the right and the Ford ricocheted onto a two track that ramped from the road into a ditch line. Cody jumped out of the cab and slammed the door. The morning was still and the brush dripped with the almost-fall night's heavy dew. She dragged her feet but got the chaps from the bed, a concession. Not worth arguing.

"We'll take it slow," Josiah said.

"You want fast, you do it." Her tongue sharp in her mouth.

Josiah had the urge to take her face in his palms and encourage, but checked himself. It was hard to know which gestures were welcome anymore. He had always loved their physical closeness. Floor wrestling, piggybacks. She climbed into his lap years longer than Louisa had. Lifting things, working together, they circled each other as laborers do, here a touch to balance, there a hand grasped to stand. He had pressed her shoulders, tapped her back without thought, until recent months. Now she leaned away.

Josiah settled for a flick of her ponytail on his way behind her and let down the tailgate and pulled the chainsaw toward him. Cody smoothed her hair in one hand and handed him the dented metal gas can, then the bar oil in its greasy plastic bottle, and he filled the tanks. She adjusted the chain tension—loose enough to spin fast, no sag to throw the chain. She snagged the cutting edge of a few teeth with her fingertip, more ritual than test, because Josiah always sharpened at the end of the last day's work. Cody learned from him how to run the round file firm over each leading edge and drop the rakers with one sure flat stroke of the bastard file. He kept the cleanest, sharpest tools she'd ever seen.

Josiah lifted the saw and let the scabbard rest on his shoulder. It was a homemade sheath of light plywood padded with foam, wrapped in duct tape. He first used them his year clearing trail in the park, where crews hiked miles with saws. With the padded scabbard on your shoulder and the powerhead resting on your pack, you could carry the saw for hours, he said.

Cody hefted the axe and followed him through the underbrush, over downed logs, snapping sprigs of yellowing mountain maple with her hands, avoiding the cow parsnip that would flare up their forearms in a bright mosaic, but for long sleeves. Josiah stopped at several trees for Cody to whack the trunk with the axe's butt, listening for the dull thump of live wood. A bright *jat* meant standing dead, dry but not rotten, and a hollow *thunk* meant standing rot, which you could also see from a sign—conchs on the trunk, moss in the roots, woodpeckered holes or flaking bark that left visible a layer of damp brown powder pressed against the wood—*frass*, Josiah taught her. Beetle-shit dust. A word for that.

Josiah squinted upward, sizing a tree for taper. You want a straight tree, where you look up the trunk like a road to the sky, he'd told her this years ago, and Cody had never forgotten it, picturing the sky as a place you could get to, if you tried. Avoid a flared trunk, no split tops. Crooked will throw off the weight, though Josiah could drop a tree opposite its lean even in a strong wind. Only once did Cody see a tree sit back on her father, who'd left the wedge in the pickup and mispredicted the lean. Tense and pissed, he directed her to run back for the wedge and a hatchet to drive it. He cut the engine and stood by the tree, spotting it with his braced arms as high up the trunk as he could reach. The saw stayed put in the back cut, bar so thoroughly pinched you couldn't pound it out if you tried. There was no wind. The most dangerous mistake you could make in the woods was to lose control of the direction your tree fell. If you forgot your wedge, you go back for it before you cut, he said. Lazy will kill you. After Cody brought the wedge and he pounded it in and finished the cut in the opened kerf, they never spoke of it again.

JOSIAH FOUND A TREE HE LIKED, finally, a larch eleven or twelve inches in diameter at chest height, which he estimated against the length of his boot at the base.

"This one looks good," he said.

"Walk me through it?"

He shook his head. "No more talking. You know how."

Cody leaned the axe against the trunk. Josiah picked it up and tested the edge against his finger while she buckled the chaps over her legs. She cinched the belt to encircle her waist, much smaller than his. Crouching beside the saw, she removed the scabbard and rolled her earplugs between her fingers, shoved them into her ears. The world eased away beyond sound. Josiah made her wear protective gear, the hardhat and glasses, the chaps and ear pro. His Park Service days canceled out his redneck ones, he said, and if he didn't always do it himself, he wanted her to wear it all. Resting the saw on her thigh, Cody ran through the steps. Chain tension, check. Choke on, pull, pull, pop. Off choke, pull again, one, two, three times, don't flood. Once fired, feather the trigger and listen—idle to full rev. Brake on.

Cody circled the base of the tree and scanned the top branches. Josiah stood back, leaning the palm of his hand into the axe handle's butt. Larch trees like this one, they agreed, were the best, the only conifers to drop their needles in fall, like leaves. In October, they lit a hillside golden and in summer the new needles were mossy green. Cody cleared the brush and small saplings around the tree, making room for herself. She indicated her escape routes to Josiah with her hand—the paths of least resistance away from the base, should it lean or twist unexpectedly. He gave her a thumbs-up. She picked up the saw, took a deep breath the way he taught her, tensed all her muscles and relaxed them. She imagined the tree's smooth fall, and the mantra Josiah had repeated so often it nearly bugged her: *It's already on the ground. Now put it there.*

But he's right, she does know, her body still knows. Bar parallel to ground, gunning sights. Face cut a third the depth of the tree. Pop out the triangle. Check for flat faces. Fix a small overcut. Wipe sawdust from safety glasses. Breathe.

He'd taught her to take a break before the back cut, to decrease the urgency and the chance of a mistake, so Cody stepped back and Josiah nodded his approval. With the saw idling loud, she watched her father as he kneeled in the brush to tie his boot. She'd spent recent months avoiding him, and she knew he noticed, knew he noted the darkness he saw in her lately, the lagged confidence. But what did he know about what went on inside of her mind? Nothing. Not about the silly high school boys, how beneath her covers at night she willed herself to picture them, pressed her fingers into her wet crotch. Not how she missed Louisa, their talking and listening, so much that nighttime alone in their room was an ache. Large parts of herself she kept distant now, when before she'd have said that her father knew her better than anyone.

Josiah smiled at her and nodded again, his arms across his chest. You'd say he was beaming. Cody resisted his pride with the thought that he was foolish, an old man making too much of small things.

Cody adjusted her chaps, fiddled with an earplug, and moved to the other side of the tree. She began the second cut, level, correcting the tip's dive. She paused when Josiah cupped his hands around his mouth and hollered, "Back cut!" His voice echoed and she chastised her oversight. She pivoted the bar through the cut until an inch of holding wood remained. The kerf did not open or close; no lean. She pulled a wedge from her back pocket and shoved it in the cut and Josiah extended the axe to her, handle first. She shut off the saw and extracted the bar, and with the butt of the axe she pounded the wedge until the lean began. She remembered to shout. "Falling!"

Together they watched the tree's slow arc, holding wood popping, until the fast end fall, when the tree leapt from the stump and hit the ground with a solid thunk. A chipping squirrel broke the quiet. The sun was higher in the sky, and Josiah and Cody stood beneath it, faces lifted. He grabbed her ponytail and yanked it soft.

"Nicely done," he said. "Not a fuck-up in sight."

TWO O'CLOCK SUN SLANTED THROUGH the trees and Cody handed her father half of her sandwich. He never brought enough food. He said he wasn't hungry but took hers when she shared, like the flirty high school girls who wouldn't eat except off their boyfriends' plates.

"How's your mom?" Josiah asked.

"Fine. You were just up for dinner."

"Yeah. But I haven't seen her much these weeks. She's busy, I'm busy. How is she?"

Cody shrugged. "She's fine. She makes dinner, she goes to the store, she visits Grandma, she talks to Aunt Dorie on the phone. I don't know what you want me to say."

"Fair enough."

"You should ask her."

They chewed quietly until Cody softened.

"Peanut butter and jam is still my favorite sandwich."

"Did I ever tell you I worked on a fire crew with a man who said he ate a peanut butter sandwich at lunch for thirty years?"

Cody thought about her father, young, before her mother, working in the woods with a gang of men. Learning things it seemed he'd always known.

"Did you ever wish you had a son?"

"Hmm. No. What on earth made you ask that?"

"Clint said it."

It had been years since that day and Cody had no idea why she thought of it, except that sawing in the woods was what a father might do with his son. Clint had said it on the bus the first day back to school, the fall she was still in junior high and he went to high school after being held back a year. She avoided him the way you'd walk around an unpredictable dog. His eyes ranged and bounced. One day he'd ignore her and another single her out. On the bus, she couldn't get away.

That same summer, one Saturday Clint was at the front door. She and Louisa never played with him anymore, only with Nate.

"I'll meet you out back, Clint," said Josiah, cleaning up from breakfast. Cody loved those mornings when he came up from the cabin for breakfast, and she found him at the counter when she entered the kitchen. It smelled like the pork sausage patties only he cooked; her mother said the pan was a pain in the butt to clean and she liked bacon better.

"Why is he here, Pop?" Cody asked. She could see Clint on the front porch. She didn't care if he heard.

"Mr. Lindsay asked if he could come and work for me a bit this summer."

"Why?"

"I think he needs a change. He's having some trouble."

"What kind of trouble?"

"The kind you don't want to talk about the details of, I'm guessing."

Gossiping, or worrying at other people's business, as her father put it, was not admired. She shut her mouth.

Clint came most Saturdays that month. Sometimes Cody worked with him on a project where they didn't need instruction, peeling logs, or sweeping up the shop. He talked nonstop one day, the next, was sullen and quiet. She never spoke to him unless she had to and tried to ignore his comments, under his breath and snide, trolling for a reaction: *No boobs yet, huh, Cody? Louisa got 'em all,* leering, hands out in front of his chest like he was holding fruit. She knew better than to respond. Clint barely had any friends. He made her organs thump around inside, like something bad was about to happen. It canceled out the good of being with her dad.

One Saturday in August, Clint didn't show. Cody didn't ask about it because who wanted him there? Bringing it up might remind someone. That fall he got kicked out of school for being drunk in science. He threw up all over the lab table, Louisa said, which made Cody remember all the times Clint had been sick over the years—normal flus and colds, the Christmas that Clint learned he was allergic to shrimp and puked chewed-up candy canes into the snow, and, in fourth grade, their shared case of chicken pox. She and Clint stayed home from school together for days, and one afternoon, they fell asleep, itchy and feverish, in the pillow fort they'd made.

By now, Cody had seen many kids drunk and kids kicked out of school for graffiti on lockers and getting pregnant and whatever you could think up in between. Even so, Clint stood out. It was downhill with him. You knew enough to stand back, or you were asking for trouble. He was the first failure she knew up close.

"I never wished I had a son, Cody. Clint wished he had a different father for a while, that's what made him say such a stupid thing," said Josiah.

Cody seized on this. "What do you mean? What's wrong with Mr. Doyle?"

Josiah was instantly sorry he put it that way. "Nothing. Not one thing. But a boy can go through a time where his own father—you wish for different. It's not personal. Maybe Clint worries that Doyle loves Nate more. It could be that, or nothing."

"Who doesn't love Nate more?" said Cody. "Clint is stupid and mean."

"Not stupid. Hard, yes. Reminds me of my brother, a little. There's a roughness about him that's not his fault, but then he complicates it with what *is* his fault. It's hard to separate."

"Who was your brother again?" Cody felt a hot rush whenever her father mentioned his family, which was so almost-never that she couldn't recall the last time.

"Henry." He didn't say more.

Cody stayed quiet and ate her chips out of the Ziploc bag she'd packed. Her father had a brother that she'd never known. And she had Louisa, so easy to know you'd have to try not to. Louisa said so herself. "What you see is what you get," she said once when Cody accused her of faking.

"I never wished for a son," Josiah said again. "I don't know how a son would be different than what I have, but I can't imagine better than you. And Louisa. I wouldn't ask for any more than that."

Cody picked up a ponderosa cluster from the duff and flossed a needle through her teeth. Until she was ten, she thought it might be better to be a boy. But she was allowed to go without a shirt, to be outside and dirty and playing ball, she had a shotgun. Boy or girl didn't matter as much as everybody said. She'd never thought about how it would feel to a father. Would you want one of what you were? Or what you weren't? Like anything, she was finding, it probably depended on the person. The older she got, the truer it appeared. Nothing was for everyone.

"Is Freddy like a son to you?" She hesitated to ask because she hated to imagine Freddy as competition, but as soon as she said it aloud, she knew she'd gotten it wrong.

"No. No. Freddy is my friend," Josiah said. He cleared his throat. "My dear friend." Margaret knew what Freddy was to him. He'd told her the first day that Freddy's hands brushed his when exchanging an armload of lumber and his body arced toward the possible like a thrown pitch. Josiah imagined telling Cody, too, almost mouthing the lines: *Freddy and I love each other*. He gathered courage as he would supplies, sharpening the best tool to describe their connection, testing the right edge to help her understand. But Cody spoke before he was ready, and the moment passed, as it always did. Shame flooded in, familiar, and covered up his worry. A certain peace in that.

AFTER LUNCH THEY FELLED THREE MORE TREES, limbed and stacked them for the next day's hauling, and on the way back to the truck Cody carried the saw and Josiah walked ahead. Just short of the forest edge he tripped—it was easy to go down to one knee when a stob caught a pantleg, or roll an ankle when a step over a log went wrong. No need to panic, you picked yourself up before you even hit. But Josiah fell clear to the ground and as he rolled to one side, his glasses knocked off. Like that, he was blind. His bare eyes in the morning were unfocused and he said he wouldn't know his own wife next to him in bed except for her smell.

Cody stopped a few paces behind her father and watched, first to give him space and then to see him, vulnerable. He patted at the ground, his hand scrabbling, fingers spread and tugging at plants and sticks. For one moment she let herself enjoy it. How small he seemed. How incapable of triumph. She shook it off just as he asked her, his voice pitched and raw, "Cody, help me, please, I can't find my glasses," and then he ceased being the pathetic one. What kind of a girl left someone on the ground and let him wallow, helpless? Who imagined her father small and weak to make herself feel big? A person who delights in others looking foolish is the fool—he'd told her that for years. Cody crouched, the saw awkward on her shoulder, and picked up his glasses where they lay in a clump of ferns, the opposite direction of where he'd been looking. She'd spotted them right away.

CODY AND LOUISA KINZLER

Sept. 9, 1992

Dear Louisa,
I am going to write you a letter a week. How is college? It's weird here without you. Mom went to Great Falls to visit Grandma and Great-Aunt Abigail and Pop's staying up here with me. Freddy says hi. We all miss you. Dad says how come everyone has to leave? I know what he means.
Love,
Cody

9/15/92

Hey Cody!
Your postcard made my day when I saw it in my little mail cubby! La Grande is pretty cool.

It's small but there are some cute guys which helps! I'm sorry you guys miss me. Dad is a sap! I'm *glad* I didn't go to Missoula or Bozeman though. Sometimes a fresh start is good, right?

I miss you too.
XOXO
Louisa

Sept. 20, 1992

Dear Louisa,
Thanks for writing back. I thought you might be too busy. A man from California bought the store. Mom doesn't care for him but she's staying on to do the books. She and Pop are talking about money a lot. Do you think we're poor?

A guy asked me out but I said my parents wouldn't let me. Don't tell Mom.
Love,
Cody

10/7/92

Hi Cody,
I am *so* glad you're not boy crazy!! I do *not* like how much I think about boys and what they think of me. It takes up *a lot* of energy. Plus, I went too far with Nate and now I'm sorry! So, listen to your big sister, ok? We all know I am wise! :) And we are *not* poor, silly. Dad worries about everything, don't pay too much attention.
XOXO
Louisa

Oct. 18, 1992

Dear Louisa,
It's pretty boring here without you. Pop and Freddy got a huge elk. Nate won 4-H in almost everything. I won a blue ribbon for a hen. A Brahma, the ones with feathery feet. I guess I'm a late bloomer cause I'm still not boy crazy. But not because you told me to, ha ha.
I miss you,
Cody

10/25/92

Dear Cody,
Once upon a time if you were my roommate, I wouldn't have to live with this girl who fills our room with hairspray and has never done a damn thing for herself! If you were my roommate, guys could come hang out in our room and I could put my feet in their laps and then you'd send them off when I didn't want them here anymore.
XOXO
Louisa
ps. Aunt Dorie invited me for Thanksgiving!! I get to take the bus to Spokane!
pps. I miss you too!!

Nov. 5, 1992

Dear Louisa,
Gross on the hairspray. I felled my biggest tree, 25 inches dbh. That means diameter at breast height. (Even though I barely have any.) It snowed and Pop's in a funk. I have more chores because Freddy went for a month to see his family. I think Pop worries that he'll stay. I can't believe I turn 17 next week. I still feel like a kid.
I miss you,
Cody

ps. Tell those boys I'm tougher than I look.

Nov. 15, 1992

Dear Louisa,
Thanks for calling on my birthday. Mom's sad since Grandma Blanchard died. Uncle Michael can't come for the funeral, he's sick with pneumonia. Didn't we have that? If you ever die, I'm coming to the funeral even if you live in Texas. Please don't though (die, I mean, not live in Texas).
I miss you,
Cody
ps. Lindsays are coming for Thanksgiving. I said we shouldn't invite Clint and almost got grounded.

12/1/92

Heya Sis,
Sorry I'm so bad at writing, I'm SOOO busy! But I'm not going anywhere—Texas or dead, you nut! Is Uncle Michael better? Let's go visit him in San Fran when I graduate, okay? Aunt Dorie canceled because of the funeral so I had Thanksgiving here with all the loners. You weren't there when I called—probably making out with Nate? Ha ha, don't kill me!! We all know you were in the barn. Gotta go study!
XOXO
Louisa

Dec. 12, 1992

Dear Lou,
You'll be home in a week! I cleaned up our room. Clint asked me at Thanksgiving if you were pregnant yet and I told him to fuck off in front of everyone and they got mad so I left and that's why I missed it when you called. I thought you'd be proud. Freddy's back so Pop is happy and when you come home for Christmas he'll be even happier. I miss my Lou, he says. Me, too.
Love,
Cody

1/15/92 OOPS 93!!

Dear Cody,
It was sooo good to see you guys for Christmas. January sucks. I'm so sick of school but let's face it, if I moved home, I would go nuts. And Dad would soon remember that I drive him crazy! Mom says you guys can come visit in the Spring! I can't wait. You'll get to meet Alex! He is older than me (not in college). PLEASE don't tell Mom. I think it will go better in person. Promise!
XOXO
Louisa

Feb. 1, 1993

Dear Louisa,
I can't wait to visit. I'm not sure if Pop can come, he says three of us is too expensive. If Freddy stays with the animals, maybe he'll come. But if it was Mom and me and you and Aunt Dorie, that would be cool—just the girls. Well, except for Uncle Merl, I guess. I've been wearing your brown suede jacket, so thanks.
Love,
Cody

2/12/93

Hi Cody,
When you come can you bring me some stuff? One, a blue folder from the bottom bookshelf, down by the magazines. Do *not* look in it, okay?! Kidding. ☺ Two, my guitar from Uncle Michael. Also, bring your riding boots. Alex has horses!! As you know, I'm not a good rider, so I want to show you off. Anything for LOVE!
XOXO
Louisa

Mar. 5, 1993

Dear Louisa,
Pop can't come because of money and his projects so it's just going to be Mom and me. I think he might get lonely but he says he'll be fine. Do you think he ever gets lonely? Hard to tell. I've got the guitar and the folder.
Love, Cody
ps. I oiled my boots.

3/12/93

Dear Cody,
I hope you get this before you come. Don't mention Alex to Mom. He's gone and he wasn't a good idea to start with. I guess I didn't know as much about love as I thought, big surprise! Bring your boots only if you want.

Give Dad a hug and tell him I will miss him.

See you soon my little moon.
XOXO
Louisa

BE CAREFUL (1993)

AUNT DORIE HAD LIVED OUTSIDE of Spokane for as long as Cody and Louisa could remember, though Dorie said when she was twenty she spent a year in Germany as a nanny for a cousin who needed help with four overwhelming children. The only remainder of those days was a cluster of German knickknacks on the mantel and a picture of Aunt Dorie in a memorable barmaid's outfit, hoisting two metal steins with a hammy smile. Her breasts pushed up at the deep scoop neck and her hair sat braided and coiled on her head like a slipping crown. In the background, men crowded around her, their faces blurry, drunk and laughing. It was hard to match that photo with Aunt Dorie they knew. The clowning fit—Aunt Dorie was "a stitch," as Margaret said—but the outfit? The men? Now Aunt Dorie wore faded jeans and an old plaid flannel buttoned nearly to her neck. Even scanning for a sign of the breasts, Cody could see only a slight fullness in the shirt, a gape at the bottom where it hung open, draped from above. Her chest made you think *shelf* more than beers and laughter.

Cody and Margaret drove six hours to get to Dorie and Merl's, icy roads slowing their climb over the passes. Louisa, on Thanksgiving break from college, caught a ride from La Grande to Spokane with a friend who lived in Coeur d'Alene and they picked her up at the Safeway on the edge of town. None of them had visited Dorie in ages; she came every few years to Montana instead. Josiah stayed home with the animals, though he loved Aunt Dorie, he always said so. Your sister is a kick, he told Margaret. The words people used about Dorie had a similar sound. A stitch, a kick. Uncle Merl called her a nag, which sounded alike but didn't ring as true.

Uncle Merl was a big man, tall and curled like a question mark, an ironic shape because he was bullheaded and less curious than a sleeping cat. His was a build often called intimidating, although the extra weight he'd put on in recent years dulled him a little. Even if he came right at you, you could outrun him, or dodge away. He married Aunt Dorie late, that's what everyone said, so even at that he was slow.

Margaret didn't care for her sister's husband, and true, Cody wouldn't have said she liked him either, but she had been fascinated by Uncle Merl, despite, or perhaps because of, her slight fear of his size and the way his teasing could take a sharper turn when you weren't expecting it. He kept bags of candy stashed all over: in cupboards, in the basement, in the console of his Buick wagon, and he was always offering some crinkling bag—gummies, licorice twists—or butterscotch discs and Skittles, a pile cupped in his palm. Never chocolate, which Cody craved. The fruity sweets didn't interest her, but she took them when he offered and gave them to Louisa. His hands looked like baseball gloves, the fingers thick and puffy, red around the knuckles as if the skin were laced too tight. As a little girl, Cody didn't like to touch his hands. To take the candy, she reached for the twisted wrappers or held out her palms.

"Your drive was slow." Uncle Merl's eyes ran up and down each of them, "and you two are getting . . . big." He cuffed Cody's head and laid his hand on Louisa's shoulder, pulling her in so their hips touched. Louisa grimaced. She was no faker. Uncle Merl had bad timing. Things said too late, hands left too long. Sometimes Cody felt sorry for him. Adults were supposed to know more than Merl did.

"I'm so glad you're here," sang Aunt Dorie. She yanked Margaret into her fleshy arms. "My biggest sis!"

Cody and Louisa went to check the swing and the creek, out of habit, as they had done since they were girls. The yard was squishy with late fall leaves piled beneath the largest trees. Dorie and Merl lived in a neighborhood with houses on either side, but their backyard opened up to several empty lots that ended in a sandy creek. Hardly a trickle in the summer, but in fall it could flood the tops of your shoes. A huge pine stretched a branch out over the creek and from a branch hung a tire swing, high enough off the ground that when they were littler Louisa had to boost Cody, who jackknifed herself over the tire and dangled her feet down so Louisa could haul herself up Cody's legs like a rope. Sometimes Cody's pants sagged if she wasn't lying right. Now that they were older it was easier in some ways, because they were taller and stronger, but also more awkward. Less room for their angled limbs and tender places. The older you got, the harder it was to wriggle.

Neither of them knew who had hung the tire. Uncle Merl and Aunt Dorie didn't have children, and it was hard to imagine them wanting a swing for themselves. Well, not Uncle Merl, anyway. Maybe Aunt Dorie. She could walk on her hands. You could picture her in a treehouse, walking the plank at the State Fair, bobbing for apples. She'd try about anything.

SPOKANE WAS CONSIDERABLY WARMER than Northern Montana had been, and by late afternoon it was mild enough to sit out on the concrete patio. Uncle Merl cracked a beer and Aunt Dorie made drinks in tall icy glasses—even Margaret with a gin and tonic in her hand. "Oh, girls, you can have one, can't they, Margaret?"

Dorie said. "I'll make it weak." The girls looked to their mother, unsure of what she'd say, but Margaret lifted her shoulders. "You're the host, Doe, your rules." Louisa ducked her chin to hide the smile that would have said, *good Lord, Ma, I hope you never guess how much I've drunk.* Cody knew, the smile and the secret, both.

Josiah hated drinking. Cody and Louisa had rarely seen alcohol at the house or cabin. For most of their lives, Margaret hardly had a glass of wine, even when the other women did at Thanksgiving, or New Year's Eve. Since Josiah had moved out, though, Margaret sometimes had a beer on a hot afternoon, drinking straight from the bottle. At first, it frightened Cody, the same way Clint did, or Louisa when she snuck in the back door after curfew, giggling and limp, smoke on her clothes. Cody did not get drunk with kids in high school or go to the parties thrown when parents were away. She wouldn't feel a buzz until she was twenty, when she'd finally give in and drink with her crewmates one summer, done with explaining. "My dad doesn't like it" or "It makes me feel nervous" sounded hopelessly square, too stupid to say out loud.

Uncle Merl drank too much. Every day. This family truth went unstated. Beer, yes, his favorite Coors in the white can, but also, stiffer stuff you'd smell on his breath but could never catch him with. He'd disappear into the basement, long enough to be odd, and he came upstairs meaner, especially to Aunt Dorie, and then everyone looked down at their hands. Josiah would confront him sometimes and stand up for Dorie—That's not called for, Merl, he'd say in his calmest voice—but Uncle Merl only got worse. It was better to ignore him, like a child saying *poop* at the dinner table. Eventually he would return to the basement, where his tool bench and an old television hunkered in the low light. He'd pass out down there—Oh dang, Merl fell asleep again, Dorie would say.

When Cody was little, she descended the stairs to the basement pantry to get a can of pineapple for Aunt Dorie and she found Uncle Merl slumped on the small orange couch, a vinyl loveseat that was too sticky to sit on in the summer and too cold in winter. One of Merl's legs hung over the armrest, so long that his foot laid flat on the floor. Cody stood behind the sofa and looked at Uncle Merl's face. His mouth parted enough to show his slack tongue and his breath came out in huffs, the air flapping his cheeks like wind in a loose tarp. Cody watched him carefully until Aunt Dorie stood at the top of the steps and hollered, "Child! Did the witch get you?" And Uncle Merl's eyes flew open, his mouth smacking and puckering around a bad taste. When his eyes focused on her, he made a wicked face and claws out of his glove hands and although Cody knew it was a joke, her legs shook as she scrambled up the steps clutching the can of pineapple. Anyone could be dangerous.

ON THE SATURDAY NIGHT BEFORE THEY LEFT, Aunt Dorie played Madonna on her pink tape deck and she and Louisa did their hair in curlers while Margaret and Cody sat on Dorie's bed and thumbed through the glossy magazines from the upstairs bathroom. *Vanity Fair, Cosmo.* Aunt Dorie brought them home from the dentist's office where she worked, so they were many months old. The covers all looked the same, so it hardly mattered. Diets, lipstick, sex. Cody perused with half interest, as if doing research.

"Ugh, don't read those in bed," Aunt Dorie squealed when she saw the magazines piled on her pillow. "They've been in a waiting room!"

"Jeez, that's nothing," said Louisa. "How about your bathroom?"

Louisa rolled Aunt Dorie's wavy hair onto the foam tubes and pinned them with brisk and confident hands. Cody's hair was way too short for rollers.

"You should be a beautician," said Cody, though once it was out it sounded a bit insulting. Louisa was in college.

"No thanks," Louisa said. "That would take every last drop of fun out of it. Maybe *you* should be a beautician." That cracked them all up.

"I can see the sign at Cody's place," said Dorie, "*Prom special—Shave your head for only $8!*"

"Yeah, or how about *Laura Ingalls braids for all ages!*" Louisa flopped back on the bed, laughing.

"Hey now," said Cody. But she didn't mind the teasing all that much. Dorie half sang, half hummed to the music—*True blue, baby, I love you*—and Margaret stretched between her daughters on the bed and rubbed Cody's leg and foot, cupping the heel in her hand.

"Isn't this nice," she said, "just us girls?"

That evening, tired of leftovers, they dressed up a little and went for a goodbye dinner, even Merl with a button-down in place of the usual baggy sweatshirt pouched over his jeans. Cody perched in the middle of the back seat leaning toward her mother and away from Uncle Merl, who liked to squeeze hard above her knee. Aunt Dorie drove and Louisa sat up front with her hair hanging in fat curls around her shoulders. She had a habit of gathering it into a pile on top of her head, holding it there with one hand. Then she'd talk and forget and it would fall back to her shoulders, shaking in a golden mass. Sometimes Cody could not take her eyes off her sister. It was like all the day's sun was caught up in her. When Uncle Merl's hand moved toward her leg, Cody fended him off with a stiff chop.

They went to an all-you-can-eat buffet, where Cody had four plates, ending with a brick-sized slab of chocolate cake and Louisa said where do you put it all, Cody, she herself wanted to throw up and why did anyone think all-you-can-eat was a good idea? Uncle Merl drank four beers and while Dorie paid the check, he wrapped rolls and cookies in napkins—against the rules—and snuck them out under his draped jacket, clowning around until Louisa punched him in the shoulder and told him to shush.

At the house, Aunt Dorie put on an album of show tunes and they packed lunches for the next day's drive and lip-synced to *Hello, Dolly!* Margaret spread peanut butter along celery sticks and hip-checked Dorie when she waltzed through the kitchen and pulled Margaret into the living room. They twisted their waists and flung out their arms in a clearly choreographed routine, Margaret with the knife above her head, slicing it through the air like a director's baton.

"Girls, we used to sing to this when we were kids, the three of us sang, so loud—Margaret, remember how *mad* Dad would get?"

"It's weird," said Louisa to Cody, watching their mother and Aunt Dorie dance. "We're two sets of sisters, but I never thought of it that way before."

The door from the basement flew open and hit the wall. "Noisy dang women," said Uncle Merl, plowing through the room with his head down like an angry bull. "It's only because you're visiting that I put up with all of this nonsense." He waved his hands in front of him in a mocking half dance.

Dorie rolled her eyes. "Ha, good try, Merl, see if you can fool them, make them think you ever get to tell me what to do."

And then, his manner turned, like milk you drank one day and spat out the next, no warning. He lurched into the living room and lifted the needle off the record with a scratch and then returned to the kitchen, his voice like someone stomping toward you.

"That's exactly what I'll make you do—shut up!" he said. "Shut up, Dorie. All of you!" He slammed his empty bottle onto the counter, where it wobbled and fell into the sink. He stood for a minute as they all looked at him. His face was somehow both angry and blank. They watched him, silent, until Uncle Merl's heavy footsteps hit the basement stairs and he disappeared into clunking darkness.

"That man," Aunt Dorie said, shaking her head. She put the record back on, but the volume on low. "Sometimes I wish he'd fall off a ladder." She laughed. "Never mind that. He'd probably get paralyzed, and then I'd have to wait on him hand and foot." Cody and Louisa saw through Dorie's bravado, another bit of stagecraft, as practiced as the dancing.

"How can you live like that?" Margaret asked. "How he treats you? Anyone he doesn't see eye to eye with?" She licked the peanut butter from her knife and set it in the sink.

"I don't know," Dorie said. "It won't last forever, mark my words. Someday I'll leave."

"You won't." Margaret's voice was resigned.

"Don't bet against me," Dorie said.

Cody opened the door to the basement. She felt bold enough to step down several stairs, her feet silent on the poured concrete treads. She crouched to see Merl with his back to her, fiddling with a knob on the television.

"Blasted women, blasted nonsense." He spoke aloud, as if to someone else in the room, but he was alone. He moved out of sight and Cody heard the door of the refrigerator—full of sprouting potatoes and random flours in freezer bags—and then the airy pop of a beer cap. Uncle Merl's boots were on the bottom step before Cody heard them, and in her hurry to flee, she slipped and he came lumbering up the flight of stairs and caught her splayed on the floor. She pulled herself into the hallway and sat against the wall. Her heart beat fast. She felt like a child, or a bug.

"Look out, girl. You be *careful.*" He sneered, standing a few steps below the landing so she couldn't see his legs from her position. "You be careful what you listen for." He waved his beer can at her and widened his eyes. "You might not want to know what people really think." Merl stepped over her legs, walked down the hall to the bathroom, and shut the door. Cody rose and returned to the kitchen where Louisa and Margaret and Dorie sang and shimmied. She went to the sink and drank a full glass of water and her heart slowed.

"Where'd you go? We need another dancer," Louisa said over the music, a little louder now. Even as they reached hands and her sister pulled her in, Cody held on to *careful.* A loving warning that could also be a threat.

MARGARET WANTED AN EARLY DEPARTURE so they could buy breakfast for Louisa's friend who'd take her back to La Grande. The girls went to bed at ten—I never get enough sleep at school, Louisa said—but Cody couldn't drift off. The clock radio read 10:41. Louisa rumbled like a beast; she went down hard no matter where she slept, but Cody never rested well away from home. Her switch stayed on.

At 11:13, Cody heard the phone ring in the kitchen. Probably a wrong number at this hour, reminiscent of the late-night prank calls with Louisa and Clint and Nate: *Is your air conditioner running? Go catch it!*, though no one they knew had an air conditioner. Voices drifted up the steps in bursts, then quiet between—Margaret and Dorie talking, no sound of Merl. Cody lay still a few minutes longer but the voices got louder, not less, until she rolled out of bed and pulled on a sweatshirt. She stood on the top step to listen. She was tired and not in the mood for further talk. Maybe it was nothing.

Aunt Dorie's voice—"Oh my, darn it, darn it all to *hell*, Michael."

Then Margaret, softer, inaudible. Crying? It sounded like someone banged on the counter with both hands. "Too late, too late! I'm always too late." A sob, cut off by coughing.

Cody rarely heard her mother cry. She peeked back in at Louisa, but the lump of her sister remained unmoved. She went downstairs.

"God, Dorie, I should have gone, weeks ago. Why didn't I go?" In the quiet house her voice was almost a shout.

"Shhh," Dorie said, "why didn't I?"

When Cody entered the kitchen, Margaret and Dorie clutched each other under the bright light, their shoulders moving in concert so it almost looked staged. Cody thought of their earlier dancing, and how many ways bodies could intersect. She stood quietly until Dorie pulled back and dragged her arm over her eyes. Her face was red and blotched, like a wet rash.

"Oh gosh, Cody. Come over here." Dorie pulled Cody into the hug Margaret had exited.

"What happened?" Cody asked, her mouth pressed into Dorie's flannel shoulder.

Dorie blew out a deep exhale and squeezed her harder. "Michael. Your Uncle Michael died. He died an hour ago. We just got the call."

"What?" Cody stepped back, incredulous. "Was there an accident?"

Dorie and Margaret exchanged looks. "He was sick. He's been sick for a while, pneumonia again," Margaret said. She leaned on the table. "I didn't want you girls to worry. Dorie and I, we were going to visit him after—after this, and then I'd know . . . what to say."

"You can die of pneumonia?" Cody felt stunned. She'd met him only once, but she thought of him so often. In her mind Uncle Michael was strong and laughing.

"Some people do, yes. He'd had it a few times. He was in the hospital. I guess—I guess it was too bad." Margaret walked to the back door and opened it a crack. "I need to breathe, Cody, I'm—I need some air." She slipped out to the patio and the motion-sensor bulb flicked on and cast her movements in a golden orb, like a snow globe made of light. Cody watched her mother through the window, on the cast iron bench with her face in her hands.

Cody turned back to Dorie, who stood still in the center of the kitchen with her arms by her sides. Neither of them spoke. The basement door opened and Merl leaned into the room. He always seemed to emerge from below in a cloud of rage and vapor, and Cody could smell him from five feet away—whiskey, vodka, whatever it was. She didn't know.

"Who's calling this late?" Merl said, rough.

"Andrew," Dorie said. "Michael just died." She lifted the heels of her hands to her eye sockets and pressed.

"Well," said Merl, "that's a long time coming." His words were slurred and snide.

"Merl, be human, for one minute? Or be quiet? He was my gosh-darn brother."

"Brother, schmother, Dorie. Serves him right. I can say what I think in my own house, when I'm asked." He turned and lunged back down the stairs. Cody willed him to fall.

"No one asked you," Dorie said to the shut door.

"'Serves him right'?" Cody asked. "What does that mean? Who's Andrew?"

"Cody, hon," said Dorie, and she approached as if to hug again, then stopped in the middle of the rug. "I'm sorry, sweetie, I need to be with your mom. I'm sorry, I'm sorry." Dorie ran across the living room to the slider. The sensor light flooded on again and Cody could see Dorie's and Margaret's backs together on the bench, the way they curled into each other and rested. Their brother. The house was silent except for the kitchen's hum. She went upstairs to find her own sister asleep, snoring, and Cody couldn't bring herself to wake her.

IN THE MORNING THEY OVERSLEPT and left in a blur of tears and hugging, Uncle Michael mentioned only briefly and so cryptically that Louisa grabbed Cody's arm in the hallway.

"What the hell is going on?"

Cody didn't understand what she'd heard the night before, or how to explain. "I don't know anything either," Cody told her.

Uncle Merl did not come up from the basement for a goodbye, a relief to all of them except Dorie, who would see him soon enough, alone, which was worse.

In the car, the doors barely closed, Margaret told the girls the story. Uncle Michael had died of pneumonia, but it was a complication of AIDS. Andrew was Michael's partner, the one who'd called the night before. They'd been together for years.

Louisa opened her mouth to ask a question, but Margaret held up her palm flat and tears ran down her face so hard, like a curtain, a stream, and Louisa said, let me drive, Mom. As they pulled over to switch places, Cody's mind rushed back to junior high, the scary magazine covers black and red with viruses and needles and huge white letters, and her questions in the kitchen where Margaret did all the talking but Cody's eyes slid to her father, who was making a sandwich, his back straight, and how he sat at the table and silently chewed while Margaret reassured her—AIDS was from drugs, the kind you shoot into your veins, or a mistake at a hospital, or when men were gay. She shouldn't be afraid. A tenth-grade girl got sent to the principal's office for saying to another kid, "I hope you die of AIDS," and the assembly that Friday was about insults, what couldn't be a joke. For months Cody had been unsettled—how small was a virus? Where would it be?—but she hadn't thought of AIDS in years.

Louisa pulled away from the curb and Margaret wiped her face with her forearm. She drew her hair into a tie and spoke again. Andrew had called—maybe a week ago?—and said the end was nearing. I'd never met Andrew, said Margaret, I meant to go, I did. My brother—I wanted to see him again. But she delayed. She put it off, thinking she'd go after the visit to Dorie, which had been long planned. Cody drilled her mother from the back seat—did Pop know? Who was Andrew, exactly? When had she last spoken to Michael? Cody could only recall intermittent phone calls on holidays, but Margaret mentioned Michael often, so easily and fondly, their childhood, what he liked and didn't. His picture hung taped to the cupboard. Why would Margaret not have gone? It was the wrong time to ask, Cody could see, and her questions lay dry in her mouth. She tried to catch Louisa's gaze over the back seat, but her sister's eyes stayed on the road, with an occasional glance toward their mother.

"I know why I didn't go." Margaret said, as if Cody had asked her aloud after all. "Yes, yes, I do. I do. I was afraid." She shook her head and the last word choked out, the tears running again, her lips and face curled into monstrous angles, puckered and raw. She banged her fist on the armrest.

Louisa grabbed Margaret's hand and held it between them on the front seat, and Cody touched her mother's shoulder.

"Mama, don't cry, I'm sorry, I'm so sorry," Louisa said, reaching for the side of her mother's face so the wheel swerved. "You did what you thought was best."

"I didn't," said Margaret. "I was a *coward*. The best would have been to go to see my brother. My parents *never* went to him, I never went. Never, not once in his whole life, and not even when he was sick! I made excuses, Louisa. I have to live with that—I did *not* do my best."

"You could go visit Andrew?" Louisa said. She pulled into the parking lot of the IHOP where they'd meet her friend for the carpool. "I know it's not the same, but—"

"I'd be too ashamed," Margaret said.

Louisa killed the engine and they sat, quiet, the car full of so much unsaid there was no place to begin.

"Taylor's here, I see her car," Louisa said. "You don't have to come in. I'll tell her you guys had to go." Cody hoped her mother would agree and they could leave, not chit-chat with a person they'd never see again.

"No, it's okay," said Margaret. "I want to buy her breakfast, a thank you for driving you. We need to eat anyway." In the morning's haste, their carefully packed lunches were left in Dorie's refrigerator.

Margaret opened her door, then swung it closed again and sat still. The girls waited.

"Don't ever be afraid of someone else's life," she said. Her voice was small and flat. She looked in the rearview mirror and ran her fingers under her eyes. Calmer, she twisted in her seat to face them. She cleared her throat and her voice came out strong. "Do you hear me, girls? Other people's lives are nothing to be afraid of." Margaret's eyes shifted between theirs, demanding, until Cody and Louisa both nodded, told her that yes, they understood, they knew. That they wouldn't be afraid.

CLINT LINDSAY

I CAN'T WAIT TO GET OUT of this fucking town. Horses, dust, people minding your business—who gives a shit about any of it, not me. The tourists come through starting in May and take their pictures in front of the train depot and the river pullouts and order huckleberry milkshakes like they're the Fountain of Youth. "Aren't you so lucky to *live* here," says one pasty lady leaning on her pasty husband while I wipe the windows of their rental car. Lucky how, I don't say, like living next to a national fucking park is so different than living any goddamn place you don't want to be. If I could leave today I would, but last time I left I came home in the back of the trooper's car and I got no money anyway, so here I am. I pumped their gas and washed their windows but I didn't smile. That guy's cowboy boots probably cost more than my car is worth, not that that's saying much. If he ever touched a horse, I'll be damned. "All hat and no cattle," that's what my dad would say, about the only thing he's ever said that I'd repeat, by the way. The rest of it is bullshit.

People think small towns are so great if they're not from one, if they drive through for vacation or on the way to somewhere else, but I'll tell you what—every single person who lives here is basically a fraud. When no one pays attention to you except to shake their heads, you can find stuff out. Just because I'm no good at school doesn't mean I'm too dumb to see who's a lech and who's a lying sack of shit and who didn't really want their kids and which golden girl gives head in the back seat of a car. Stick around if you want to know who's who.

For starters: My father's a "great guy"—and also, a jackass who thinks he's better than everyone else, a perfectionist jackass who hasn't asked me a question in ten years. And my mother! He doesn't ask her anything either, except do you need a hot water bottle, or what can I bring you? Those aren't the questions she's hoping for when she lies in the dark with her back to the door and her room smells like old flowers and slept-on hair. What I would ask her is, what did you want, Mama? I think I know her answer—no more let downs. But I've never asked, which I am totally aware makes me just as bad as good old Doyle. Chip off the fucking block.

My brother Nate is a decent guy but he's so busy kissing ass. He thinks he's hot shit because he got to third base with Louisa, big deal. She was probably too drunk to go all the way. It *is* true, Cody, oh yeah, sorry, who do you think's bought her vodka? Who's taken her home when she's shit-faced and left her at the end of your long-ass driveway so she could crawl home and pretend she wasn't rescued by the neighborhood fuck-up who knows exactly how to drive drunk? I thought so.

And Cody, you and your goddamn father, the two of you like a special club no one else can join? I know it's the quiet people you have to watch out for. They have all kinds of opinions, and no one's good enough to hear them. They're never the fools.

I could wreck their world. I could wreck Cody's world in under ten words: *He isn't who you think he is*. I can about see her face—she likes to think she's tough but she worships him, and the ones who love that much are the ones you can hurt. Mrs. K, she might be the only true story in this town. I'm sure she's got a fault—who doesn't—but she's always been kind to me. She asks me stuff—what's next for you, Clint?—when I barely passed high school, as if I had options. Or, how do you like this? she'll say, arranging daisies in a jar, as if she wants my opinion. Sometimes I wanna tell her exactly what I know about everyone she loves. Then I think of her questions and those flowers. It's so easy to hurt. So far, I don't say a word.

PERFECTLY NORMAL (1994)

A GREYHOUND BUS RIDE from Kalispell, Montana, to La Grande, Oregon cost $12, for a barely flushing toilet, three breaks at dusty rest stops, and eighteen rows of sticky and restless people without enough money to fly. Cody and Margaret had visited Louisa at college during her freshman year, but this was Cody's first time alone. Rumpled and famished, she stepped down the steep stairs into the windy parking lot of a McDonald's. While they waited for the driver to pull her luggage out from beneath the bus, Louisa told Cody she was having an abortion. That weekend. Tomorrow. Happy spring break, she said.

"Jesus, Louisa," said Cody. "Can you wait for my bag, I have to pee."

Cody fled to the bathrooms—cleaner than the foul stall on the bus, where everyone could hear—and splashed water on her face to zap her bloodshot eyes. When she returned to her sister, they sat in a once-shiny booth for hot fries, large and shared, with a limp apple pie for dessert. Louisa had scheduled the appointment so Cody could go with her. "I'm sorry to drop this on you, Cody, there's only two days a month they can do it, and I didn't want to wait. I meant to tell you on the phone but . . ." Louisa twirled a strand of her coppery hair around her finger. "I was afraid you wouldn't come."

"Louisa, for Pete's sake," said Cody. "Like I wouldn't come."

"I know, I know. It's a long story," Louisa said. At a party she'd met some guy visiting from Seattle. She got a little drunk, which she usually didn't do anymore because of her so-called shitty judgment. He was sweet enough, Louisa said, but we were both idiots. No way around that.

Cody had not kissed a boy yet, as a senior in high school and by her own measure barely a woman, flat-chested and slim. Even now, visiting a college, her hair was in braids and she wore running shoes and a hooded 4-H sweatshirt. Kissing was on her mind, but sex was totally unimaginable, except when it came to Louisa. Her sister had always been miles ahead.

"Of course I'll go with you," Cody said. "Don't even ask."

Cody hardly slept and they woke early. Louisa had to be at the clinic by 6:45 a.m. and neither of them was hungry. The morning hallway in Louisa's downtown building was silent. An old house partitioned into small apartments full of college kids, its stairways and porches overflowed with bicycles and hockey sticks and ashtrays. Everyone was asleep and the girls snuck down the steps, careful not to knock over the empty beer bottles on every rail and landing. The clinic was only six blocks away so they walked; the streetlights snapped off as the sun rose during the time it took to get there. In the waiting room hung a poster of the twenty-eight-day cycle, the reddish cells of ovaries like fish roe. Eggs, Cody thought. It's all eggs.

"Remember your first period?" Cody asked her sister as Louisa filled out paperwork, rubbing her chin with a pink feather taped to the end of the pen. Loose hairs from her ponytail strayed around her face as if she were wrapped in a fluffy shawl, and the purple moons under her eyes were as dark as makeup.

Louisa had told her the story when Cody was too young to understand, so it made an impression. Louisa was fourteen, staying with a friend at her family's cabin on Flathead Lake. Jaclyn was the girl's name, which to Cody sounded like a doll. Jaclyn went to high school in Whitefish and Louisa met her at summer camp. She was a flouncy, giggling girl, "like coyote shit," Louisa said, "all powder and hair." But Jaclyn invited Louisa to the lake and who said no to that? The cottage next door was full of boys, preppy boys from Missoula, a rich family with a fancy house, not a cabin at all, including a boathouse down by the lake and a shared wooden dock too smooth for splinters.

The bleeding started the night Louisa arrived and it soaked the sheets and her underwear. In the morning, she hid in the bathroom for almost an hour, rinsing the heavy wet cotton in the tub, and crying. Even she agreed it was a little dramatic. Finally, Jaclyn's mother came in and took her by the shoulders. Enough was enough. While Jaclyn flirted outside with the neighbor boys who'd come to ask if the girls could go out in the rowboat, her mother dug out a tampon and unwrapped it for Louisa, held it out like a candle, Louisa said. But Louisa couldn't get it in. It was dry and rough and much too big, so Jaclyn's mother knelt before the toilet seat where Louisa sat with her legs spread. She put her hand over Louisa's and pushed it in, the angle desperately wrong. Louisa almost threw up it hurt so much.

Once Cody thought the memory all the way through, she was sorry she'd brought it up, here, but Louisa was unfazed.

"Oh god, yes, how could I forget my first period. Maybe I'm doomed, all my womanly milestones are bound to suck." She turned to Cody and whispered, her eyes wide behind her slightly sticky lashes, "That bitch who rammed that thing up in me! Can you imagine? And remember the rest, those boys, the lake?" Louisa out in the rowboat, all of them having a go at the oars, and when her turn came it got windy and the boat began to rock on the crests and falls of the waves. By that point, one oar was loose from its lock, broken in a flirty tussle between Jaclyn and the tallest of the boys—my dad will kill me, stop it, you ass!—and the neck of the oar slipped along the gunwale, the blade slack and useless in the water. Louisa was anxious and she didn't row well, a ranch girl who'd hardly been out in a boat before, and they spun in circles, out of control. Louisa was not one to panic, but she was scared.

One of the boys took the oars like he was a rescuer. Lucky you're so sexy, girlie, you sure can't row, he said, and Jaclyn turned on Louisa then, mocking as hard as the boys did, worse, even. Louisa thought, I got my period and my crotch is on fire, you little traitor, and anyway, she hated to be rescued, ever. She took care of herself. The boys teased her the whole ride back, one spinning the boat in circles just to make her mad. Louisa could be easygoing, but not then. When they got to the dock, she scrambled out first, hauling the loose oar with her, and shoved the boat away with her foot. Fuck you all in your stupid boat, she said. Give me a horse any day. She didn't even like horses that much.

It took the boys ten minutes to row the boat in because of the wind and no oar, Jaclyn crying—faking, Louisa knew—and at the end, the biggest boy had to jump in and swim, towing the boat to the dock by the line at the bow. He swallowed water and panicked like an idiot, and acted enough like he might drown that Louisa had to throw him the life ring from the post of the dock as Jaclyn's father came storming down the planks so they flexed, and shoved her out of the way. He hauled the boy in, pulling the towrope hand over hand, and helped the rest of them out of the boat. Jaclyn cried and tattled on Louisa and her father said, "Don't invite her kind, then."

I never forgot that, Louisa said. My kind.

She would have walked home right then but it was two hours away by car so she kept to herself. Alone in the upstairs bathroom, she pulled out the swollen tampon and bit her tongue to keep from screaming. Louisa wrapped an extra sock around the crotch of her underwear and avoided everyone. She skipped dinner and filched the pantry for packaged peanut butter crackers with the tiny red stick. "Aren't you hungry, dear," Jaclyn's mother asked, "we have real food," and Louisa shook her head. She read on the porch late into the evening—a mildewed copy of *The Thornbirds* she'd found on a shelf, the memory of which she'd masturbate over for years—even though it was so dim she had to squint and mosquitoes bit her legs. The boys called, *Hey, cowgirl* for the rest of the evening and after Louisa got home the next day she threw two bloody socks in the burn barrel behind the house. She never spoke to Jaclyn again, though she pointed her out to Cody when they played opposite each other in sports, Whitefish High in their fancy jerseys and the C-Falls kids scrappy and smelling like manure.

A STOCKY NURSE WITH drawn-on eyebrows emerged from a door near the front desk and called Louisa's name. Cody went up with her.

"Well, who's this?" the nurse asked. Her tone was sweet, more like a children's librarian than a nurse.

"My sister. Can she come?" Louisa adjusted her bag on her shoulder. Cody could tell she was nervous.

"Are you a minor, dear?" the woman asked. Cody shook her head and started to get out her driver's license but the woman motioned for her to put it away. "You can come back in a few minutes, hon. But first I have to speak with your sister alone. That's the law, dear." She smiled again and took Louisa by the elbow. Cody returned to the chair Louisa had sat in, the seat still warm.

The waiting room was empty except for a petite girl with wispy hair and a boy that could have been her brother but was probably her boyfriend. On the floor at their feet sat a car seat much too large for that girl to carry easily, with a baby slumped in it like a bag of chicken feed. The boy rocked the seat with his foot even though the baby was not crying or making any sounds. You could hardly see the baby at all, only a lump of colorful fuzz. It seemed like a bad idea to rock a baby that was not crying. Cody tried to think of a strong opinion then, about Louisa keeping the baby and her taking care of it—a niece—but she couldn't make up a position worth saying out loud. Everything was just a guess at what was right.

The nurse returned and invited Cody through a different door that closed behind them with a heavy huff. The woman led her down a bright hall past a row of rooms, their doors open to sharp metal tables and shiny sinks and empty chairs. Her shoes squeaked against the white tiles and Cody hurried to keep up. In the last room off the hallway, Louisa sat on the edge of the exam table in a baggy blue paper gown that gapped below her collarbones. The nurse explained the procedure in diminutive terms—a small shot, a little tugging, a short time—and then helped Louisa lay back on the table and lifted her socked feet into the leather-covered stirrups, which Cody had learned about a few months before at her first "lady parts exam," as her mother called it. Cody would not have guessed that a clinic and a barn would have much in common, but stirrups, those she knew.

The doctor was old and gentle with spiky white hair and he looked over the tops of his glasses as he spoke. "Everything down here is perfectly normal," he told Louisa, who laid on her back with the paper sheet tented over her legs and held Cody's hand. The first nurse disappeared and a new nurse with two wheaty braids entered the room and immediately began to open drawers and unwrap plastic supplies.

She stopped at the table, shifting the doctor's metal cart on its wheels to get closer to Louisa's side. "Sorry to switch nurses on ya, hon, I'm Lindy, and I'm going into doctor's assistant mode here," she said to Louisa, "so get my attention if you need anything emotional." She wore green scrubs and a button with a yellow cartoon dog: "Give Blood or Go Home!"

"Here comes the anesthetic," said the nurse, loosely gripping Louisa's upper arm.

The doctor pointed the needle away in the air and pushed the plunger until liquid squirted. "Now you're going to feel a little prick," he said.

"That's what got me into this mess," said Louisa.

The doctor tucked his lips and Lindy laughed out loud. "My goodness, I don't think he'll say *that* again!"

Cody stood at Louisa's shoulder and looked down at her sister's face. Under the florescent lights Louisa's regular beauty dulled a little—she was usually the brightest thing in the room—and Cody could see the tiny creases at the corners of her eyes where the mascara pooled, and the small pores where her nose sloped down to her cheeks the way a ridge drops into a creek. Each freckle stood out like it had been drawn with a marker. It made Cody think of Raggedy Ann, whose floppiness had always frustrated her.

The procedure was shorter than Cody had imagined it would be. The doctor pressed a foot pump and the small, square machine started with a low hum, the innocuous sound of a bathroom fan. Louisa squeezed Cody's fingers tight like a rancher's handshake and took short sucking breaths. Small beads of sweat popped out on her forehead, sudden and round as raindrops on window glass. The room smelled of chemicals and underneath that, the sweetness of bodies, and Cody leaned down to Louisa and chanted what came to mind, a song of almost nonsense, the way you'd calm a scared horse: *hey now, tshhh-tshhh-tshhh, it's okay, girl, hush-hush, almost over, shhh.*

When the vacuum stopped the room was quiet until the doctor pulled out a rattling shelf and removed Louisa's feet from the stirrups to place them there. He tucked the wrinkled drape around her legs.

"Any questions for me?" He patted Louisa's knee.

"Is it over?"

"All over," he said.

"We told you it was short," the nurse said over her shoulder, in constant motion—trash can, plastic again, a paper towel swiped across a cart.

Louisa pushed herself up on her elbows. "Thank you," she said to the doctor. Color came back to her pale cheeks in two round splotches below the hollows of her eyes.

"You are so welcome, dear. Please take care of yourself. And come back for your follow-up. Okay?" He looked right at Louisa, then at Cody, nodding. "Promise me. It's very important."

"I will," said Louisa. "It's hard to picture right now, but I usually do what I'm supposed to."

The nurse laughed again. "I like this girl. What a darn good sport."

It was true. Cody would say the same. It was amazing how, in fifteen minutes, under not ideal conditions, people could see Louisa for who she was.

The doctor and nurse left the room—more squeaking shoes. Cody helped her sister up and Louisa stood with bare legs and pink socks on the linoleum and wiped between her legs with the wadded-up paper sheet. A drop of bright blood hit the floor and Louisa dabbed it with her foot. "A souvenir," she said. When she dropped the paper away from her waist there was more blood, and Louisa stooped to wipe it.

"I'll get it, Lou," said Cody. "Don't clean."

When Lindy knocked to reenter the room, Louisa was dressed and sitting in the chair, her eyes a little off, but as far as Cody could see, no worse for wear. Lindy led them both down the hallway to the aftercare room, where Louisa sat in a Lazy Boy with the leg rest kicked out and a heating pad on her lap. Twice, another nurse took Louisa's vital signs, "as normal as normal can be," she said. In between checks, Louisa dozed with her eyes closed and Cody ate the animal crackers and paged through old magazines. After half an hour, Lindy returned. "Let's get you on out of here," she said. "Up and at 'em." Louisa might be hungry and could eat whatever she wanted. "Have a hamburger. Take some Tylenol for the cramps. As far as bodies go, this is no big deal. Except for no below-the-belt until after your follow-up."

"Or ever," said Louisa.

"Easy to say right now, hon. That's why—" The nurse punched her arm into the air and jostled a rattling paper bag in front of her like a pom-pom. Louisa made no move toward it so Cody took it and peered inside. The bag was full of condoms in shiny colored wrappers you could mistake for candy. Lindy shook her finger, then squeezed Louisa's shoulder. "Good girls."

They went out for chocolate milkshakes and Louisa swallowed the pills from the packet the nurse had given her. "It's weird, isn't it? Something can be hard or scary, whatever, but in your body, no big deal."

"Were you scared?" Cody pulled the shake through her straw and her throat went cold.

"Not really. Nervous, I guess."

"Are you sore?" asked Cody.

"A little. Not that bad."

"Are you sad?"

Louisa sipped through her own straw and looked at the ceiling. "I feel older, I guess. But in another way, extra, extra young."

Cody nodded. She could see exactly why. She thought again of a niece—nephew did not occur to her, though if pressed she'd admit to liking small boys better—and she kept it to herself. Over the years, she'd think about the niece more than she'd guessed she would have, the little girl alive in her mind if she felt lonely or misunderstood. Not quite the same depth of character as her imaginary friends from childhood, but akin to that. A person just for her.

Louisa had cramps off and on all weekend so they laid low, no visit to the antique store where the year before, Margaret bought Louisa a fur stole for a Great Gatsby party and Cody a halter dress which she'd never worn, and thank god, no sneaking into Lyle's, the downtown bar with a Johnny Cash cover band and bouncers that didn't check IDs. In the bathroom after a shower, Cody pinched a couple condoms from the clinic's paper bag. Louisa's roommate was out of town so they watched old movies—pulled the shades in the middle of the day and ate pepperoni and mushroom pizza out of the box and turned the volume up loud. *Breakfast at Tiffany's, The African Queen*. Louisa dissected the costumes, and Cody was riveted by lives she had never imagined. Boat trips. An apartment with a balcony. She ate more than her half of the pizza but Louisa never minded.

At the end of the weekend, they walked to the bus station, and as they hugged Louisa whispered into the air over her sister's shoulder, "Thank you."

Cody told Louisa, I like your kind.

A CUSTOMER

AT THE T WHERE RANCH ROAD meets the highway, there's a wooden sign tacked to a telephone pole. I'd seen it for months and then once I pulled over and read it out loud. "Handmade Furniture, 4 miles," with an arrow and a number, 1154. Later that fall, I had to buy honey for my wife. She knew a woman who kept bees and when the kids got sick, we tried it all. Honey from local pollen was supposed to be good for asthma, that's what they said, and it made sense to me, curing yourself with what was around you. My wife said it's up Ranch Road and I remembered that sign about the furniture, and I told her I'd go.

The man I met, Josiah Kinzler, that was his name—he was not what I expected. Maybe I'd made up a mountain man in my mind, I don't know. But he was smaller than me. He had a beard, not tidy but not wild, the kind you had to take some care with. Even with sawdust on his jeans and his hands by no stretch clean, the guy managed to look neat. He let me into his shop, and I considered what I wanted him to make for me. I knew as soon as I got inside I was going to place an order.

Another man and an older girl—Kinzler's daughter, you could see it in her face—worked at the back of the room. She raised her hand in greeting when we entered, but she didn't speak. My girls were noisier.

"How'd you learn this trade?" I asked.

"A man who worked for my father taught me some. Some from odd jobs. Mainly the wood'll show you." He shrugged. "Screwing up, trying again."

What I wanted to ask but had no way of saying was, how do you do this, make something I have never considered? A table that looked like a tree, a box that could have grown from a pinecone. The wood teaching him seemed possible, another idea that had never crossed my mind.

"You're an artist," I told him.

"Exactly," said the other man, an apprentice, I guessed. He was younger, and eager to please.

"I don't know about that." Josiah said.

I fancied I knew about artists. My father painted landscapes; one hangs in the museum in Kalispell. He painted the same basic western scene a million times: cattle, horses, fields, sun, sometimes an elk. What he knew. But when he died, we found a closet full of paintings of naked women. On water, on land, in clouds. Mermaids, angels. An entire other life in his mind. How about that, my brother and I said. He knew more than we thought. We got rid of them before my mother could see, burned at my brother's barn in an oily smoking pile. Maybe my mother wouldn't have minded. They were mild, barely pornographic. But a secret, that can rub you the wrong way. I didn't want her to have to think about my father picturing women who weren't her. Burning them may have been wrong, considering his reputation. But they weren't good. I thought I was protecting him.

"I wouldn't say artist," said Josiah. I thought for sure he wouldn't offer more. He was a type of guy I was used to, didn't care for talk about himself. So, I said, "Beautiful wood," touching the surfaces, to fill the space. But then he surprised me. Started speaking at the same time as I did, and he said words I've never forgotten: "People think of trees as wood, but there's spaces in trees. Between the limbs, around the trunk, how the top hits the sky. I leave the spaces in my things. So you think of branches. You think of living under trees."

"I'd like a table," I said. It was doubtful I could afford it, though not impossible. I was better off than lots of people at that time, what with the mills closing and the ranches getting split up into condo land, Californians coming in all over, though not as fast as they would ten years later, old Montana families barely hanging on and the Indians pushed even further to the edges than that. I knew what I was asking for would cost a pretty penny. A table, I said, making it up right there out of my mouth, a family-sized table where all of us can sit. It was 10 at the time, my wife and me, our three, my brother and his wife and boys. But I said 12. He nodded, glad, I guessed, for the work and the money it would bring. A big table like that, it was a thousand bucks, easy.

We bullshitted a little longer, about the wintery teeth in the air, when the first snow might come. I took out my checkbook, offered five hundred dollars down.

"I'll take your word," he said, holding up his palm as if to stop me. I should have insisted. Coming out of my mind like that, a table I had never even once wished for before that moment, when it became all I wanted? Money was the only way to make that real. But he shook his head and started moving boards around, so I left.

His apprentice followed me to my car and said, "Thank you, sir."

"Oh sure," I said, thinking he meant the order. "Thank you."

"I don't know what you did to get him to say that—the trees, the spaces? He's never said that to me. And I'm glad to have heard it. So, thanks." I knew what he meant. As I said, it's stuck with me.

At the mailbox where the driveway hit the road, I saw the girl in my rearview, jogging to catch me, her eyes cast down. I stopped and rolled open my window and waited for her to arrive. She took a second to catch her breath and pushed her hair out of her eyes with the crook of her arm how only women do.

"We could use that check," she said. I felt awful. I knew her father hadn't sent her running. I took it out of my pocket, scribbled the amount and handed it to her.

"Thanks," she said, and walked back up the driveway.

I forgot the honey that day. At home I had to tell my wife I'd spent jars and jars of it on a table instead. I waited almost a year for it to be finished. He had to plan in advance for a slab that big. And I knew it took time to make what he did. I didn't mind waiting. It gave me a chance to set the money aside. I paid the rest when I went to pick it up. It took four of us to load that table onto the trailer, my share alone heavy as anything I'd carried in my life.

In our dining room, the table looks like a big boat moored at a small dock. When we brought it in and put the chairs around it, the rest of the room disappeared. It was like a table with windows, like we were eating outside. When it rains hard and you sit in a chair with your back so close to the plate glass, you can imagine your shirt soaked, the fabric all flat to your skin.

I went back for the honey later. It didn't cure the asthma, but it tasted sweet.

PART TWO

\\

Barn's burnt down—
now
I can see the moon.

—MASAHIDE (STUDENT OF BASHO)

HOTSHOTS (1995)

CODY KINZLER AND JESS MCCAFFERTY acquired their third dog in October, on the way home from a trip to the Oregon coast after fire season ended and a wad of cash in a pocket was the beginning of money instead of the end. The dog approached at a gas station outside Klamath Falls when they were road-stiff and tired of each other's company. It sidled across the parking lot as Jess pumped gas and Cody searched her pockets for bills. Her wallet was missing in the heap of the truck's bed and it was her turn to pay.

"Hey, pup," Cody said as the dog dipped its face into a bucket of windshield washing fluid. "Don't drink that." She tapped the pail with her toe and the dog licked its lips and backed away.

"Who's he?" said Jess, glancing up from the pump, out from under his shaggy bangs. He always watched the numbers scroll by and stopped on the exact dollar, or fifty cents if he missed, unless he was distracted.

"Actually, I think she's female." Cody squatted and ran her hand under the dog's belly. The dog licked her forearm. "I think she's had a litter. Her teats are hanging."

"Did you find money?" Jess returned the nozzle to the pump. He leaned against the truck and lifted his face to the low-angle sun.

"God, Jess, look at her coat. She looks like hell." The dog licked her face, pawing and sniffing. It rolled over on its back, exposing swollen nipples. Cody ran a light finger along a shallow cut up the width of its midsection and the dog yelped and flipped over. She stood up and the dog walked around the back of the truck and sat down. It eyed her and when Cody approached it again, it whined and moved forward. Cody circled the truck twice, the dog two steps ahead and looking over its shoulder. It didn't run, though, and when Cody clicked her tongue softly and stopped moving, the dog stopped too.

"Come on, Cody. Let's pay. We should get going." Jess opened the driver's door and put his booted foot up. He stretched his arms over his head and gave her a half grimace, half grin, trying to provoke a smile.

"I want to take her." Cody scratched behind the dog's ears again. "I'm sure she's a stray. You can see her ribs."

Jess let out a breath. "Cody, she's wild, we can't take her. She'd rather run free around here anyway. What the hell would we do with her? She'll piss in the truck." Cody rolled her eyes and went into the station.

"Pump six, I think, the red pickup." She leaned on the counter and glanced at the man behind it. He was obviously Native, and reminded her of a busted-up movie star, craggy and sun-bit, with a face she wanted to sneak another look at.

"You like that dog?"

Cody showed her surprise. "Yeah. Is she yours?"

"Nah. Stray, rez dog. Lives off what people feed her. Donuts. Hotdog buns from the trash. Little beggar. Easier than gophers."

"Think anyone'd mind if I took her?"

"We'd get over it." The man looked right at her. His mouth was still and yet he was laughing.

The register totaled $18.56—Jess distracted. Cody laid the bills on the counter and came up with a quarter, a dime, and three nickels from her pocket, and one sticky Tic Tac and a tube of lip balm.

"I need six more cents, hold on." She started to the door.

"I got it." The man emptied six pennies from a green glass ashtray behind the counter. "Adoption fee. We pay you." She had never encountered someone who projected such amusement while his face showed none.

"Thank you," Cody said.

"Headed north?"

"Montana, actually. North of Kalispell. How'd you know?"

He shrugged. "Plates."

Cody knew the tribes in her part of Montana, the Blackfeet on the east side of the park and the Flathead along the highway to Missoula. She'd known a couple of Native kids at school, though not well, and her friend Boz, a sawyer on the fire crew, was from the Rocky Boy Rez, out east of Great Falls. He was an ace at saw repair, his nickname, "The Surgeon." "I'm an Indian," Boz said that season to the new crew boss, a skinny chain-smoker from California who called them all "dude." "You can keep your Native Americans in your museum," Boz told him. Cody didn't know anything about Oregon Indians. She realized she'd spent four days in their terrain and had never considered them at all. An awkward guilt rose up in her along with the wish to connect, to assuage it, and she said to the man, "You know, my dad's hero, he has a picture he ripped out of a magazine, above the table in his shop, it's Chief Joseph." *Dumb, Cody,* she thought, *shut up, shut up.*

"Huh," said the man.

"He's—" Cody struggled for words beyond "Indian," an actual name—"Nez Pierce, I think?" *Perce,* she thought as soon as it was out, not Pierce. Her junior high teacher's exasperated correction. "Nez Perce."

"Your dad is, or Chief Joe?"

She looked at him and now he was laughing at her outright. Not unkindly. She deserved it.

"Chief Joe," she said.

"Don't know him."

She twisted her mouth to mock herself but the man wasn't looking anymore. He gestured out the window toward the dog.

"She's wild, you'll hear her howl. Part coyote, maybe."

Cody pushed open the door with her foot. "Thanks again. I'll take real good care of her."

He nodded. "You're welcome, kemosabe." The man saluted, ending with his thumb cocked and two fingers pointed at her, a smiling gun.

CODY FIXED HERSELF FOR AN ARGUMENT, but Jess was in the bathroom and the dog already in the truck bed, scratching at the tailgate and circling the mattress where the two of them slept. When Cody peered into the topper window the dog whined and sat on its tail, as black and curled as the heavy rubber snake from her childhood toy box.

Jess knew what mattered when, and this was one of the first things Cody had loved about him, besides the look of his slender ass in Nomex pants when he hiked in front of her on the fire line. The first day the crew met at the Forest Service office in Columbia Falls to fill out paperwork, and they recognized each other at the same time and at the same time said each other's names. Jess McCafferty? she said, and Cody Kinzler, said Jess, holy shit! There was a half step when they each decided what to focus on—Louisa's old boyfriend? Cody's school-girl crush, could he have known? That knife he'd stolen, she'd never told—until they settled on more obvious and neutral terrain. How'd you get the job, what had happened to whom in the time since Jess's family moved to Billings in his senior year.

The beginning of fire season there was so much downtime, the standing around not yet turned to the hurry-up-and-wait and then the ramped-up flash that characterized the middle of fire season. Jess told Cody about high school on the east side of the state, learning to break broncs in 4-H but deciding not to join the circuit like half the boys he knew. His family stayed there but he missed the mountains. Cody said not much was different on her end. Same land, same deal. Louisa had left college and moved to Missoula, Josiah in his cabin and Cody with her mother in the house. Jess had seen a flyer for Josiah's business pinned on the bulletin board at the post office—"Handmade Furniture, call for appointment."

"I was glad as hell to see there were still Kinzlers around," he said, a little shy.

When they ate meals in fire camp, Jess let Cody ahead of him in the food line with a hand on the small of her back, though on the crew men and women were supposed to be treated the same. They looked alike in their green Nomex pants and brown leather belts and their dark red T-shirts saying "Flathead Hotshots" with a goofy lakes-and-hoses logo some hippie college kid designed the year before. They didn't have to wear the yellow Nomex shirts when they weren't on active fire line, and their arms and necks tanned brown as Boz's while they played hacky sack in gravel parking lots all across the county and waited for the first big burn.

Cody knew early on, but did not admit until a few weeks in, that her childhood crush on Jess still had teeth. Her lone experience even close to love—and also to sex, which didn't always go together, she knew—had been a late senior year boyfriend. They rescued each other from graduating as virgins and he was the only guy up until that point who had made her feel what was different about being a woman than being a person. Jess did that, too. Around him she tugged at the hem of her T-shirt to loosen it, aware of the way her chest curved it and caught his eye.

For the other guys, Cody felt a sibling's kinship, like suddenly getting the brothers she'd never had, and she loaded in and out of the trucks with them, rolled hoses and sharpened saws and ran laps with full packs side-by-side without a thought of where one left off and another began. But if she ended up tight with Jess in the front seat of the six-pack, her leg where it leaned against his blazed. She walked differently if she could sense him looking, and sometimes just by getting up, she knew she'd draw his glance. He'd smile and look down and she would busy herself with a pointless task, any excuse to rush away.

Chemistry, Louisa called it when they talked on the phone. "My favorite subject, ha ha!" Cody didn't mention any names.

THE DRIVE NORTHEAST FROM OREGON was hot and long. Cody and Jess decided to take the round-about route home, eschewing the straight shot through Spokane for the southern route along the Lochsa River and through Missoula, though Louisa was in Bozeman that week with her new boyfriend so they couldn't visit. Cody hadn't met him. It could be hard to keep track of who or what Louisa loved.

Road construction in three different states slowed them even more and they spent an uncomfortable night in a noisy paid campground in the Clearwater Forest because it got too dark to find a pullout. Tension rippled under flat sentences. Jess resented paying for what he thought should be wild, or free, and Cody was sick of arguing about trivial things. She craved a big holler, or quiet. They cooked on the tailgate, each performing the duties they fell to. Cody, water. Jess, stove. Cody chop and open, Jess boil and stir.

The new dog sat at the bumper tied up with a hank of old climbing rope from the emergency kit, meant to be used for a tow. The mutt walked out to the end of the line and stood still, face pointed toward the dark brush lining the edge of the site. Every so often a small whine, but otherwise focused and motionless. It could have been a sentry, or an assassin. Then a brief argument about whether to let the dog sleep in the back with them—Cody sure, why not, and Jess no way, she could have lice—and when they slid in together and pulled the topper window shut, they heard the dog scratch herself a spot in the dirt beneath the tailgate and drop to the ground with a sigh.

"She's already staying close," Cody whispered. "We're her family."

Jess pulled Cody into him and their legs kicked free of the unzipped nylon sleeping bags and found each other, scratched and dusty and warm. What they could agree on.

SUMMER HAD STARTED SLOW and the crew stayed in-state working projects and managing small lightning fires. Then there was a hot, quick start in the Kootenai and they fell on it with the pent-up macho verve of a lazy wet June, and money in the budget to burn. One afternoon Cody and Jess were left behind at a helicopter pad while the driver took the short green school bus to pick up the rest of the crew at the base of the ridge, an hour away by a rutted Forest Service road. The crew had dug line downhill while Cody and Jess had drawn the job at the top of the ridge, awaiting a drop of a second saw to replace one that blew a cylinder. It was overkill, an expense that would never fly later in the season, but a new pilot needed a training run, so—. Except for a stationed lookout, they always tagged a job in pairs. Cody and Jess had not yet been placed together. Usually the rest of the crew padded them with an easy vibe in which to hip-check and piggyback or grab and swing, the easy physical camaraderie of a gang.

Alone, their job was to wait, which, in lieu of urgency or mission, turned into lie on your back on the ridgetop and watch the clouds pass overhead. The ground was dusty and bare, plants and duff cleared away to make a safe zone devoid of flammables for a landing pad. The gravelly soil rolled rough and warm under their bodies. Cody lay spread eagle on her back like a gingerbread cutout and windmilled her arms and legs.

"Did you ever make snow angels?" Jess asked. He lay back and mimicked her, a few feet away. They swept at the dirt with flat jumping jacks. Lazy game.

"Yep. And snowmen. Louisa called them snow friends because she didn't know why they had to be men. She liked to make them with boobs." It was out before she could think of how embarrassed she'd feel, Louisa and boobs out of her mouth in front of Jess, who'd groped her sister's chest, she knew. But he didn't note it. They both quit waving on the ground after a while and lay still, the hot wind gusting in the afternoon. Their hands spread toward each other and when they stopped moving their fingers touched.

The chopper approached from the north. They could hear thwacking from far off, giving them time to stand up and brush off each other's backs. Cody put her hands on Jess's shoulders from behind and ran her palms down the back of his yellow shirt to wipe off the grit and then she stopped at his belt, holding on to it, brave fingers tucked in between the leather and the waistband—bare skin, fine hair. They stood like that. In front of them the dirt remained swept into their touching shapes, like evidence.

"Cookie cutters," Jess pointed.

"Dirt angels," said Cody.

The heli came in hot and the prop wash lifted dust into the air and by the time it flew away and left behind not one saw, but two, and they got the call to hike down the line and meet the crew at the base, their outlines had disappeared, swept up in the wind. They talked loud and blunt to stave off the unspoken.

THE KOOTENAI FIRE EXPANDED, wolfing up crews until the whole state was in, the Initial Attack crews from the Rez and the mixed-agency Type 2 crews made up of odds and ends from the National Park, the Forest Service, the State. Up the North Fork, a remote cabin was threatened and Cody and Jess were sent to sweep the trail—the crew boss could not have guessed, could he, or he would have split them?—their assignment to escort hikers out of a backcountry campsite before the fire spread and pinned them there. But when Cody and Jess arrived, the campground was deserted. No sign of campers gone for the day intending to return, no stuff sacks hanging from the bear-proof food pole or nylon tents left set up with rain-flies taut and faded. They spent longer than they should have looking, up the trail toward the pass and down another spur to the lake, but despite the permit office's records, there was no sign of a camper anywhere. Above the lake to the west, a funnel of smoke morphed and swirled.

With no campers needing protection, the mission evaporated and all urgency with it. A flight crew wouldn't come in to lay hose around the cabin until the next day, and it was too late to safely hike out before dark. Even though fires usually stepped down at night, it seemed wisest to stay put. "Avoid country not seen in daylight," Jess warned, parroting one of the fire orders, shaking his finger with a grin. While he climbed atop the outhouse roof in search of a clear signal to radio their location to dispatch, Cody unlatched the cabin door and pulled off the bear-proof cover, a plywood board driven through with outward facing 16d nails, pointed as medieval spikes atop a castle wall. The packrat under the cabin rumbled and scratched and finally waddled out to piss on the woodpile stacked under the eave. It bared its yellow teeth.

The evening folded. Tactics, mission, operations, all suddenly moot. Aloneness and proximity charged the air like a new lightning strike. They passed each other closer than they needed to. Unpacked their backpacks so their hands brushed. Rolled out two bags on the twin bunks, a sleeping-apart charade. Cody hardly spoke for fear she'd say something voracious. She guessed Jess was thinking that too, but she couldn't be sure enough to dare.

Cody lifted down the fishing rod hung on nails above the cabin door and Jess caught a trout in the lake. They pan-fried it in a skillet on the two-burner Coleman that flared up in a burst of orange oily smoke. The MREs stayed in their packs. After dinner they sat on stump seats out in front of the cabin and watched the sun, obscured all day behind the smoke, setting in the thick dusk, the colors brightened by ash in the air. Jess stood up on the ends of two upright cut log rounds, one foot on each and legs spread wide.

"How do you like the cabin I built for you," he said, gesturing with his hands at the place. Cody smiled. Like she and Louisa used to do, a game out of nowhere, imaginary and without explanation.

"I love it," she said. "I can't believe you built it all for me." The lilt of Little House in her voice.

"For us," he said. She crossed her legs and cocked her head at him.

"I got the windows for trade," Jess said, hopping down from the stumps. "Another homestead up the way, the family moving on, starved out, and I traded the man three windows for a side of bacon and a flask."

"Empty or full?"

"Full, of course." From the side Jess grabbed her wrist and held it in both of his hands, then raised it to his lips and kissed it, mouth open a little way to taste her skin. She stayed on her stump and closed her eyes.

"I'm sorry to be so forward, miss, but I can't help myself," Jess said, voice low.

"No one can see," said Cody, pretending herself a lady she wasn't, dressed in petticoats instead of sweaty clothes, one thought on her reputation and the rest on his slightly chapped lips.

"I'd wait until we marry, but I haven't yet asked your father for your hand."

"It's my hand, not my father's," Cody said, her own self sneaking back in.

It was nothing like a date—the lake, the smoke, the woodpile—and that made it easier. After the first slowly undone buttons they pulled and clawed at each other so Cody had red scratches on her ass where Jess's fingers dug into her. "A wild beast got you," he said after, tracing the streaks with a light thumb. Later they'd look back and laugh at themselves, that silly game it took to rouse their courage. Fucking like rock stars and talking like pilgrims while the packrat snuffled under the cabin.

Until it got too cool, they lay in the dry grass out front of the cabin with their Nomex half-off and sticky skin and Jess whispered in her hair, "Will you marry me, my darling, and bear me twenty sons?"

THEY NAMED THE DOG MAGGIE. Cody intended to find her a home but it's hard to give up what you think you saved. Maggie never left her wild days entirely behind. The mange went away, and the nits, and her nipples shrank up and healed, but the sound of the train's whistle always made her howl and a barking dog that ran up fast triggered a nasty snarl. An east wind off the prairie carrying sage and she'd sit on her haunches and sniff, nose drilling the air. Several times Maggie ran off, gone for an hour or a day, long enough that her return was a surprise, well after they'd quit looking.

Cody's room was at the back of the first floor of her mother's house, private and cool. She thought she'd have left home by now, but she wasn't in a hurry to change. Margaret loved Jess and didn't mind him sleeping over, as long as he didn't move in. If Josiah came up for dinner and Jess was there too, when the evening got late, she'd use Josiah's old joke: Cody, let's turn the lights out so these people can leave.

Dogs in the house was different than men. Jade was almost sixteen years old and finally mellow enough to sleep inside, collapsed in a heap by the woodstove for twelve hours at a stretch, the slack lip over her teeth flaring with each breath. Jess's heeler, Sara, lay curled between the two of them. Cody's dog was Lear, a shepherd-husky cross, named for the jet and the king, though Lear was young, not old, and always hungry and he paced the rooms, his nails clicking on the kitchen planks. Maggie slept on the rug in front of the door, ready to go out and run should anyone give her the chance. She went from deep sleep to lightning speed faster than any dog Cody had ever seen.

In her green chair, Margaret scratched at a crossword puzzle and let her legs swing over the arm like a teenager. Cody knew her mother sometimes forgot they were there.

"Let's go out this weekend, let's sleep out a night. We haven't the two of us in a while." Jess picked up a strand of Cody's bronzish hair and ran his fingers to the ends, letting them drop.

"Can't. I told Dad I'd help him get wood in on Sunday," Cody said. She lay on her stomach with her head on crossed arms, her voice drowsy and soft.

"I'll help if you want." Jess adored Josiah. Admired his skill, that was easy to do. Jess's own father was in insurance. But most, he envied Josiah the focus with which Cody loved him.

"Yeah, maybe." Her voice was noncommittal. Jess let out a deep breath through his nose. He moved his hand from Cody's hair to Sara's coarse fur and worked a bur loose with two fingers. Sara pulled her head away. Jess waited until she laid it back down on her paws and resumed fussing with the knot. Sara sighed so her ribs expanded.

Jess had a problem, and he knew it. He loved Cody in the way he'd heard was possible but didn't guess would happen to him: almost painful, a sickness you didn't want to go away. At first, he'd loved her because she didn't need him; now, having found other qualities in her to love, he wished she did. Around her, his natural patience gave way to grasping, as he pushed and Cody edged away, not turning her back, exactly, but shifting to the side. It was a dance, in a way, and Jess couldn't disagree that it charged them, made the times when she faced him straight on electric enough that he craved them, like a man close to finishing a task in the dark wants a few more minutes of day.

That night, when Cody went to the bathroom Jess said to Margaret flat out what he'd been biting off for months. "You can probably tell by now, I'm in love with your girl." Talking made him braver. "I need some advice."

Margaret lowered her magazine and let it rest in her lap. "I'm not much for advice. What's up?"

"Does she even love me a little? Even a tiny bit? Has she ever said?" He shrugged with a plaintive face, making himself foolish so she'd see how serious he was.

"That's not advice, Jess! That's giving away a secret. But she wouldn't tell me anyway. It's not like her to say."

"I know," he said. "That's exactly it."

"Just wait it out," said Margaret. "If she loves you, there's no rush. If she doesn't, well, you'll find out soon enough."

"Did you know right away, you and—?" He stopped it halfway. Jess respected what Margaret and Josiah had made, spacious and, to them, unremarkable. He'd never talked about their arrangement with Cody, and perhaps there were sore spots, places to be careful pushing on. But Margaret seemed unfazed.

"I would say I did, yes. Josiah, I'm not sure. He keeps his thoughts to himself. Cody's like him that way. But knowing now or later, it doesn't mean much. It doesn't save you either way. It's the growing into each other you do after that matters. Some people grow faster than others."

Maggie let out a high-pitched whine in her sleep, and Sara lifted her head, looked at Jess and licked his face. He leaned his head back and let her cover his neck with her slow tongue.

"That's advice after all, Margaret. Pretty sneaky." Jess eased back to the floor and pointed his toes, feeling his tight muscles go taut.

"I guess it is," she said. "Take it or leave it."

"Leave what?" said Cody, entering from the hallway. She wiped her wet hands on the tails of her open shirt.

"I'm not leaving," said Jess. He grabbed her shin and pulled her leg to him, biting her calf through her jeans.

Cody shook her leg free and poked his ribs with her bare toes. "You're a nut," she said, "and I'm going to bed." She half shut the damper on the stove.

Lear came from the kitchen, finishing a lap, and his wagged tail brushed Jess's face. Cody opened the back door a crack and all the dogs heard the latch click and made for the door. They squeezed through over top each other, a moving pile, Maggie leading the way with a yowl, Jade at the rear. Jess got up and stood behind Cody in the doorway, beyond them the waxing moonlight and three streaking blurs.

"You're my pack," he said. He made his arms a loose leash, clasped in the front of her. Cody leaned forward on his weight. If I were a dog, she thought, if I were a dog. But she pictured herself alone. She watched the dogs charge off, barking, into the autumn dark.

AS CODY AND JESS SLEPT TOGETHER at the Forest Service cabin, entwined on one lumpy mattress too short for the fold-down twin bunk, the fire jumped the creek and burned over the trail only a few miles away. The cabin had no reception inside so they didn't hear the overnight radio chatter of Boz on lookout to Incident Command, the Com Center taking stock of who was where and realizing that Kinzler and McCafferty were bunked a mile from the leading edge of the fire. Their morning radio call-in from the outhouse roof was terse, with broken reception, so they had no idea how close it came until the next day, after they'd hiked out and driven the truck back to Headquarters to check in for their next detail.

"Thank the Lord," said Kathy, the wiry-haired dispatcher who treated the crews like they were all her kids. "That sure was a near miss," she told them, Forest Service lingo for "close call," which they'd first heard in early season training. *A near miss is actually a hit,* Jess whispered to her, sidelong and smart as hell. They both snorted loud enough to draw the ire of the instructor, his wad of chew pulsing against his cheek like a vein.

Even Boz cussed them out as they gathered up at the end of the hitch. "Fuck you guys," he said, snatching Jess's cap from his head and hucking it overhand into the truck bed. "I thought I was going to watch you stupid fuckers sizzle."

Early in the season Boz had said he liked lookout best of all the jobs, solitary, sometimes in an old fire tower like the Washburn, out the ridgeline from the Kinzlers' house, now unmanned. Cody asked him why he liked it so much, all alone, no crew, no help, nothing.

Boz shrugged. "My ma said we have an ancestor, some famous Cree sentry, maybe that's where I get it." He stuck his flat hand over his brow and pretended to canvass the distance in the ironic tone he used when talking to white kids—half-proud, half wishing he didn't have to explain. "Or maybe I just like being by myself and Indian's got nothing to do with it."

"Are you ever scared?" Cody asked him.

"Nah. What's to be scared of? Looking out over the country? I can see it all coming."

His words, months prior, came to Cody when she thought of someone watching them out at the lake. Boz had been too far away for details, but still, she pictured what he might have seen—not the close call, the singed trees on the far lakeshore less than half a watery mile from the cabin, but instead, the more explosive thing—Jess' hands on her bare back, the twisting pair of them, a braided wick. Like Boz would even care. He chose his own watching.

The morning hike out had been a slog, her body sore from long miles and the kind of sex she never realized required endurance. The radio blurted chatter until the battery died and in the quiet she lagged behind Jess to avoid conversation. A couple trail miles from the cabin they crossed the burn line and hiked the last six to the trailhead in the black, fallen trees every which way, their footsteps crisp in the smoking char.

"It's sort of like hell," said Jess, but Cody thought heaven. Still, dim, surreal. Her first week on the crew she learned about *the black*—burned-over places where nothing left to catch fire meant a safe zone—and *digging line* scratched out in the duff to stop the leading edge of a fire. Of course, she'd thought of her father, the trenches Josiah had dug in the grove behind the house when she was a little girl, and the fire he'd lit, letting it burn hot and high enough to frighten her and trusting those strips of turned-up dirt would keep his lesson within a perimeter. He'd taken a risk, she could see that now. No matter how well you knew it, fire could surprise you. A strong spark in a damped-down stove would fail to catch, but a single flash from an engine could burn down a forest. The dotted line between hypothesis and wreck you could almost, almost touch.

NATE LINDSAY

WHEN I RAN INTO CODY last week in line at the IGA, I hadn't seen her in ages. Cody and Louisa aren't my sisters exactly, but like cousins, at least. I don't remember a time not knowing those two. My mother watched them at our house when we were little, before she got too sick. And all those holidays spent together, Thanksgivings we traded off, one year at our place, the next at the Kinzlers'. I always liked it over there, with piles of books and papers and shoes all over the place, this friendly clutter that made you feel welcome. Our dinners were huge, so much food. Man, Cody could eat, I'll tell you that. She was the garbage disposal, forget the teenage boys. The Kinzlers never had a dishwasher though. That was not so great. Us kids had to wash up piles of greasy plates. One year, we sneaked the dirty dishes in a sled to pull it up to our place and load the dishwasher there. But their grandma caught us before we got far. You must be kidding me, she said, and both of our mothers laughed their heads off. By the time we unloaded all the dishes and carried them back in, it was more work than it would have been to wash them in the first place.

Cody is a little younger than me and so I taught her stuff, like how to make a slingshot and forge our parents' signatures. Louisa, I never taught her anything. Me and Clint both used to dream about her. She was hot, but not so out of our league as to be stupid to dream about, not like Cindy Crawford in her calendar swimsuits. Louisa was real. You knew you'd see her at the bus stop. You might get sent to the Kinzlers' to borrow a fence puller or a stick of butter and if you saw Louisa at her house with her hair mussed from sleeping, you'd have what the other boys didn't. A picture for later. Not her careful school face. A few moments like that in a year were worth a lot of Kleenex. To be honest, I still think of Louisa like she was back then. I have a girlfriend now and no complaints, but there's a kind of girl who appears when I need a fantasy, and she's pretty much Louisa at seventeen.

My brother talked like they'd gone all the way, but I knew it was bullshit. Clint is full of it. I am not the first one to say it and I won't be the last. I'm not sure when he turned into an asshole. I have some good memories, as kids. I used to think he'd invented everything. But I've never understood Clint very well, and I've spent a long time trying to figure what turns him on a dime from the best person in a room to the one you have to watch out for. Not that I'm perfect. I have a temper same as Clint's and when I'm mad it's hard to talk any sense to me. I can be lazy. I put off what needs doing longer than I should. I am seeing that part of what it means to be grown is pushing against your nature a little. I wish Clint could see it. It's hard to love an asshole, but when he's your brother, and you know there's more, you keep on trying.

My girlfriend and I have been out a few times lately, at a movie in town, around my folks' place, and we'll see Cody and Jess. He moved away and then he came back, and I like a guy who comes back here, who gets that it's not just a place to leave behind. Jess and Louisa dated in high school for a few months, nothing serious but memorable if it was your hobby to keep track of Louisa. Seeing Jess and Cody together now, I think how funny it is. When you're a kid, it's easy to fall for the obvious, what you think you should want. But later you might get braver and figure out what you want on your own.

I don't know what Clint figures. He admired Josiah an awful lot, used to tell our father he'd trade him in a minute for Josiah. But now? Say his name and Clint'll spit at the ground. It's like the whole family did him wrong somehow. Louisa is a tramp, Cody a snob. Only Mrs. Kinzler avoids his scorn, at least out loud. My father wouldn't stand for that.

When I see Cody around, I get this feeling inside, a cross between déjà vu and telling the future. Kind of like the view of the hills that have been out the kitchen window all your life. You know the flowers and when they bloom—bitterroot first, then lupine, fireweed after a burn—and you know what belongs, if you're apt to see deer grazing one place, or where the coyotes walk, and past that, there might be wolves. You know the hills, but still, they're far away, and wild. There's places in them you'll never get to. If you even think to try.

IN THE WOODS (1996)

JOSIAH WORKED ALL OF OCTOBER up Fielder's Road, cutting trees and stashing the wood in piles, firewood rounds here, project logs there. People bought up Josiah's pieces as fast as he could make them. Tables, chairs, bureaus, cabinets, all the mainstays, but also tool handles, dollhouses, picture frames. Whatever he could think to build, someone wanted. His pieces were so unusual they stood out, and this was how his customers came—word of eye, he called it. Friend a Eldon's, a guy would say, saw the table you made him and I'd like a desk for my wife. She's starting up her own business. Just a simple thing, a few drawers. Then they gestured, sketched out plans on blank sheets of paper until they arrived at the details between them. Josiah's clients came to him for a certain unevenness, a true grain, splinter in the hand, some subtle imperfection that had become difficult to find.

It was nothing Cody had planned, but when fire season was over, after a week of sleeping in and resting her achy joints, she joined Freddy and Josiah in the shop. One afternoon she walked down and skirted their edges, offering to lend a hand here or there, stacking boards, cleaning up, but careful not to intrude. A week later, a big order came in—twenty end tables for the fancy rooms at the Belton Chalet—and she was part of the crew. Josiah wanted to pay her, but she wouldn't let him—room and board is enough, I'm fire rich, she said. Josiah was glad for her help, and more than that, how she'd returned to him, so glad that he hid his pleasure for fear that too much attention, as always, would send her darting away. Freddy was the finisher, with a knack for sanding and oils and grain. Fine-fingered, with a grip as still as a surgeon's, he loved the meticulous. Cody preferred larger movements. Swinging an axe or striking a chisel and most of all, working with her father under the trees. October was for shopping, Josiah said. It was his favorite month in the woods. Cody's too—the coming cool and golden needles. Elk bugling. The going light.

I'd like to help you guys sometime, Jess said. He had been around the Kinzlers long enough by then to see that working in the woods was how you got to know them. Cody preferred the days alone with her dad and usually it didn't bother Jess, but now and then he wanted in. He wanted to be welcome. He wasn't proud of this, how he shouldered himself forward like a kid left out on the playground. But he kept on until Cody said yes, okay, firewood on Saturday. Jess drove because Cody's truck needed work.

Fielder's Road was half an hour from the house. The cab was sun-warmed when they rattled across the cattle guard and there was Josiah's rig off in the trees, facing them, the driver's door open. As soon as Jess came to a stop, Cody flung the door wide and rolled out of the truck in one motion. Jess let the dogs out of the bed, slammed the tailgate and arched his back, his hands at his narrow waist. When Cody neared Josiah's Ford, she shoved the door shut with a flat palm.

"Pop," Cody called. It was a soft day, the bright sunlight dimmed through gauzy cloud cover, the wind gentle but steady. No sound of the saw idling or running. Quiet.

"Hey Pop!" she hollered again. Lear's tail wagged from the back of the truck. As she rounded the rear bumper, there was Josiah, slumped against the side of the truck, his neck leaned on the tire, one leg tented up and the other stretched in front of him at an odd angle. His eyes were open and his skin was pale and wet. His glasses lay in the dirt beside his lap.

"Pop. Fuck. Jess!" Cody shouted, hating the crack in her voice, the panic before there was even cause. She knelt in front of her father.

"Ah, Cody." Josiah spoke before she could. "Glad you showed up. I was about to be a *Reader's Digest* hero, chewing through barb-wire fences and dragging myself home." He laughed and winced as he did. Cody looked down at his jeans, ripped and bloody, and again, the leg skewed out below his knee.

"Shit, Pop, what happened?" The strong press of nausea surged in her throat and she looked from his leg to his face. "You look bad." She laid the back of her hand over his forehead and it came away dripping. Her own skin was dry and cool.

Josiah jerked his head behind him at the load of wood scattered in the truck's bed. The move unsteadied him and he shut his eyes. "The stack rolled on me, I went over the side. My leg got caught, that's what did it. I would've been all right if it hadn't got pinned." His eyelids flitted shut against his waxy skin. Cody saw him faking. He needed help more than he'd say, possibly more than he knew he did. Josiah was stoic, not prone to drama. He feigned whatever he needed to so you might look away. When Jess approached, he found them sitting amidst wood everywhere, wherever it rolled, spilled and jacked like pick-up sticks. A spot in the dirt where Josiah fell, darkened with blood.

Jess's first aid training kicked in and as he took charge, Cody felt foolish, so undone by her father's flat face that she'd forgotten what to do. Vitals, questions, all of it, out of her mind. She sat next to Josiah, glad for Jess. He probed for Josiah's pulse. He counted his breaths and peered through the tear in the pant leg without touching. To Jess's precise questions Josiah said yes, he could move his hands, no, he never passed out, he didn't think so. About an hour ago, maybe? He'd forgotten to look at his watch right away. He'd stopped the bleeding with his tight handkerchief—not quite a tourniquet, he said, don't worry—and inched himself upright into the position he sat in now. He landed on his neck and left shoulder, twisted the caught leg, maybe it broke. He couldn't move it. He couldn't feel his toes. He said the pain was a four, which meant eight.

"At least the saw was off. If the saw had been running . . ." Josiah winced again.

"Shh, Pop. Too much talking. It's bad enough." Cody looked at Jess. "We shouldn't move him. You go get someone and I'll stay. Call Doyle."

Jess nodded. He put a hand on Josiah's shoulder. "Okay, Josiah, Cody'll give you a few painkillers. But sit tight, I'm going to get help. Don't move, all right? Take it easy?" He stood up. "Both of you." He laid his hand on top of Cody's head.

Her throat felt solid, as if a thick snake filled her from mouth to stomach. Jess took her hand and peeled apart her clenched fingers. He ripped open two small pouches from the first aid kit in the truck glove box and put four white pills into her palm.

"He should drink, try to get some water down him with these. Keep him calm. Don't let him move, keep his back and neck straight." Jess ran for the truck, parked nose out, a habit ingrained by Forest Service work. Always back in for a quick exit. No three-point turn necessary if you're on the run from a fire. Or for help. The truck's engine lagged, then caught, and Jess skidded the tires on his exit. The noise of wheels on gravel faded and grew again as he descended the road's switchbacks.

Cody gave Josiah slow sips of water from the cap of his thermos, which smelled strongly of coffee. He seemed more alert than when they'd found him, but Cody wasn't sure that was good. She worried he'd tire himself. She held his neck steady with her sweatshirt and had him shift his position a little. He was in pain, Cody could tell, because he took the pills she handed him without comment and swallowed them with another slow gulp of water. She didn't think she'd seen her father down a pill in her entire life. When he settled again, she stood to give him space—he hated hovering—and she shoved the wood that had rolled to the edge into the bed and shut the tailgate.

"How do you feel?" Cody said. She heard the dogs barking at the edge of her senses, Maggie's high, wild yelp above Lear's deep woof and Sarah's hound-yowl. Josiah puckered his lips and closed his eyes again. "So much for a day in the woods, huh? If this is broken, you're going to be doing a lot of stove wood for your old man."

"Forget the wood," Cody said. "Christ, Pop. You have enough wood stacked for six years." The leg was obviously broken. One look at him suggested metal rods, concussion. Cody inventoried the damage, both possible and escaped. Plenty of folks had been killed working in the woods by lesser hazards than a pile of rolling cordwood. Boz had an uncle smashed by a widow-maker, he lost an ear. A man from West Glacier died two years prior when his pant leg caught on the branch of a downed tree he was limbing. He lost his balance and fell onto another branch, which impaled him in the stomach. He died of blood loss hours before anyone found him.

Josiah's eyes closed, and in a few minutes his features slackened as the pills kicked in. Cody crouched beside him and watched his face in repose, the lips turned under, a lid flutter, moving in all the small ways a face can move that you don't realize unless you're looking at it straight on. She scanned him, the hairs in his beard and mustache, some graying. The wrinkles at the corners of his eyes and how one brow grew a little thicker than the other. When she was a kid, they had reminded her of caterpillars. *Don't die, Pop,* she thought, and stopped herself from whispering such nonsense. She resisted the urge to touch him, so he could rest.

Sooner than she expected, Cody heard a siren up the dirt road, and the cattle guard reverberate under tires. Josiah's eyes opened and stayed glazed for a second before he caught up with where he was. Doyle Lindsay's truck first, backing in and out of the tight spot to park nose out. Jess got out of the passenger side.

Doyle crouched next to Josiah, one elbow leaned on his bent knee, the other hand on his friend's boot. Josiah put his own hand on Doyle's arm and let it rest there, and in the small gesture Cody saw the long trust between them.

A station wagon cruiser pulled in with Marcia Stiles from highway patrol, and a medic Cody did not recognize. He climbed out of the front, carried a collapsed stretcher under his arm.

"Hello, partner," he said. "I'm John Helms."

"Pleased to meet you, John," said Josiah. "Hello there, Marcia." He gave her a small smile and raised his hand. John laid the stretcher out next to Josiah and collared him with a foam C-spine in thirty seconds. The four of them gently and stiffly lifted, then settled, Josiah onto it, while Cody stood by his head and watched his face for any register of discomfort. Marcia counted Josiah's pulse, checked his color. "Show me your gums, you old horse," Marcia said and she put one hand on each of his cheeks and stroked his face back to his ears in the tenderest way, reminding Cody that her father had lived here all his life. He and Marcia and Doyle had gone to grade school together. Josiah tried to rise and straighten himself, but Marcia stopped him with a hand to his chest.

"You big oaf," she said, though she was taller and broader than he was. "Don't you dare."

"Hangin' in there?" Doyle asked Josiah as they carried the stretcher to the car. Josiah nodded, his eyes still closed.

"Hey, Joe, thanks for not crawling out of here yourself," Marcia said. No one ever called him Joe.

Josiah smiled. "I was just considering my options when Cody found me," he said. "That's my girl."

On three, they lifted the stretcher to the rear of the cruiser and slid Josiah in. The old white station wagon had been used for the VFD ambulance so long, Cody remembered a kid taken away in it when he broke his collarbone on the playground in kindergarten. The trunk smelled the same, musty and old, with shagged carpet glued to the back walls.

"It's broke for damn sure," said John, launching a shot of chew spit out the gap in his front teeth. "We'll take him to Kalispell. One of you ride along, one follow in his rig?"

Cody felt suddenly restless and crowded. "You go, Jess. He's okay, I'll follow you. His clutch is weird." She pushed Jess towards the wagon and leaned in the back door. "Pop, I'm going to follow in your truck, okay? I'll call Mom and pick her up, we'll meet you there. Jess has your glasses."

Jess put his hands on Cody's shoulders from behind and squeezed them hard, pouring his calm into her. They couldn't see Josiah's face over the bill of his cap, but his voice was stronger, lying down. "See you in the city."

Cody laughed. When she was a kid, Kalispell felt like the city, but even though it was bigger now than it had been then, calling it that made Josiah sound naive.

"Keep me posted," Doyle said, hugging Cody to his hip. "I'll swing by the hospital in a bit. Holler if you need me sooner."

When the station wagon was gone, Jess and Doyle on their way, Cody checked the load to see that the wood in the truck was secure. She paused at the logs on the ground, hating, even in a crisis, to leave the work undone. As she considered hoisting the fallen logs into the truck and salvaging a full load, she thought of the dogs. She couldn't recall seeing them since the ambulance arrived. She whistled loud, yelled each name, clapped her hands. Two minutes went by with no rustling underbrush and no tags rattling, no dogs spotted on the periphery, close by all along but up to their haunches in a ground squirrel's hole or fighting over a shin bone from last season's gut piles. Cody whistled again, two fingers between her teeth. Nothing. She climbed into the front seat of the Ford; the steering wheel was tacky with spruce pitch. When she started the truck, the diesel exhaust covered the smell of pine and the engine's rumble blocked out the sound of the cattle guard as she passed over it. No dogs. She couldn't wait.

JOSIAH'S CONDITION WAS STABLE but the leg was broken below the knee and his ankle shattered, requiring the surgical insert of a metal plate. Jess, Cody, and Margaret watched him in the hospital bed, tan against the white sheets, his legs like logs under snow. The drugs made him chatty and loose.

"I got to keep it elevated, stay off it for five weeks, crutches a couple months, if I'm lucky. And get X-rays along the way. It should heal up, the doctor says, no biggie. He's getting ready to treat these breaks all winter, from the skiers." Josiah snorted to imagine himself in the company of snow bunnies who gassed up their vehicles in Whitefish.

"The part nobody tells me so far," he said before they left him to sleep, "is how I'm going to pay for this." He leaned back into his pillows. Cody pressed her lips into his forehead and inhaled, the scent of saw gas and woods still on him strong, resistant to antiseptic and the smell of cafeteria food. Margaret smoothed his hair to the side behind his ear and kissed it.

"Will you please call Freddy," Josiah said as his face relaxed and his voice began to drift. "He'll worry if I'm not there in the morning." Cody promised.

"If I fly I'll set off all the detectors," he mumbled. Josiah hadn't been on a plane in years.

WHEN SHE WOKE THE NEXT MORNING to rain hard on the metal roof, Cody thought first of the dogs and then of the cut wood lying in the rain. Last night after they left the hospital it had been too late to drive all the way back, but now it felt urgent. She rose and in the empty kitchen left her mother a note—*Mama, I'm in the woods, Fielders Loop, be back late lunch, don't worry. Did you call Freddy? —C*

Cody gunned Josiah's truck and pictured him, not in the hospital bed, but teaching her to drive a stick shift on the winding roads behind their property, with plenty of hills and little traffic. Then, Josiah in the shop with Freddy, one on each end of a beam, pivoting around the space to find it room. Strong, uninjured, no glimpse of even the possibility of weakness.

By the time Cody reached the pullout, the rain had tapered and a weak sun winnowed the damp in the air. She walked the perimeter of the clearing first and shouted for the dogs by name, but there was no sign. She lifted the saw from the back of the truck. Though the chain was fine, she got out a file and ran two strokes over the teeth. She topped off the tanks, fired the engine, put on the chain brake and let it idle to warm. Fifty yards into the woods she found the last tree he'd downed and began to cut up the rounds, her chaps soaked from busting through brush.

Cody didn't know any of the projects that were in Josiah's mind, couldn't see the jewelry box for Margaret for Christmas, or the straight limbs he'd use to turn new handles for the broken tools cached in an aluminum trash can in the corner of the shed. She didn't know about the money, her father's stash, her mother's marked-up columns, or how they'd pay for the surgery, and the drugs. She cut without thinking, letting the chain pull through the wood, the chips firing out and covering her chaps. As the log rounds fell away beneath the bar, the chain tugged sharper on one side, her fault, the slightly arced cut making the butt ends less than flat. He'd square them later. A plumb cut was the first rule of building, she knew that. It didn't matter—piano bench, music stand, crate. Even a curve started from plumb.

She'd left her gloves at home and the saw pulsed under her vibrating palms. It felt like a way to undo his injury, or at least the helplessness of it—finish the task he meant to. Cody worked until late afternoon, the logs cut into rounds small enough to move and stack herself. Sappy fluid coated her palms. The truck was too full to fit another stick of kindling. Still no sign of the dogs, though she called and called, stopping between tanks of gas to walk a loop in a different direction. She stood still and stretched for a few minutes, her hand on her lower back, arching one way, then the other, a bent hang to not quite touch her feet.

Far off, she heard a truck engine, and then the cattle guard as Jess came to join her, bringing a peanut butter sandwich. Together they walked the near forest, spread out in a grid like a search for a missing person, alternating the called-out names. No sign of any dogs, and once they stopped shouting, the forest was quiet again, even the squirrels and birds still in the peculiar heat.

That night, Jess stayed over. In bed he seemed sad and boyish. Cody cupped her body around him, her bent knees behind his knees, one hand rested on his stomach.

"You were so good yesterday. What would I have done without you? They probably would've found me and Pop both stiff three days later." She homed in on Jess so her own fears—her father gone, the frailty of bodies—eased away. She smoothed the hair off his brow and rubbed the cowlick behind his hairline, stiff as bristle. He didn't respond for a minute or more. She sensed in him a closed-off self she knew so well, but usually it was hers.

"Did you see Freddy today?" she asked.

"Yeah, at the shop. He was headed to the hospital when I left."

She pushed up on one elbow and looked over Jess's chest to his face. "What's the matter?" He was mostly easy to read. Cody was unused to guessing what was in his mind.

"Everything leaves," he said, almost under his breath. "No one ever stays for good." Jess had spent all evening looking for the dogs, back way after dark.

Cody flipped onto her back and rubbed his stomach. The dip of his navel swirled like an eddy line at the edge of still water. Jess breathed deeply and held it in, his torso tautening under her hand.

"They hadn't been there since we left. I could tell." A pause. "I've had her since I was a kid." His words cracked and she thought of him at fourteen training Sara, his higher voice, a boy half turned to man.

"I think they got on a scent, an adventure. They might show up. They'll be okay." It sounded hollow but she believed it as clearly as if the three dogs were lying on the floor next to the bed. They were absent, but they didn't feel gone.

"Sara's so old," Jess said. "She's not as fast as the other two." In his voice the worst, whispered fear. His dog would fall behind, unable to keep up, eventually alone.

"She might surprise you," said Cody. "I think she'll find her way."

Two of the three dogs would return, turned up the next day when Jess went back to search—Sara and Maggie asleep on the tire tracks left in the mud. Only Lear never came back, but he'd always been prone to jaunts, young enough to survive on his own, and that wolfish thrust to his muzzle, the stand-up ears and yellow-green irises, those consoled them that he'd found someplace wilder.

But that night in bed, they didn't yet know who would remain and who would go. Cody left her hand to lie on Jess's stomach, his breath lifting and sinking her palm. She imagined herself in the forest, every companion she traveled with gradually leaving her behind. Louisa ran ahead of her between dark trees, her hair flicking in and out like a flag at the stern of a boat disappearing into fog. Her mother at a steady pace, arms swinging, and her father slightly ahead of that with his stiff-legged gait. Uncle Michael, his hair draped over his collar, the Lindsays and Freddy, and last of all Jess, who turned and held out his hand to her but she could not reach him and before long he vanished, too. When the last person was gone, Cody sat under a tree and waited until the dogs came and circled her and rested, one in her lap, one behind, one draped on her feet. Pressed in the space between them she was warm and could sleep until morning. Jess tossed and turned.

DR. BRIGGS

A YEAR AFTER I FIXED HIS LEG, Josiah still limps. I feel badly about this fact. I did the best I could at the time, and though it was a major injury, it wasn't as bad as it could have been. I would not have predicted he'd have lasting effects. That's one of the marvels and the dangers of the human body—nothing is certain. Any doctor who promises otherwise is fooling himself or you. For the most part, I see Josiah from afar now. I suggested a physical therapist, but I don't know if he went. I have my doubts.

Josiah still carries himself well, but the limp ages him. He hesitates to fully weight it, as if anticipating a fall. I have pains, too, hitches in my get-along, as we say, so I recognize the way he moves. But I am a good twenty-five years older than Josiah. Older enough to have known his parents. I treated his mother, and when she was only fifty, I diagnosed her cancer, which she asked me to keep a secret, and I did, and managed her pain, but not as well as I hoped.

When she killed herself, I regretted my silence and the help I failed to give. In any case, I have seen Josiah's entire family burn out and disappear. His father couldn't walk straight and his mother laid down and his brother lost his balance. That may be why his limp catches my eye.

On his last visit to my office, I asked him, "Are you all right, Josiah?" He had a heaviness, not his weight, but his spirit. His gaze evading mine, his answers a bit . . . remote, I suppose, is the word. The mind is not my area of expertise, and I hate to burden a patient with a large diagnosis for what may be just a hard week. Too many make that mistake, I know. I offered Josiah a prescription once, when all the drug reps were leaving freebies with my nurse. Maybe a pill would have helped him. How could he know unless he tried? He wouldn't take it, though. Not surprising. Josiah hasn't let the dentist use Novocain since he was twenty. I don't like the feeling, he says. With a family like he came from, I guess he prefers outright pain to any kind of fog.

Some patients stick in a doctor's mind. People I see around town, working at the diner, at the post office, in my mind they are fixed in time, as they were during the injury or sickness that brought them to me. Last week I was given a citation for a taillight out and the policeman who stood outside my window I knew as the boy who would have gone to MSU in Bozeman on a football scholarship but for the prom night he got hit by a teacher, of all things, driving drunk. They say I saved his life, but that's a stretch, as you can't ever predict which bodies will heal. I did the best I could. I don't think he remembered me at all. I was pleased to see he'd shaken off the worst of it, as far as I could tell. He was chipper and polite, his bearing upright but not too altogether full of himself like the boys you know chose police work to keep some inner urge in check: a hunger, or a powerlessness, which are near the same, in my experience. Josiah is like that boy—he sticks in my mind.

I have always tried to see my patients, I mean really look. It's easy to focus on parts, when that's what they come to me for—a stiff back, a cough, a mole that's grown. Taking a pulse, you look at the wrist, or at the wall clock, counting in your head. Feeling for a break or a lump, you look at the limb, or the place where the organ lies beneath the skin. Makes sense. But I do try, whenever I can, to look at their faces, right into their eyes. I remind myself that they are people, not just bodies. Possibly I want to remind them that I am a person, too. There is a moment sometimes, in my office, where it settles on you both, the doctor and the patient, so heavily—what will become of every last one of us—that you have to look away from each other. You don't mention it. Either one of you. You talk about prescriptions, or prognosis, or the weather, or their child in the army, at college. You don't mention the looming thing.

I should tell Josiah what I wish I'd told his mother—no one should try to bear their griefs alone.

FAMILY DINNER (1998)

RANDY'S STEAKHOUSE LOOKED as disgruntled as it ever had. A tightly notched decrepit log building perched at the back end of a gravel parking lot you entered over an awkward, too-steep lip, it brought to mind a pretty kid from a small town, ready to pick the shit out of her boot treads and find a limelight. Out Highway 35, set apart as it was from the restaurant strips in Big Fork or Kalispell, you had to mean to get to Randy's. Most people meant to, either for the long slab-oak bar with every kind of glinting liquor bottle lined up behind, or for the famous steaks: "Best Rib-Eye in the Northern Rockies," said the hand-painted sign propped up against the front porch railing, now half blown in with snow. On Valentine's Day or prom night at C-Falls High, the lot was packed.

A weak squall threw light flakes against the windows and Cody waited in the lobby for the rest of her family to join. It was late March, and Louisa hadn't been home in months. They were gathering for her—a college degree, finally, in communications, her natural subject. She'd split from Oregon after her junior year and drifted through massage school, at-a-distance classes and one final seminar at U of M in Missoula. She'd completed her last semester of credit before Christmas, and the diploma finally came in the mail. I'm ready to celebrate, she told them.

She was driving south with a new boyfriend she'd met in Missoula, a man from Browning, on the Blackfeet Rez—Earl Heavyrunner was his name—and Louisa had gone up north to meet his family. Passing through on their way back to Missoula, the timing was right to convene for dinner. Josiah and Margaret, Jess, even Freddy, all on their way. Her parents were proud of Louisa, the first one in their family to go to college. Margaret would liked to have gone, but it was a further stretch back then. Cody had taken a few courses at the community college, but except for an art class where they sketched outside, she'd hated it. She couldn't understand the draw towards more time at a desk under bright lights with people pretending to know what mattered, but she did salute her sister for sticking it out. Louisa deserved a toast, all their glasses raised.

Cody had not been inside Randy's in years but when she sat down in the waiting area the red leather seats gave a familiar airy huff that shot her back to childhood. She and Louisa used to bounce on the seats to make them gasp unless Mom or Pop grabbed an arm with a firm pinch and a best-behavior glower. Growing up, a restaurant meal was a luxury their family couldn't afford, and they rarely ate out anywhere but the diner in Columbia Falls. Once in a great while they'd gone to Randy's for a special reason—a perfect report card, a big birthday—and then Cody and Louisa whispered in the car, planning who would get a burger, who would get chicken strips, the cheapest items on the menu. They pretended they wanted those meals most, which sometimes they did. Back then Josiah ordered a baked potato and a bowl of chili. The girls added up the bill in their heads. Louisa was fast at math, could figure a tip in a snap. Ten percent is too easy to think, she said.

Cody had rarely been in Randy's as an adult, not since an early date with Jess. Never with the fire crew, not even with Louisa. Other places had cheaper burgers and live music and Cody didn't care about single shots of expensive whiskey or an excuse to wear fancy shoes.

Margaret and Josiah arrived first, arm in arm. An antique sleigh bell sashed the door handle and clanked as they entered. Margaret's cheeks were winter pale and her eyes tired, but she smiled and stomped the snow off her boots. Josiah took her jacket and shrugged out of his own.

"She here yet?" he asked Cody from the tiny coatroom off the lobby.

"Just me so far. Jess is running late. Freddy's not with you?" Cody hugged her mother and swiped snowflakes from her hair.

"He'll be here in a bit. Coming from town."

A hostess led them to a long table in the back, set with lit candles and a bouquet of flowers at the head. Louisa's seat, her father pointed. The three of them clustered at the other end, Josiah and Margaret together on one side, Cody across. Although Cody lived at her folks' place, she spent most of her time in the shop, or at Jess's, or out on the land, and it felt oddly formal, sitting across from them at a linen-draped table, her mother in faint lipstick. When had Cody eaten out alone with her parents? Years? Ever? She couldn't recall.

"Tell me something, dear," said Margaret.

Cody hadn't meant to bring it up, but asked outright, there was nothing else to note.

"I drove to Spokane last week to see the AIDS quilt."

"The AIDS quilt?" Josiah asked. "The big one, from Washington?"

"Yeah. It travels, pieces of it, all over the place." She'd never told anyone how she'd written to Andrew once, a few months after Uncle Michael died. I made Michael a square, he'd written back, but the quilt was new then and she couldn't quite picture it. When she saw the story in the paper about the quilt coming to Spokane, well, it was only five hours away. Cody loved to drive by herself.

"What was it like?" Margaret asked. "Where did you stay?"

"It was at a high school, last weekend. I drove there and back the same day."

The parking lot had been packed, like for a tournament or graduation. Rows of cars for acres, and she had to park at a fence overlooking the football field and walk the length of the lot to enter the gym. On the curb in front of the doors, picketers stood with signs stapled to wooden stakes. "Abomination!" one said in red paint like blood dripping, and "God Hates Gays," held by a small girl with pigtails and very white teeth. She smiled and waved at Cody, as if in a parade.

Inside, voices echoed off the high gym rafters. The quilt squares covered the middle of the floor, spread to hide the stripes in the center of the basketball court. The hoops floated in the air above the crowd with open nets hanging down. The squares were arranged in rows with aisles between so people could approach each one. Men and women and kids bent down everywhere, some kneeling alone, others in small groups. Many read the names and phrases on the quilts aloud so the gym had a hum to it, a wash of sound.

Cody followed the aisles. Each panel was 3 feet by 6, the brochure said, to mimic the size of a grave. Some were sewn like a bed quilt, others painted or glued fabric, or made of scraps—the seat of a pair of jeans, a pillowcase. Lots of tarps, in all colors. Many had photos, and names in large letters. Messages, some short: "Best Daddy in the World. I love you forever. Baby-doll." Others crammed so full of stitched or markered letters, they were almost too small to read: "Nick was my Neighbor. He liked Art. He was a computer programmer. We rode the El to work together almost Everyday. He was a great cook. He was a loner. He never said he was sick . . . He died alone. I'll miss you." Cody didn't know any computer programmers. She wasn't sure of Uncle Michael's job. The names jumped out: Gerd Wagener. Gus Arnette. Joseph Tucci Jr. Most of them were men, but also, Baby Jessica and Queen Christine. In the aisles, glitter gritted beneath her feet.

Josiah and Margaret listened as Cody told them some of it, but not all. Once she started talking, the details were too much somehow, like she was making a story out of it, but smaller than it was. The names in particular—she remembered so many, but listing them in a litany sounded crude. She felt like a child saying memorized lines.

After she'd been in the gym a half an hour, Cody found herself in the middle of a row, people close on all sides. She guessed there were more folks in the gym than lived in her entire town. It was hot, and maybe because of the virus, silent but alluded to, other people seemed dangerous, like touch was a threat, though she knew that wasn't how it worked. She tamped down a small panic and looked for the closest door. Worming for spaces between groups, she found an exit and fled the gym into a hallway. It was quiet and dark except for the EXIT signs glowing at each end of the corridor. She walked down the hall until she saw a bathroom, GI LS, the "R" missing, and pushed open the door and went inside. She sat in the stall for a while after she'd finished. She soaped her hands twice and let the hot water run long.

Halfway back to the gym entrance, Cody passed a trophy case. Against a velvet background, bubbly cutout letters said STATE CHAMPIONS and GO WOLVES. Some pictures were faded, black and white, others brand new, from this year or the last, yearbook shots with braces and dangling earrings and sprayed-up bangs. High-school portraits brought Louisa to mind, her soft cascading hair suited to photos.

"State champs, huh."

A man stood next to her, a few feet away, and instinctively she stepped aside, opening a distance between them.

"A bit overwhelming in there." He jerked his head toward the gym doors. He had close-trimmed hair and wore jeans and a polo shirt tucked in tight. His glasses were dark-framed and his eyes swam a little behind the lenses.

"Are you here for the quilt?" He had the affable way of those people who want to connect.

Cody found her voice. "Yes."

"Me, too. I'm here for my brother. Max Perkins." The man smiled, his lip bitten in. "He was kind of a son-of-a-bitch, actually. Pardon my French. I didn't put that on my square."

Cody wasn't sure what to say. Everyone could be a son-of-a-bitch at times.

The man kept looking at the trophies. "Max played tennis in high school. Doubles, state champs." He tapped the glass near the bottom of the case, under his finger a gold plaque engraved with names. "If you saw him play, man, you couldn't walk away."

Cody's lack of offering hung stark even to her, so she spoke. "I didn't know my Uncle Michael very well." What could she say? He'd left home before he finished high school. Her grandfather wouldn't speak his name. The Little House voice. How she'd leaned against him that night she was lost.

"He gave me my first saddle," she said. Outgrown years ago, it still hung in the barn. "And my mother really loved him." Cody felt then she should have asked Margaret to come. Why did she always choose to be alone?

Cody and the man made their way back toward the gym entrance and when they reached the painted line at the edge of the court, she realized she'd been holding her breath. The two of them stood beside the drinking fountain, watching the crowd. Such a large group, it struck her again, this big united mass and also, every one of them with a hole its own shape, a geometry that no one else could know.

"You take care of yourself," the man said. Two kids ran up to the fountain, parting them, and she raised her hand in a wave as he walked away. The bigger kid lifted the shorter one up for a drink and Cody moved into the crowd.

She walked the gym for another half an hour, staying at the perimeter this time to avoid the pressing bodies. She looked at the index, and the map, but Michael Blanchard's name wasn't there.

THE WAITRESS HUSTLED OVER THEN, a tiny busty woman with a Southern drawl who had worked at Randy's forever. "Y'all ready?"

she asked, unpocketing her notebook from the hip of her tight Wranglers. While she explained the specials, Jess slid into a chair beside Cody, the cold air clinging to him like damp cologne.

She and Jess told her parents a funny story about that hostess, who'd waited on them one time they'd been in on a date. They'd ordered pie for dessert—Randy's was famous for that, too—and the woman cocked her head and asked, "You want that with mode?" Jess laughed, but the woman waited and arched her eyebrows, the question hanging there.

"Ice cream, Cody?" Jess asked, and they agreed, yes. After the waitress left, they discussed whether she knew that *mode* didn't actually mean *ice cream*, or if she did and was being ironic, the joke on them. It was hard to tell, and funnier for that. Since then, she and Jess called it mode, even at home. "Anyone for a bowl of mode?" she'd say after dinner.

"What *does* it mean?" Josiah asked. "I always thought it meant 'with ice cream.'"

"I guess, well, it does, but not literally," Cody said. "It's French for, I don't know, what is it again, Jess?"

"It means 'in the manner of' or something like that. Basically, it's French for 'this is how you should eat pie.'"

"And indeed, you should," Margaret said. "I'm having a glass of wine." She leaned across the table toward Cody. "Thank you for telling us about the quilt," she said, quiet enough so there was nothing more to explain.

THE RESTAURANT SLOWLY FILLED until the noise of people dining drifted to even the empty corners. A jukebox played old jazz on low. Freddy joined in his subtle way, no talk as he sat down opposite Josiah, then looked up to smile at them all. Everyone was relaxed and laughing when Louisa finally arrived, the boyfriend they thought was staying up north a step behind her, his hand on her lower back. They shifted chairs so Louisa sat in front of the flowers and Earl sat beside her. His thick black hair looked wet, the tooth marks of a comb swirling at his temple, and a tiny silver hoop in the lobe of each ear. Leave it to Louisa and her boyfriend to turn all the heads in the room.

"Hope it's okay I crash your dinner," Earl said after shaking the thrust-out hands. Cody hated introductions. Awkward and boring. Better to sit and watch, then shake later, once you meant it, that's what she thought. She was curious about a man who managed to snag her sister, a guy she'd been hearing about for months longer than usual. He gets me, Louisa told her. I trust him.

"Anyone who brings Louisa with them is always welcome here," said Josiah.

"Oh, Dad," Louisa said. "Leave it. Only praise for me tonight! No giving me a hard time." Josiah took Louisa's absences hard, though it wasn't personal. Louisa concentrated best on what was in front of her, and that wasn't home anymore. Cody found it funny: one daughter hardly returned, and one had never left.

Everyone ordered steaks except Freddy, who chose pork chops. Cody reminded Louisa about their chicken fingers pact.

"We each tried to be cheapest," Louisa said, "so you wouldn't be stressed about money."

"Considerate girls! No chicken fingers this time." Margaret raised her wine glass with a wide smile and a drowsy gaze. She rarely drank and Cody found her giddy looseness sweet. A real celebration.

Cody listened to laughter and talking and drifted above, as she often did, catching the current of voices more than the words. Louisa and Earl skirted in and out of a private world, one minute in the midst of the table's joke, the next, Louisa teasing and flirtatious, Earl a bit shyer, with a half smile. He rested his arm along the back of Louisa's chair and Cody watched his fingers trail the ends of her hair, same as Cody had done herself for so many years. She could almost feel the glossy coil, the way the strands cut into her skin like floss. Under the table she rested her own hand on Jess's knee. A family, she thought. That's what this is—a big old pile of us, all our pasts and futures and what each of us thinks of the others, all overlapping. Mostly love. In that, they were lucky.

Cody excused herself from the table for a trip to the restroom. The men's and women's doors were marked as they had been for years: Stallions and Mares. At the back of the hallway, in the dim light, she saw two figures standing so close that she had the instinct to turn away. Even as they came into focus it took her a minute to make sense of it: Bobby Watson and Clint Lindsay. She hadn't seen either of them in ages, Bobby in years, Clint months, at least. She'd thought he was gone again. Doyle had mentioned Idaho the last time he'd been up to the house.

Bobby pushed a mop and bucket into the narrow hallway and Clint followed him with his hand hovering at Bobby's back, a gesture so intimate Cody again felt a pang of intrusion. After a few moments of their slow shuffle and then Bobby's face visible in the crack of light as he opened the men's room door, Cody saw it—the blank, slack look of a nearly emptied mind. Clint's voice its kindest register, "You got it, Bobby?" and Bobby did, he entered alone and Clint backed out into the dark and let the door close against the tip of his boot, leaving a slight crack so he could hear.

"Jesus, Clint. What happened to him?"

Clint visibly jumped and the door swung shut. "Christ, you scared me." He focused on her—"Cody?"—not just a customer in the hall. "What the hell are you doing here?"

"Dinner, bathroom, you know. The usual." She gestured with her hand toward the Mares. "What happened to Bobby?"

"Bar fight."

"Bobby?" she asked. He was one of the sweeter boys she'd ever known.

"Not his fight. Got in the way of a tussle, took a bottle to the head. Hit the off switch, they said. Didn't think he'd walk again." An apron hung around Clint's waist, spun so it draped the back of his jeans. Bobby clanked and banged behind the bathroom door.

"When did it happen?" It was hard to believe she hadn't heard this news.

"A few months, maybe. Four months?" Clint moved to edge by her.

"Did you—" she asked and then Clint was in her face, not touching, but as close as a lover would be.

"I wasn't here, Cody, I was in *Idaho,*" he said. "He was like this when I started." She could see the broken capillaries around Clint's nose and taste the last break's cigarette on his close breath. A brief fear tensed her chest, like a small animal sighted quick, then darting away.

"*Fuck* you, Cody. Every wrong turn in this town is not because of me." He swung the bathroom door open—"You good, Bobby?"—and when Bobby answered yes, his voice high and almost childish, Clint shoved himself away down the hall toward the kitchen, rotating his apron into place.

When Cody returned to the table her hands shook and she pinned them under her thighs to steady them. The food had arrived, pink bricks of meat leaned on piled-up onion rings and mashed potatoes with buttery divots.

"Better eat that steak, Cody, or I'll trade it for my pork chop after all," Freddy said.

Outside the windows the snow settled, this March layer the latest drift in a winter as heavy and cold as any in recent memory. The windows steamed at the edges and a little girl in a front booth traced faces and initials in the glass. Cody watched her and finished the meal without speaking. Jess gave her a sidelong look. He could sense when she was off balance, but she didn't explain. Bringing up Bobby now would be wrong, like inviting a street drunk into a kid's birthday party.

After they'd ordered dessert—a whole peach pie served in its glass pan—Doyle entered the dining room and waited at the bar. He didn't see them until Margaret called out.

"Doyle!" she said. "What on earth!" Doyle approached the table smiling as big as he ever did, but beneath his expression Cody saw a hesitation. He had to pick up Clint, he said. Clint was working in the kitchen now. Cody stared at the table, hiding that she already knew. Clint had been gone, now he was back, Doyle said. Working, that was good, a good thing.

"He was in Idaho?" Margaret asked. It was hard to keep track, Clint was always coming or going. There had been rumors about new trouble, harder drugs—Iva's pilfered oxy traded up for heroin—maybe even jail in Coeur d'Alene, but now he was trying to straighten out. He's not allowed to live with us unless he works, Doyle said. There was a DUI, though, so he needed rides.

"Enough about that." Doyle put his arm around Margaret's shoulder, ducked low and kissed her cheek. "How's my dear friend and her dear family?"

"Sit, Doyle, we ordered a pie," Josiah said. They shifted their chairs to let him in.

"With mode!" said Margaret, and half of them laughed so Cody and Jess had to tell the story again. Earl and Doyle shook hands.

"Good to meet you," Doyle said. "You rescued the elusive princess." He smiled at Louisa, who stuck out her tongue. She hated her sweetheart reputation, but you couldn't change what family friends thought they knew.

Earl shrugged. "She didn't need rescuing to me," he said.

If Louisa was the reluctant princess, then Cody thought herself the odder daughter, an archer on horseback, a loner roving the country with a string of furs tied to her saddle. And Clint, Clint was in a dungeon, clanking around in his self-forged chains. Maybe he'd grilled their steaks, though more likely he was washing dishes, or cutting carrots in rounds for the salad bar. If Clint glanced out the swinging door or peered through the long window between the kitchen and the dining room, he'd see them all. Louisa, his years-long crush, her leonine hair, long black wool dress scooped deep, a scarf around her neck in a way nobody else wore. Next to her Earl leaned back in his chair, long-legged and striking, his Chuck Taylors crossed in front of him, as relaxed and confident as Clint was skittish. There was Clint's own father, sitting among his old friends—Josiah and Margaret, Freddy—clear that he belonged. If Clint came up right then, there'd be nothing to say. Even imagined, the silent gap hung leaden in her mind.

After dinner and the check (Louisa figuring the tip, fast) Doyle walked them to the foyer and held Margaret's coat while she wriggled her arms into it. Her girlish buzz had turned to sap, and she kissed faces wetly, palms on cheeks, which, when Doyle's turn, he held there, pinning her small hands under his large ones.

Josiah and Freddy stood on each side of the door like guards. Josiah extended his hand. "So good to meet you, Earl. Come out to our place next time you're through. Bring Louisa." He laughed.

"I'd like that," Earl said. "I've heard a lot about the land from Lou."

"Let's be honest, I ought to leave it to you when I go," Josiah said. "By rights, it's more yours than mine."

Earl didn't smile back. "Mr. Kinzler, I do appreciate the impulse, but please don't make a gesture you don't intend to keep." He did not seem angry, exactly, but he didn't look away. "I've heard enough empty words from kindly white folks to last me a good long while."

Josiah's face registered the surprise of that, such straight talk about what no one ever said out loud.

"Fair enough," he said. "I'm sorry to have made light of it."

"It's all right," Earl said. His smile returned as easy as it went. "You can think it over and tell me again if you mean it. Or maybe I'll marry your daughter and make it moot." Josiah shook Earl's hand pressed between two of his own. "Glad you came."

Josiah turned to hug Louisa goodbye. "Glad you brought him."

"You better be, Pop. He's sticking around." Earl gave a single nod.

"Good night, gang," said Freddy. Josiah walked with him to his truck. He stood at Freddy's open door talking until his brown coat was covered in snow.

JOSIAH DROVE MARGARET UP to the main house and escorted her inside, their elbows crooked together. In the kitchen, still in their coats, Margaret faced Josiah and laid her hands open on his chest. They were nearly the same height and, in this position, she knew just what the phrase meant, seeing eye to eye.

"I'd like to see that quilt sometime," Josiah surprised her by saying.

"Maybe it will come to Missoula," said Margaret, the only place in the state she could imagine it. "We could all see it together." She thought of Cody going alone, what she was willing to take on.

"We have good girls, my dear," Margaret said, hoping to snag him on a proud thought, a truth they could rally around.

"We do," he said. "We do."

Josiah squinted and looked at the floor. His thumbs hooked the back pockets of his jeans and his fingers drummed. Doyle's hands were in his mind, clasped to his wife's face.

"Margaret. Doyle, as you know—he's like a brother to me. Do you—"

"Shhh," she said, and touched his lips with two fingers.

They stood, quiet. The only light in the room came from the hood of the stove.

"Have I kept you from a happier life?" Josiah said.

"No one gets everything, Josiah." Margaret's voice was clearer, the wine's grip diminished without the group's bustle to buoy her. "Whatever you kept, you've given plenty." She laid her head on his shoulder.

They leaned against each other in the dark until the snow melted on their clothes in wet patches and they took off their coats to stay warm.

NEIGHBORS

WE APPROACHED THE HOUSE IN PAIRS. We came as couples who'd known the Kinzlers our whole lives, we came one by one, we came in clumps until finally we were a stream, indistinguishable even to ourselves: "townsfolk" or "neighbors," like extras in a movie. Josiah was our star.

We came in office clothes, in overalls, ranch coats, or our Sunday best. We changed our clothes to honor him, or we came in whatever we were wearing, and that haste honored him too. We wore Stetsons and faded ball caps that we removed to expose hair flattened at our pale parts. We brought deviled eggs, muffins in a tin, we brought casseroles, the foil-covered pans our grief made tangible, tucked tight around the edges and offered still warm.

The way word spread after the crash disoriented us. Most of us never heard straight out "I have to tell you, Josiah Kinzler was killed" or "I'm sorry to inform you, there was an accident." Most of us did not receive the news from a speaker who cared for us to know, but instead as an undercurrent, a wave of knowledge that coursed through town like a flood-stage stream. Josiah Kinzler's truck, rolled three times, wet road, herd of elk. Last night. Out 133 by the old Thorpe barn. The news brought up floating logs and jammed them in our lawns. It drowned us.

We opened the door he'd made and we greeted Margaret and their girls, boyfriends by their sides, silent and tall. Louisa, we hadn't seen in years, Cody looking so much like her father it startled us. We'd come to feel the loss of him, but he was there in her face, the first thing we saw. We hugged them and muttered *so sorry* and *how awful* and shook our heads; we hugged everyone. When had we last touched so many in such a short time?

In some places, "neighbor" connotes distance, a relationship notable only for proximity, not quite a friend, but here, it can also mean an abutting presence, a shared fence. A neighbor is a separate self, close enough to note a loose cow or a new truck, a hurt dog or a porch light left on too many days. Keeping watch.

We moved through the house, past Josiah's furniture, touching each surface. We laid our hands on the tops of bookshelves. From the stand he'd made, we pulled out the canes he'd carved for himself after he wrecked his knee, and we leaned on them. Two fingers dragging along the edge of a table—we wanted to touch everything. Truthfully, some of us were only there to gawk, those who were not close enough to have been invited inside the house before. Margaret and Josiah kept to themselves. Those of us who knew them felt a proprietorship, eager to show we were closer than others, while those of us who knew them distantly were perhaps more respectful, because the house was opened for a brief moment right as it was closed to us. We had nothing to prove. A few were so intimate that proof or access or the lack of it never crossed our minds.

We passed the coffin, which remained closed. We guessed that Josiah's face was wrecked, his neck was broken. The roof of his cab had been crushed. We were relieved not to see him, but also, grateful for his body among us. We knew his body. We knew his straight back and his cleared throat, his late limp. We knew his forearms, wider than they should have been for only a moderate-sized man. We knew his eyes that were watchful behind his glasses and his rough lilted laugh, as welcome as it was unexpected, and his beard, the browned thatch that might have reminded a bird of a nest. We watched the undertaker stand beside the plain pine coffin and wondered if Josiah had made it himself. We did not know you could lay a body in your home like this. We had never thought to ask.

We ate and drank, and the drink made some of us cry. Both the crying and the soothing made us tired and afraid of ourselves. Afraid of what could happen to anyone. After a while, we left. We left in pairs and in families that had not come together but needed to leave as one. We tried not to leave alone. The girls and their boyfriends and Margaret shut the door. What next? We drove home carefully to our own families, to our own houses, where we shut our own doors, and felt buoyant and guilty: relieved.

CROSSING THE FENCE LINE (1998)

AFTER JOSIAH DIED, Dorie wanted to help. Please let me come, Margaret, she said, and though Margaret craved nothing more than solitude, she agreed. She thought a visitor might help her, and Cody, someone outside their insular world, the one absent Josiah. When Margaret was a girl, their beloved family dog had died. The day after, her father moved the dog's bed from the porch and shifted the chairs around. A change was easier to live with than an empty space.

Dorie didn't come to visit often and for years had bunked at their parents' house. The first time she stayed with Margaret instead, she had come to help move their mother to a home in Great Falls. Mrs. Blanchard didn't know one daughter from another anymore, and the house she lived in with Aunt Abigail was too much for them. But Abigail was still sharp and wanted to live with her sister just down the hall, so one weekend Dorie and Margaret rallied together and moved their mother and Abigail into the home. Before they left her in the new room, they surrounded her bed and held her hands and Mrs. Blanchard smiled blandly. The nurses said she was a lovely woman, so sweet, no trouble at all. The sisters nodded at the nurse's praise and didn't say what they knew. No trouble was trouble of its own.

After their mother was moved, Dorie stayed a week. Margaret had not had a daily sister like that since she'd left home after high school. They listened to old records that reminded them of being teenagers. The phrase "riotous laughter" was made for Dorie. One evening while Margaret cooked dinner she could hear screaming and stomping from upstairs and when she went to ask Louisa to set the table, she opened their bedroom door to a pillow fight right out of a sitcom. Feathers floating, Dorie collapsed in giggles on the bed and Cody jumping so high her bouncing ponytail almost hit the ceiling. Coming, Mom, said Louisa, but Margaret hated to make her leave all that fun.

The last time Dorie stayed was after she and Merl split up, before Josiah died. Margaret anticipated then that Dorie would need comforting, because her voice broke on the phone when she called with the news—Margaret, I've done it, I gave Merl the boot. Sixteen years of marriage and then Dorie wanted him out and once she told him, she couldn't stand to wait even a day, so while he moved into his brother's basement across town, she drove to Montana and stayed a week. Margaret thought Dorie would arrive ragged and sad and she would cheer her like an older sister should, but Dorie was the same as always. *Unflappable* was the best word for it. Not a tear, and none held back. I told you I would leave and I have, she said. Enough is enough. Nothing bruised about her at all.

"I can afford to send him packing," Dorie had said, "because John gave me a raise, where Merl's been laid off for months." Logging had dried up then and Spokane's big mills were closing, like all over the forested west. John owned the dental practice Dorie had managed for decades, and surely he was a little in love with her, an excuse for the raise. Dorie without Merl was a prospect that would have crossed many minds.

Before Dorie went back to Spokane and her empty house, she and Margaret camped out together for the night, the two of them. They took the horses and one mule, Onion, with light loads on each side so Margaret could lead Onion and Dorie could ride free. Josiah and Freddy came up to help them load. Margaret could do it herself, but she hadn't in years and Josiah was particular about the tack. He didn't mean to meddle, but he wanted to see what was rigged how and give the animals a slap on the rump and send them off. Margaret didn't mind. "Have fun, sisters," Josiah said.

"Hand-some," said Dorie about Freddy when they were far away enough from the barn, and Margaret had to laugh. Dorie on her own was going to be an event. In high school all the boys fought over her, who could ask her out and when. At one point, Dorie made a schedule, Margaret reminded her of that, how they'd taped it to the fridge.

"Oh, that was a riot, wasn't it," Dorie said. "Frankie and Roger and Bo, they each had a turn. And then I got to decide who to give a second chance." She curled her neck back and hooted. "Whoever gave me that much power! I never had it again, that's for darn sure."

Dorie didn't seem to Margaret like a woman who'd just left her husband. Trouble didn't stick to her—it never had. Not like Margaret. She knew she carried things a long time.

They built a fire in a stone circle at the camp spot their family had been to over the years. Summer weeks, she and Josiah came after they were first married, before the girls were born, and then later on, all four of them. They'd cooked potatoes and hamburger wrapped in foil pouches and slept in their sleeping bags bundled in the canvas manties they wrapped the loads in, Josiah and me in one and the girls in the other, Margaret told Dorie. They brought a tent, always, but Margaret didn't think they'd set it up once. They picked times it was unlikely to rain.

"You have a good life, Margaret," said Dorie as they lay side by side in their bags, looking up at the stars. Onion and the horses sighed nearby. Margaret pictured her life as her sister might—the land and the house, full of what they'd made or earned. The girls, eager and laughing, their selves strong. Josiah in his own cabin didn't bother Dorie, though Margaret worried what she'd think. Dorie didn't mention it except once, and not right out: "You have space for yourself here. I like it."

Margaret held on to her sister's approval for years, even more so now that Josiah was gone. She remembered the room that had opened up around her the first year after Josiah moved down to the cabin. All the time she'd spent dwelling on his needs, she could turn to her own. But now that the gap was bigger, it no longer felt like freedom. Josiah gone, his needs gone, his weight gone, but also his light. On a good day, the light of him, the way, when he turned to her, it was like unfiltered sun. Sometimes the thought of that, gone for good, made her unable to breathe.

Margaret did not consider herself anxious, but what else to call it? That night out, the trip she'd taken with Dorie, she had woken hot and restless. She wouldn't have said panic, but it did feel like an attack, the way her thoughts struck at her. How could things change so quickly? You go to sleep contented beside your sister and then you wake—was it a sound, or your own mind?—and some quality of your life stops you short. The longer you stay awake, the worse it gets, until you can't imagine the person you were when you went to sleep. Why didn't you see it before, how foolish you were, how intangible every last thing you thought you loved? Even though Margaret knew it was the night that made it worse, the dark, and the expanse of what you don't control, she couldn't set back the refrain. Reason wasn't the tool for those times. Dorie slept soundly beside her, so Margaret shrugged out of her bag to pee and hoped to settle her mind.

She walked to the edge of the small lake a few hundred yards away. Mallards paddled near the shore, one of them giving an occasional squawk in the dim light cast by the stars and a three-quarter moon. What must it have been like, she thought, when the entire world was like this? Quiet, except for storms or howls, sudden wing flaps and hooves on rock, but no road noise, no planes overhead, not even a house to go into. Any creature that lived, lived out here, like this, getting food and rubbing up against another when it needed touch. Where you knew the time of day or night by the way the air or the light or the dark fell on your skin.

Margaret let the world nurse her until she calmed. She snapped a tip of branch from a fir and rubbed it between her fingers. She watched the ducks paddle down the shore, four ducklings scrabbling in the wake of an older bird, and when they were out of sight she crawled back into her place and slept. In addition to the memory of dread, Margaret held on to this: the way you saw your life could change depending on the light you saw it in. She was consoled by the thought that this must be true for everyone. Not just for her.

NOW, WITH DORIE ON HER WAY for the first time in years, Margaret had to take stock. The house was a mess, Cody mute. The weeks after Josiah died had been a blur. Grief mussed her like she guessed a drug would, time collapsed or endless, an odd taste in her mouth, a vagueness to the days. Chores helped. Margaret dusted behind furniture and vacuumed rugs, cleaned the refrigerator and returned the neighbors' glass pans that had sat stacked on the back porch for weeks. She weeded the garden and trimmed the first greens. Cody washed the dogs tied up at the outside hose and turned the compost bins. When Dorie arrived, Margaret's mind cleared a bit, as if having a witness helped her better remember her own self. Even Cody roused slightly, staying at the table after they finished eating and lingering before she disappeared on a horse, in the truck, to her room. A week passed this way, then half of another.

The day before Dorie planned to leave, the sisters walked to the Lindsays'. I need to do this while you're here, Margaret told Dorie.

Will you go with me? Yes, of course she would. There was a difficulty between her and Doyle, which Margaret did not name, but implied. "I need to talk to Doyle about. . . a hard thing," she said. "I've been putting it off."

For weeks it was never the right time. First, Margaret was too shattered and later, after the initial visitors had trickled, being alone so much had made her wary of company. She couldn't imagine talking or laughing, no social effort worth the energy. Lately Doyle had begun to stop in again for a short hello, sometimes only a hug. Last time she had seen him, before Dorie arrived, Iva was doing poorly and for the length of Dorie's stay, Margaret had used Iva's privacy as an excuse to avoid a visit.

But now Margaret was ready to see Doyle. Dorie in the house had helped with that—company she didn't have to seek out or hide from. Another person, near, made other people seem possible again.

On the way to the Lindsays' place, Dorie commented on everything they passed or saw, a red-tail hovering in the sky—*what's that bird called again?*—or lupine blooms *gorgeous!* dry on a stalk, or trash blown up against the fence—*why don't they outlaw those goll-darn straws.* To Margaret it was such a habitual trek she hardly noticed details, though familiarity was a kind of seeing, she knew. Ten minutes across the paths through the field, down the dirt road at the property boundary, through the gate, then up the hill and past the beech trees to the house, approached by a long sloping yard. So many trips between these two homes over years of neighboring, Margaret couldn't begin to count. Josiah and Doyle playing in the fields as boys, then their own children back and forth from house to house. Borrow an egg, buy milk, share the torrent of zucchinis, return a horse. Sometimes they drove, in a hurry or with a heavy load, but often as not, the walk was part of the event. In winter, they'd visit for an evening dinner, carrying a Pyrex dish in a picnic basket covered with a towel. The dogs sprinted ahead and Josiah pulled the kids on a sled. They kept a trail stomped out in the snow.

The Lindsays' house was unusual for the area, standing out among the slapped-up or hand-hewn. It had been built in the early 1900s by an odd-duck lumber baron who forewent ostentatious but splurged on architectural details reminiscent of his Carolina-Victorian roots. Dorie waited with the dogs on the porch, wide and shaded as a southern veranda, welcome in the growing heat. Dorie pulled dead heads off the geraniums and whistled to herself. Margaret went inside.

"Doyle? Iva?" Margaret called out softly into the empty hall. If Iva was in bed Margaret did not want to rouse her. She liked Iva, but it had never been easy between them. Iva's ill health and a remoteness that resisted care made her difficult to know. It would have been hard, Margaret thought, to have another woman not a sister, in and out of your home, doing the jobs a wife would do, if she could. Doyle was different, as warm and breezy as the front before a southern storm. He put you at ease. Even Josiah had been lighter with Doyle. But the house was quiet. Clint was out of state again, last Margaret had heard, and Nate gone to Bozeman for forestry. I hope he'll move back, Doyle said.

Margaret had her hand on the doorknob to exit when Doyle surprised her from behind, coming down the hallway at the back of the house. He greeted her with his arms open and she leaned into him, her sturdy friend. Once she began to talk, it was not as difficult as she'd dreaded. She had known Doyle for so long, he had context for whatever she might say. Details about how Josiah had died that she'd never spoken out loud to anyone, but needed to try, to see how they fit and how he'd respond. Money came up, Doyle making her feel like a child when he promised to take care of her.

"That isn't what I meant," Margaret said.

Margaret looked out the front window at Dorie sitting on the porch swing and her sister's so-familiar bearing brought it home: she had not properly considered Doyle's loss. Her own had been enough. But Doyle had known Josiah all his life, like a brother, a mirror. More than twice as long as she had known him. Margaret sensed all her lacks and gaps yawn beneath her like the open air at the edge of a cliff.

Doyle put his hands on Margaret's shoulders and spun her to face him. They both looked down at their feet, hers quite small in blue sneakers, his offset between hers in his creased leather boots. He pulled Margaret to him, the full front of her body up against his, and in her ear he said, so low it was more of a thought than a sentence, "Come to me, Margaret." She made no response, but stayed in his arms for a moment, her body not quite resisting, not giving itself over either. She was warm, but not warming. Then she moved away. She turned to the sink and washed her hands. She pumped the soap and lathered in the purposeful way she performed a small task. Margaret could not have known how much Doyle loved this attentiveness. Her pragmatism. She wiped her hands on the front of her jeans.

"Well, I should get back," she said. "Dorie is waiting for me." She turned to Doyle and her face didn't betray whether she'd heard him and chosen not to answer, or if his words were spoken so softly she could pretend not to hear.

"Thank you for listening, Doyle. You're a good friend," Margaret said, and as she passed on the way to the door, the nearest she got to him was a bent arm's length, her hand laid flat on his chest. To him, the foot she kept between them was vaster than his whole acreage. A day's travel, at least.

On the walk home, Dorie ranged around from this to that, asking a question and then stopping to note a flower and hunt around for the name. A lousewort, spirea? Did Margaret want to go out for dinner, did she think Cody would go back to fire this summer? She'd heard a storm might blow in, two weeks and she hadn't even seen a good storm. Margaret walked beside her and gave short answers. Dorie could fill space when it was needed, and Margaret was grateful for that. She opened the gate on the fence line and they stepped across into her own fields, Josiah and Doyle both strong in her mind.

LOUISA KINZLER

POP, I'M GETTING MARRIED, and Mom will walk me down the aisle to meet my Earl, but I wish I could go between the two of you. Mom on one side, Pop on the other. Like how you raised me. It's awfully soon after a funeral for a wedding, I know. I've had some time to wrap my head around no you in the world, but I still can't. The first months, I was so pissed, Pop. How could you die in a truck wreck, of all the damn things, you who taught me how to drive so careful and quick, how to judge the distances and drive smarter than any other oncoming fool? I meet so many grown women who can't drive a stick shift, too scared to even try, when to me it was no big deal. Every guy I know says I'm the best driver they've seen. How do you teach your girls that, Pop, and then roll your own truck three times? I know, the elk, water on the road. But we've passed a million animals in the road at night. You see it coming. You steer into the skid like you taught me. Don't overcorrect. Hands loose on the wheel. Were you sleepy? What startled you?

Cody, she needed you even more than I did. You were her best friend. Sometimes I thought I was, but now that you're gone, I can see it was you all along. There's something wrecked in her that might not get fixed. If I had to say, it was like her heart was broken. I thought only romance did that, but now I see that's silly. Anything that opens a heart up can close it when it disappears.

Anyway, I'm pregnant, Pop, which was an accident but not a problem, and now it's the night before my wedding and of course I'd think of you. Even though Earl and I have lived together already, we're doing all the silly rituals. He hasn't seen my dress. I won't lay eyes on him until tomorrow. Most of his family is coming, his mother and sisters, uncles, aunts and cousins, lots of whom I've met. It's funny, isn't it, we joke, that all those years we grew up practically next to each other, him in Browning and me in Columbia Falls, with only the park between us, but it's like we were from different planets. Well, we were. Part of me wanted to get married up at home, a skyline we both know, him from the east and me from west, but really, let's be honest—the way we found each other was we had to leave the place we came from. I went to Missoula to be a hippie. You saw me! Uncle Michael got the idea in my head and I had to try it. And Earl went to Missoula to be a lawyer, but he got sidetracked by kids, and now he's a social worker in the public schools.

I'm glad you met Earl, Pop, but I wish you'd really known him. You'd say he was a good man. It's the Indian kids he sees first and looks at longest, as he should, but Earl notices anyone that isn't getting what they need. He recognizes a look, a smart kid, or even a dull one, any child who wants more love or less wound, someone to look up to. After their brothers die in car wrecks—the crosses on Hwy 93, two of them were Earl's cousins—and their mothers get too sad to move, Earl listens. Not everyone agrees with us marrying. Some people in his family think it's another kind of tragedy for him to marry a white girl, one with stupid feather earrings, probably a dream catcher in her house, made in China. Some of my friends think it's dumb to marry a Blackfeet man. They don't know any Indians but the ones outside the Missoula Club where their frat boyfriends get drunk, and how that's any different I don't know.

This is why I have you in my mind, Pop, because of something you said once, in passing, almost under your breath like some of the best lines you'd say. It was the spring break I was home, after Uncle Michael died. You were talking to Mr. Doyle, something about Andrew, who we'd never met. Doyle said, "Josiah, it doesn't feel right to me, a man living like he's married with another man. I can't get myself around it." You were rinsing your coffee mug and I was silent and leaned toward what you'd say. "If someone is lucky enough to find love in this world, Doyle, I surely won't say who it can or cannot be." I think about that, Pop. I told it to Earl when we talked about getting married the first time. It's what I could give him so he'd understand something of you, even something small. If I had known you'd be gone, I would have brought Earl over more. You take time, and so does he, and I thought we had it. I don't know why I stayed away. I needed space back then, but I don't need it anymore.

I'm not taking Earl's name. I'm Kinzler, for better or for worse, I guess. Louisa Heavyrunner, that's silly, with my blond hair, like some powwow hang-on girl. I wouldn't feel right. Earl understands. I worried he'd think I was ashamed of his Indian-ness, resisting making us into a family, but he told me, "I'd never take your name from you." When they put his mother in a boarding school they changed her name and the teachers twisted her tongue if she said a Blackfeet word. Earl says getting married means that part of our job, our whole life, will be to try and say exactly what we mean. Like you and Mom did, I told him.

TAKING STOCK (1999)

A YEAR AFTER HER FATHER DIED, Cody moved out of the family house and into Josiah's cabin. Margaret tried at first to dissuade her, worrying that more isolation would warp Cody's already ardent grief into an intractable darkness, but Cody persisted. One afternoon in May Margaret watched her dogged girl haul boxes and a duffel bag across the fields to the cabin. She navigated the rutted gravel path with the same yellow wagon she had used to haul lumber scraps and rocks as a kid. Different objects in the bed, but a similar bearing, arms towing the handle behind her. The same march toward solitude that she had exhibited since she was young.

Once, soon after Cody had started kindergarten, Margaret watched her daughter walk up the driveway from the road where the school bus let her off. Her posture—slumped and slow—told anyone who looked that she was sad. A bully, a bad game—Margaret prepared herself to console, but fifty feet from the porch Cody squared up her shoulders, lifted her chin, and her body morphed from an inward turn to a small swagger, a façade that claimed the unmentioned sadness for her own. If Margaret had asked what was wrong, Cody would have said, nothing. Do you need to talk? No thanks. And she'd be off, to the barn, to the creek, to her room. Then, as now, Margaret let her go.

Her first weeks at the cabin, Cody kept to herself. She never left the property once, though she visited Margaret every couple of days, and Jess stopped in often with a random story from town or a plate of muffins. Sometimes he spent an hour on the couch and rubbed her feet while she dozed. They didn't talk much, coming back together slowly after Cody had all but pulled away. I'll wait, Jess had said. I'm here. Cody knew Josiah's death had unmoored Jess, too—he'd never missed someone more, he told her—but she couldn't forgive anyone for *living*. Not her mother, not herself. Most days Cody spent alone. She woke in the morning and fixed a cup of tea, ate breakfast, watched out the windows. She read a few pages or swept the porch or listened to music on the radio for ten minutes before shutting it off when a broadcaster's voice interrupted. Words irritated her.

Outside, she found she could concentrate longer. Cody rode Daisy, who did not mourn or try to comfort, for hours. She walked the property and collected varying objects—small, round stones one day, seedpods another. She carried them in her palms and pockets like she had as a girl, when her childhood bedroom was rimmed with collections. A seed would sprout or mold on a sill—it smells like compost in here, Louisa would say, and make her sister drop the mulching item out the window. Now Cody scattered her handfuls off the porch before she came inside. Gathering, not keeping.

In the third week of walking past it, Cody opened the shop for the first time. She pushed the door open and stood on the stoop before she entered. She'd come once before, soon after the funeral, but then she couldn't cross the threshold. Now, she stood inside for a full minute before she had to leave. Then, a little longer each day, like how she'd learned to swim, holding her breath and counting underwater first to five, then ten, then a minute, until she could do a lap in the high school pool without coming up to breathe. In the shop, she dusted the surfaces of tools. She swiped woodchips to the ground to sweep them up. She emptied the ash from the woodstove, snaked out the stove pipe and split kindling to fill the bucket beside the front door.

Cody began the first project only to finish a piece her father had left midway—a wardrobe for Bob Mitchell, half paid for and all but done. She saw the undelivered project like Josiah would have—a handshake gone back on. So Cody busied herself with the last steps: attaching the doors, buffing the wood with oil. She'd helped Josiah long enough, and watched him close enough, that she knew what to do. One hinge she wrecked when she forgot to prop the door and it sagged before it was hung. Sandpaper fixed the small gouge and she tried it again. When she called to tell Bob Mitchell the wardrobe was finished, he came to pick it up with his teenaged son and Cody helped them load it into the back of his truck. He paid the remainder in cash. Cody shoved the fat wad into her pocket without counting.

"I was surprised to hear from you," Bob Mitchell said. "I didn't want to ask."

"It's a lot of money not to get what you paid for," Cody said, unsure if it was timidity or respect that could make a working man leave hundreds of dollars unclaimed. Maybe both.

"Well, thank you again for finishing it," Mr. Mitchell said while his son hung back and ejected small cobbles from the gravel with the toe of his boot.

Cody shrugged. "I didn't do that much."

"Your father's work is very fine," said Mr. Mitchell.

"He has some pieces left," Cody said, gesturing at the shop. "Quite a few."

"Well, you inherited them then," he said. They shook hands and as he drove away a burden lifted from her as sure as if she'd carried a pack and set it down.

The next day, Cody returned to the shop and took stock. A bookshelf, a piano bench. A set of four stools with odd-sized oblong seats cut from an old-growth birch that had come down in a windstorm. She remembered severing the fat stump from its tentacled roots, left behind in the dirt. There were no notes or plans. Cody had seen her father sketch buildings and rooms on his gridded sheets, and occasionally a client would draw out an idea, but Josiah kept most designs in his head. She had no idea who, if anyone, the half-done pieces belonged to. She'd only known Bob Mitchell because the receipt from his deposited check was taped to the top of the wardrobe. Cody wished she could ask Freddy, but he was long gone. He'd disappeared before the funeral without a goodbye or a forwarding address, compounding her loss. The unclaimed pieces made an easier entry. No pressure of a face or a promise. Only the wood and the evidence of her father's hand and whatever she dared to add or try.

Taking a break on the porch that first week, Cody shielded her eyes against the late afternoon sun. She had never talked to her absent father aloud, never uttered the *fuck yous* and the *help mes* that the counselor said would be normal in the months after he died. Cody did not believe that Josiah looked down on her from somewhere else. She had inherited, among all the other qualities they shared, his disinclination toward an afterlife. But now, she tried it.

"You left a lot of stuff undone, Pop." It sounded like a reprimand. No one answered.

"I'll finish it. Since I'm still here." The clenched-up fist of her voice, accusing—*you left me.* But in "still" a quiet persistence. And "here" was the meat of it, really, what her father knew, too: a place you chose, and what surrounded you. In front of her, uneven ground, dry dirt heaved by groundhogs. A low sun, tall grass meadow full of insects all lifting and landing. An empty bottle sat on a flat rock where Jess had left it after an evening beer, and at the edge of the ponderosa fringe the sound of the creek filtered through trees.

CODY DECIDED TO TAKE a season off from fire—some life insurance had come in so she could. The crew hadn't been sent out yet so Jess was around. He didn't always call before he swung by the cabin, and some days Cody returned to a note on the table. *Sorry I missed you*. Other times, a loaf of sourdough bread from the bakery in Whitefish, which she'd never buy for herself but ate in one day. Once, only a flat stone with a heart scratched in chalk. Her days in the shop were a private respite she didn't share even with Margaret, though Cody thought she'd probably guessed, from the wood smoke above the trees. She hadn't planned it the night she told Jess.

"I've been working on Pop's stuff," she said while they ate pizza out of the box he'd brought.

"What do you mean," Jess said, chewing.

"He left some pieces—a couple stools. I'm trying to finish 'em."

"I didn't think about that, that there would be . . ." He looked at her and paused. "When you're ready can I see?"

"Tomorrow, maybe," she told him.

The next day Cody looked out the window to see Jess making his way down from the main house, slowly, as he balanced a mug in each hand. She shut off the sander and removed her earmuffs. He stepped on to the porch and she opened the door, nursing irritation at the unannounced drop-in. Jess held out a mug with steam curling from the top. "For you," he said. Cody took it and the heat warmed her palms.

"Hot cocoa?"

"Yep. Spilled it all over myself."

Cody studied Jess. Her favorite drink, from milk, not a powdered packet, and he'd made it for her and brought it down. He had gone well out of his way. It struck her then, how often he rearranged his steps to approach her.

"You didn't bring this from home, I'm guessing. How's Mom?" Jess often visited Margaret before he came to find Cody, or when she wasn't around.

"Good. I didn't tell her. About the shop. I figured you would, when you were ready."

"I'm guessing she already knows."

They walked the room and Cody explained her progress. The Mitchell wardrobe that had lured her in, how she might never have thought to start if it wasn't for the receipt. Here, the final resin coat on a bookshelf. Those godawful stools, their legs still had a slight wobble.

"It'd be easier to learn on three legs than four," she said.

"Three points make a plane."

Jess touched everything. The furniture, the hunks of wood—boards, posts, curved willow branches waiting to be stripped—even the tools. He'd lift a hammer, tap his palm, then set it down.

"It's weird, isn't it," Cody said. "All his stuff, but he's not here."

"How long did it take to get used to?"

"Not yet."

He rubbed the back of her hand with a finger, and she didn't pull it away.

"I inherited it, Mr. Mitchell told me."

"Can I help you somehow?" Jess asked. Eager to make a space for himself, careful not to push.

"Actually," Cody said, surprising him, "can you hold this, put pressure on the seat so I can finish sanding? It keeps sliding."

"The human clamp," he said, pinching his fingers together. Josiah's old joke. She smiled. Jess leaned on the stool, weighting it to the floor, and she turned on the sander. The whine and hum drowned out the quiet, showering Jess with fine powder until he sneezed and she flipped the switch off. Cody shucked her glove and brushed dust from his nose, then his lips, and he held her fingers there. She leaned in toward his mouth, a kiss, sad but open, another first time.

LOOKING ON THE BOOKSHELF in the cabin through Josiah's manuals on woodcraft is how Cody found the letter. She pulled out *Fine Cabinetry* to read about dowels and two handwritten pages leaned against the next book. Josiah's penmanship so distinctive, she'd recognize it anywhere, scrawled but readable. The paper was creamy and thin enough to see through, so he had written on one side of two pages.

My dear girls, it read, *I should have given this to you while I was still alive*—and her guts lunged at his voice, as clear as if he spoke aloud. Looking again she saw the date at the top, years before. She would have been twenty when he wrote it, the spring before he broke his leg getting firewood.

Cody turned both pages over, then back, ran her flat hand over the sheets and the embossed places the pen left on the page. She handled the paper a hundred ways before she read on, and one line in, she heard it, the odd formality he'd always had when writing—*Dear sir or ma'am, Please pardon Cody from this absence as she was ill in the morning and I was unable to transport her later in the day*—the diction in those notes a contrast to his easy, rural speech. She guessed it was a result of the way his generation learned to write, practicing their cursive by copying the Bible, some rhythm fluent to their fingers that had never entered their mouths.

March 24, 1996

My dear girls:

I should have given this to you while I was still alive, but I am a coward in many ways. I have loved you both, so much. Your mother may have told you that I was not keen on having children. We did it anyway, and I have never been sorry. You girls have been two bright spots in my very ordinary life.

I always have had a troubled part of me. I cherish the times we had that were not colored by this fact. I had many of those moments, enough to make a good life of, but I worry I did not readily enough share them with you. What's broken in me was so long before you. It comes from my family, an inheritance I pray I have not passed on (this is one reason I did not plan for children). Your mother has seen my dark times, but not my worst. I think I protected you all from that. I have been lucky to have friends and good work and of course the three of you.

Louisa, your bright ways are from your mother and I cherished them even when I worried I would tarnish you and I know I sometimes left you too much alone. Cody, you are more like me, and I found you a comfort, though perhaps at a cost to you. It seems one of you I have driven far from home, and the other I have kept here too long. Maybe I weigh myself too heavily and count my influence where there is none. I hope so.

I am sorry for the ways I have let you down, the many ways you realize I have faltered, most of all, this last one. I would have been a more contented man if I could have chosen it. I have always believed, and told you this, that mind can take you a far ways over matter. But it humbles me to realize that despite my efforts some things I have been unable to change.

I love you both.

His signature crouched at the corner, squeezed in where there was barely room. The ink at the period blotted the page, as if his hand had rested there.

Cody laid the letter back on the table. Her hands ran again over the sheets, up, down, up, down, the imprint of his words veined under her palm. She could not make sense of it. A letter written years before he died, as if he were about to kill himself? Had he tried? The letter never given, never thrown away, tucked away in a book as if it were forgotten, a scrap. Had her mother known? Or Freddy? Her mind wandered down one path and another with the panic of someone lost. It was hardly thinking, more like jumping rocks to cross a stream, but the bank got farther away. It was almost dark when Cody came to herself, her hand lying still on the paper and her mind on her father, on the failures she could see an outline of—*perhaps at a cost to you*—and the wounds that rang familiar—*a troubled part*—though if asked, she could not have named them, or said why she knew they were true.

Through the window above the table, she scanned the meadow in the evening light. The sky to the west settled into a warm autumn sunset, the pink and orange display a gaudy pleasure. The sky carnival, Louisa called it. Cody wished her sister were near. Her own favorite view was the night sky to the east, more subtle than heavenly. A bright inky blue that deepened while you watched it and folded the day up inside.

MRS. LINDSAY

YEARS I HAVE SPENT WATCHING. From my bed, out three windows I can see trees, and beyond them, a square of sky. Blue or gray, cloudy, rain on the screens. Birds in the upper branches much too high to notice from the ground. Once I saw a pair of songbirds build a nest from scratch as if they were a small crew. Every few minutes I'd look out and see it had changed. I don't know what kind of bird it was—small and yellow. Not a robin. Not a finch. The names don't really matter to me. I know them when they come.

The headaches move in like fire and settle like fog, the exhaustion afterward so complete I almost prefer the pain. To survive all these years, I have had to hold still. Sometimes it works—I rest long enough and the ache behind my eye lifts for a few hours, a few days. When I was pregnant with the boys it was gone for months, such a long relief that I forgot. When it came back, with babies to care for, so many days I wished I could disappear. I have missed out on one life. Being still, I have had a different one.

Most people don't watch closely because they are busy. Flitting from one task to the next. That's what it means to be well. To move. Only if you have been frail, then you learn how to relax into what can't be changed. We are the ones who know about watching. If a body slows down enough, the eyes become the fastest moving thing. Most people don't know who their families really are. They can't spot the way their sons move from a distance. Which boy runs with his arms out wide and trusting and the other with his head tucked down like he is going to knock over a wall. Which one is flailing and which one will be all right in the end. People don't notice who their husband really loves by the way he holds his body when that one comes near. People don't know where their dogs go when they aren't watched or how young deer with the tiniest of antlers practice crashing them together so that when it comes time to rut, they will know what to do.

I have watched all of this—dogs, husband, birds, deer, neighbors, sons—and while it is not the life I have chosen, I have made the best of it. The doctors say that my headaches may diminish as I age, that new treatments will come. That someday I may get up out of bed with no thought at all to the years I've lost. I imagine myself moving fast like people do—running around, to and from places, buying, helping, laughing in the bright light with one leg in, one leg out of my car, awaiting a friend. I don't recognize her. If that happens someday, the ease will be a relief. But who, then, will I be?

Who would any of us be when what we think we know changes? We cling to what is familiar, and to the explanations we can understand. For example—the pain in my head is neurological, a bright genetic misfire. It's a tendency I can't control any more than I can change the color of my skin. The workings of my body are an invisible mystery, like yours, like anyone's. Pain, comfort, revulsion, desire.

I do not judge. If there's one thing I know in this life it is that everyone has a burden, and everyone has a task. One's task is to build and another's to tear down. One's task is to make friends and another's is to put people on their guard. One's task is to remain loyal and another's is to test loyalty. One's is to need, another's to give. The burdens, they are less clear. We hide them or explain them away. But another truth I know is this. We all get attached to something. Some of us to sickness and others to health, some to beauty and some to ugliness, some to success and some to failure, depending on what's closest at hand.

SISTERS (2002)

LOUISA'S TWINS WERE three years old and still nearly identical. Girls, blond curls tendriled at their temples like pea vines, and almost-black eyes, a combination so unusual as to make even a parent look twice. The hair was clearly Louisa's and the eyes from Earl, so together the features were striking and unexpected—were they pale brown girls, or brown pale ones?—especially in double, and strangers commented on them so reliably (in grocery carts, at story time) that from the start, Louisa felt the urge to protect them from assessment.

Sometimes Louisa herself could not tell Lily and Iris apart. Before they were born, she thought the sheer heft of maternal gravity would grant her expertise, at least in knowing who was who, no matter what. All the books said it. Before they came you couldn't predict how you'd feel after. It would be instinct. A bear knew which cubs were hers.

But she wasn't a bear. She did know them deeply, their smells slightly different, Lily's sweeter and Iris's mulchy, and their personalities distinct, though overlapping. From the front she knew their tiny apple-shaped faces, one nose more upturned, a faint mole on a cheek. In profile she knew them, too. But across the yard, or looking down at each hugging one leg, there were times when Louisa thought not only *who is who* but also, *are you mine?* Post-partum depression, a friend told her once when she admitted it. It was common, the connection not always easy. But Louisa knew that wasn't it. This far in, the bond was clear, no sadness in sight, so she didn't name it at all. No reason to. The love she didn't doubt, only the knowing. What was possible to expect?

Earl, she knew. There was no one to mistake him for, the only man in the house, the only person Louisa had ever known who helped her vault over the hurdles that usually tripped her. If she ever worried about her parenting, Earl shook his head. To him, family was bigger than who birthed you or lived in your home. He had seen every kind of mother—father, too—from fierce and delighted to glassy-eyed ruin, and all that fell in between. You won't be the best and you won't be the worst, he told Louisa, mouthing her neck with a rumble, half farce and half desire. His trust buoyed her.

Louisa planned Cody's visit for a month in her mind, thinking out the possibilities. Which cafe for lunch. Take the girls to this park, that trail. Help me organize my closets. Tell me what's too small, what I'll never wear again. Cody had always been good at clothes. Not the wearing—for her, only a version of Carhartts or coveralls, a sweatshirt and sneakers—but the seeing. Cody had a "flair," Margaret called it, that she never used on herself and Louisa was happy to borrow it. They were so different and most often far apart, but what one sister offered, the other would take.

With Earl, Louisa copped to nerves about Cody's visit, how her sister couldn't commit to any plans, as if hedging her bets, which made Louisa doubt Cody's intentions. Earl listened while she ticked off the worries, small and larger. Would Cody like yoga? Should she find a sitter some weeknight for the twins so they could all go out? Would her sister show up at all? Twice in the last year Cody had canceled at the last minute, couldn't leave home because of a piece she was finishing, or wanting to stay put. A sister's worst fear: what if she didn't *want* to come? Louisa waited. When Cody finally arrived, the week was blank.

Since Cody's last visit, when the twins were a year, Louisa and Earl had bought a house and she was proud of it, ready to show Cody the life they'd made. Louisa bought special cheeses, and flowers for the table in the extra room, Cody's futon wedged in next to a tower of boxes draped with a sheet. The first days after Cody's arrival they hung out in the tumbled jungle of a backyard where the tomato plants outgrew their cages and you could hear the neighbors argue. They watched the twins jam their cheeks full of raspberries growing through the next-door fence, pricking their fingers. *Owie*, Iris would cry, and stuff her fingers into Lily's mouth. For a day or two, that was enough. Iced tea in afternoons and Cody reading to the girls—they could listen to stories for hours, riveted to the pages and their limbs tangled. Francis the badger and Arthur the aardvark and Ferdinand the bull and Frederick the little poet field mouse. All the best characters were unusual animals with old-fashioned names. For dinner Earl grilled elk steaks or pork ribs—Cody's favorite—and evening meant walks with two rattling strollers. The twins kicked and shrieked at every dog.

Near the university, volunteers had built a new playground complete with wooden boardwalks and a fountain and a slide like a dragon's tongue. We can easily walk, said Louisa, and that was their first morning away.

"Do you want to use the stroller?" Louisa asked Lily, and Lily said, "Does Iris?" Iris shook her head. "Walk," Lily said.

They left the strollers in the garage and the girls ran ahead, stopping at road crossings. "Both ways," they crowed, two little birds. Missoula in summer was bicycles and farmer's markets, the students all but gone and the road-trip Deadheads passing through and staying for weeks longer than they'd planned. They tossed their Frisbees in the green open parks along the Clark Fork and pressed their sunned skin up against one another. Piggybacking girls in homemade patch sundresses clung to the shoulders of bare-chested boys and the scent of pot smoke drifted from park benches and clumps of river brush near any eddy wide enough for swimming.

At the park Lily and Iris went straight to the slide. The gaping dragon was a magnet. Fear repelled them but fascination drew them in. After Cody helped once, her hands hovering behind their skinny butts, the twins climbed steadily up the ladder on their own, one behind the other, and then down the dragon's neck and out the mouth, spit off the forked tongue like watermelon seeds. They arced their little backs and landed in the sand in a giggling pile and they orbited the only other child on the playground in their own universe, unaware of his persistent efforts to play with them. Cody and Louisa laughed about what it was like to be romping sisters, everyone else peripheral, barely even moons.

"You were such a little pistol," Louisa said, "they must get it from you."

"Oh, not from you, delicate flower."

"Hey," shouted Louisa when the little boy shoved Iris and sent her sliding down before she was ready. "No pushing!" Lily waited for her sister at the bottom and took her hand. Cody was impressed at how long the girls played together without guidance or intervention, how sturdily they pursued an idea only they could see. They were so small, but big enough to make a world between them. Cody and Louisa half closed their eyes in the sun and talked in a wander about their mother—older, slower, but softer somehow—and what to have for dinner. Pork chops, voted Cody. She could smell the cut grass that dried in a loose layer along the edges of the pavement.

"Earl is a good guy," Cody said, thinking of him at the grill, how he'd air guitar with a rake and then set it back against the house straight-faced, not performing, just following a sudden urge. He was hard to peg, which Cody liked. She found herself too predictable.

Louisa smiled at her sister, sidelong. "I'm so glad you see it," she said. "He is good. Gooder than anyone else I know." She twisted a dandelion stem between her fingers.

After a while Cody got up the nerve to say her own news. "Jess and I are getting married."

Louisa sat straight up. "Oh my god, honey, that's huge! Why did you wait so long? Finally! You love him? You totally love him, look at your face."

Cody smiled, her eyes still closed. She adored him, but she never said it out loud.

"He is the only person in the world who might deserve you."

What could Cody say to that? What anyone deserved was hard to know.

Louisa stood and pulled Cody up from the bench and folded her into her arms. Cody was surprised, as always, how delicate Louisa seemed, like she could break. Cody felt her own torso thick in Louisa's arms—her sawing biceps iron, her stomach muscles like boards tucked into her jeans. Louisa sat back down and held Cody's arm, turned her body so their faces looked straight on.

"I never slept with him, you know."

"God, Louisa, shut up, I know that."

"He told you?"

"That was high school, Louisa. We hardly talked about you. It was weird for one minute, then done. Everyone is different now."

Louisa waved her arm. "Did you tell me first? Did you tell Mom already? All this time, getting married! Are you going to stay in Dad's cabin, live apart like him and Mom?"

"No, you dummy, we'll live together up in the house. The shop, we'll share. The furniture, you know we've been doing that, Jess is getting really good. We'll build our own place in a few years." She did not mention her work, the sculptural pieces she was becoming obsessed with. Her private experiment.

"We have to celebrate! Stay here, watch the girls. I'll be right back." Louisa shot off toward a clump of grungy boys playing hacky sack, two white with perched dreadlocks, one brown without. Their legs were skinny out the bottom of ragged cutoffs, bare feet below that. All the boys looked the same, rangy, loose-limbed, their clothes baggy and bright. Cody wondered if you could be a hippie boy if you were chubby, with a crew cut, or soccer shorts. Probably not. Even to free spirits, uniforms came easy. The boys gradually circled up around Louisa and Cody watched her sister's body language, the way she could flirt and demand at the same time. She was back in two minutes.

"Two bucks!" she said, holding a joint low and discreet in front of her. "Shh. Let's celebrate." She lit it with a book of matches the boys must have included with purchase and they shared a few drags, Cody's tiny and almost pretend. She hadn't smoked pot in years.

"Here's to marriage. To my little sis marrying the best kind of guy," Louisa said, forcing smoke out her clamped lips in a thin stream. "Will you bring him down next time for a visit? He and Earl will be brothers."

Louisa was a little stoned when Iris fell. She was climbing halfway up the ladder, and they saw her plummet, arms out to the side like a bird flying the wrong way, then flat on her back and quiet. Not even a cry. Cody sprang straight at her and by the time she reached the base of the slide and the pushing boy had slid down and crouched next to Iris, she finally began to cry, a welcome, jagged sound. Louisa hunched beside her, her palm closed around Iris's leg, a foggy haze between her and an honest assessment.

"Don't lift her," said Cody, remembering her annual first aid training from years of fire crews, and her father at the tailgate of his truck. "We have to check her spine." There was blood where the sand had scraped Iris's cheek. When the little boy tried to speak Louisa freaked.

"Shut up, shut up," Louisa screamed at him, "you little punk. Where's your goddamn mother?" She scared him, and the boy began to holler. A small circle of people had clustered close enough to listen, and one woman ran over. Iris tried to roll and when Cody saw her move she hefted the little girl into her arms. Even the boys stopped hacking and watched from a distance.

"He didn't push her, Lou," Cody said, low. "I saw it, he was already halfway down the slide when she fell." Cody had a warring impulse to care first for Iris, who lay limp and bleeding on her shoulder, and to shepherd Louisa away from a threatened mother who might find in Louisa's loosened face a thing to focus on that wasn't her son's fault at all.

"Fuck him," said Louisa.

"Come on," said Cody. "Take Lily's hand." Lily stood next to her mother with silent tears running down her face, as if her twin's quiet hurt was contagious and the fall had knocked the wind out of them both. Louisa picked up Lily. The weight in her arms brought her back to herself and she bucked up for the walk home. The woman gathered her son and Cody could tell from her face and her gentle voice—"Come over here, Sam, leave that family alone, the little girl is hurt"—that she didn't want in to their troubles. A relief.

More relief at home, when Iris lay on the couch and let Cody look in her pupils and undress her and check her body for bruises or breaks, a hand up and down each calf and thigh up to her undies, printed with turtles and shells, and over her narrow back and neck, each vertebra a tiny stone. Lily kept solemn guard beside her sister while Louisa made them lunch in the kitchen and cried, drops peppering the sliced ham. Cody said Iris looked okay. Besides the scratch, a shallow cut on the back of her head, the hair clumped with sweat and maybe a little blood. They should probably take her in.

"Oh my god, Cody," Louisa said at the table while the girls ate the sandwiches cut into triangles. Iris ate half, listless, a crust dropping from her hand onto the floor. "We cannot tell Earl that happened. Please. Please don't tell him I smoked that pot. I haven't done that in . . ." Louisa trailed off. "Please don't tell anyone, okay?"

Cody shook her head. "She fell, Louisa. It could have happened anytime. It had nothing to do with the pot." Which was true, but even as she said so, it didn't make a joint on a playground seem like a great idea. The doctor's office said come right in—from the sound of it she was probably fine, but it couldn't hurt to be sure. Louisa washed Iris's face with warm water while Cody strapped on Lily's tiny shoes.

CODY AND LOUISA HAD LOTS OF SECRETS, things only they knew they had done. Some they told later on, some not. Louisa had taken Pop's truck once in high school when she was grounded and he had left the truck parked up at the house when he walked down to the cabin. Their mother slept too soundly to rouse, but Cody woke when Louisa pulled in, the truck crooked in the driveway and her jacket redolent of smoke and spilled beer. Cody went out in the dark to straighten the truck so in the morning no one would know. "Oh, *thank* you, goody two-shoes," said Louisa, her voice following, too loud and slurred, its edge mean. By the time Cody came back inside, Louisa had passed out upright on the bedroom chair and Cody untied her shoes and slung her into bed, as limp as a just-shot deer.

Another secret was visiting the morgue to see their father. The night after Josiah died, Cody wanted to see him. I can't let you, Margaret had said, too scarred herself by what she had seen, the last she'd know of Josiah his smashed-up face, the caved ear, hair full of blood, one eye a puddle. I know you don't like to be told what to do, Cody, but a mother has to protect her child. Please let me do that. Cody promised, and she meant to keep it, but the next day she talked Louisa into going to the funeral home, at least driving by. She was too frightened to go alone, so together they drove there and then Cody was inside, asking the man to let them in. He isn't ready yet, and it'll be a closed casket anyway, the man said, but he gave her a chair to pull up to his body, covered on the table under bright lights. Louisa waited in the car. Mom is right, she said. I don't want to see. So Cody sat there alone. At the last minute she trusted her mother and instead of drawing the sheet all the way back, she sat by her father's side, tucked the sheet around his arm and took his hand. Cold and unbending, which she expected. She had buried cats, birds, watched autumn's deer and elk hang stiffening from barn rafters.

Cody knew it wasn't her father under there. It was just her in an empty room, not at all like when she was with him. She sat and held his undamaged hand, which felt like enough. But as she left, she had an almost ungovernable urge, at the door, to rush back in and throw off the sheet after all, and that's when Louisa helped her. Having someone to return to, in the car, waiting, was what she needed. She thanked the funeral director, seated in the front room full of coffins and gilt, and then left.

"How was it?" asked Louisa.

"I didn't look. I just sat with him." She looked straight ahead. "Please don't tell Mom we came here."

"I won't," said Louisa.

"I let her protect me," said Cody. "I did."

They'd have other secrets later, years of them. But as they sat parked on the street in front of the mortuary, they both knew while it was happening that here was the start of something new. It was an adult secret, not a child's, not a teenager's. A quick bird landed on the hood of the car, then flew away. The sky grew dark fast in the manner of late spring, when light lasted forever until all at once you couldn't see.

"Do you want to tell me more about it?"

"Drive," Cody said. Louisa did.

THEY WERE BACK FROM THE CLINIC with hours before Earl came home, and the day stretched out long, no naps. Not for Iris, who had to be kept awake until later that night in case of a concussion—unlikely, said the doctor—and so not for Lily, either, who wouldn't sleep without Iris beside her. They walked for blocks around Louisa's neighborhood, checking to be sure the girls didn't conk out in their strollers.

As they rattled down the gravel slope to the riverside trail, Louisa said, "Once I talked to Dad about my abortion."

"Really?" Cody couldn't imagine bringing it up, but Louisa was another story.

"Yeah. It was right after Earl and I moved in together. I was pregnant then, the time I had the miscarriage. I hadn't told Earl about the abortion before, I didn't think it mattered. Then, when I got pregnant, all this shit stirred up, and it was weird that he didn't know why. I was anxious all the time. Then I was visiting home, I had hardly been in years, and Dad asked me if everything was okay, if I was happy."

Cody could not recall if her father had ever asked if she was happy. She thought not. He'd already know that about her, or else would not have put her on the spot. Louisa was different. She would say.

"It all came out to him, the whole story, about the abortion in La Grande, and you helping me, but also how I felt about it right then. I didn't want to make it into a big deal, but I knew I should tell Earl. My mind wouldn't let it go."

"What did Pop say?"

"I will never forget it, actually. He said, 'Sometimes what you don't say out loud for long enough becomes a secret even if you didn't mean it to.' That's exactly how I felt. *Exactly.* It was so weird, that he gave me the words. If you had asked me would I tell Dad about an abortion before Mom? No way."

Cody peeked over the stroller awnings and the girls sat looking ahead, their legs stuck out straight and faces slack. They were tired and so was she. She couldn't think of a response. It was Louisa's story.

"He said, 'Tell it, Louisa, give it to Earl to help you hold.' And I did. When I got home, I told Earl all of it. And Dad was right. I've hardly thought about it again, not in that way, like a loaded gun in your purse. If you carried a purse, I mean, ha, that would be the day." Louisa laughed.

"Anyway, Earl listened to me, and we talked about it, like it mattered, but he didn't make it too big. He heard me, and then we moved on. It wasn't a shame anymore. It was a rough patch—like a breakup, or letting someone down. Just part of the deal."

Cody was still unsure what to say. They sat in silence until Louisa broke it. She was always the one to speak first.

"I'll probably tell Earl. About the pot, I mean."

"Yeah."

"You were so good with Iris today."

"Well, I doubt you would have gotten stoned if I hadn't been there," Cody said.

"It's just, I get so flustered. When stuff happens with them, even a little thing, I don't know what to do." She stopped pushing. She turned to Cody and held her arm. "Do you think I'm a really bad mother?" Louisa could be so dramatic.

"No. It's probably easier to take care of what isn't yours. You can love them without owning it all."

"You are so fucking wise, Cody," Louisa said. She took her sister's hand and they walked the rest of the way home like that, pushing the strollers with one arm.

"Don't you fall asleep, turkey lips," Louisa said to the girls, rattling the handles until she heard Lily giggle, "Stop it, Mama!"

EARL READ THE TWINS a bedtime story and Cody heard his low voice pitching up and down for different characters. Cody came from her room into the kitchen, where Louisa was wiping up dishes.

"I brought something to show you," she said. Louisa walked to the table with a plate and towel in her hand. A paper shopping bag sat next to Cody's feet, and she lifted it onto the chair between them.

Louisa leaned forward expectantly. She had always loved surprises. Cody took a box out of the bag and set it on the table. Louisa knew it right away. They both did. The size of a large jewelry box, but it looked as if it belonged to a man. Rich brown and smooth, no shellac but the oils of hands. Cody ran her hand along the top. The box had sat on Josiah's desk in their parents' bedroom. Even after Josiah had moved out and Margaret slept in the room alone, the box stayed on the roll-top, tucked into one corner and lined up with the glass jar of pens and a stack of envelopes and a tight roll of stamps. Cody would sit on the chair with the red upholstered cushion and roll the desk's top up and down. It's your father's, Margaret would say when they asked if they could open the box. I don't even know how to unlock it.

"I found this," Cody said, touching the tiny metal key in the lock. "It was in Dad's cabin, on a ring of odds and ends. The Master lock to the barn door, the keys to the panel boxes on the Ford. It took me a while to figure out what it was for, but then I was like, of course."

Louisa lifted the box and shook it slightly. "What's in it? Did you open it? Please tell me you're not too holier-than-me to open it. I couldn't wait two seconds." Her voice grew louder, excited, and Cody had the urge to quiet her so the girls wouldn't rouse, even though they were down the hall, their door half-closed and Earl's voice layered over any noise.

"I did open it. And anyway, I'm not holier than you."

"So? What's in it? Open!" Louisa bounced in her shoes. Cody turned the key and picked the silver clasp with her fingernail and lifted the lid. She felt almost guilty for prolonging it, but she wanted Louisa to go through the same stages she had. The lid stood stiffly, upright, as if the hinges had rarely been opened. The box was empty.

"Did you take something out?" Louisa put her finger inside, traced the gray satiny edges and the tight lapped corners.

"No. I opened it, and it was empty. Like this. Do you think I should ask Mom about it? If there was supposed to be anything in it? If she knows?"

Louisa knit her face as she did when she was thinking. "I don't think Mom knows."

"What do you mean?"

"She doesn't know what was in it. If anything ever was."

"How do you know?"

"I just do." Louisa was quiet for several seconds. Cody knew her father and her sister in such different ways. Sometimes it was hard to remember they'd known each other, too.

Earl entered the room and stood behind Louisa and bent to kiss her ear. He was taller than her by nearly a foot, wide shoulders and a narrow face with dark slivered-moon eyebrows that could change his expression with the slightest move.

"Book finished. Down." Earl mimed a plane landing with his hand and sank into an empty chair. Neither sister spoke and he looked at them, raised his brows.

"What are you two up to?"

Louisa pushed the box toward him on the table. "Cody brought this—my dad's," she said. "It was always on their bureau. Mom didn't even have a key."

Earl opened and closed the lid. "Ash," he said. "He made it?" Louisa nodded.

"Beautiful work," he said. "Nothing he couldn't do, huh."

Louisa took his hand and lifted the back of it to her neck below her chin, holding it there.

"There was stuff he couldn't do," Cody said. It surprised her. She wasn't sure what she meant. "What makes you think there was nothing in it, Lou?"

Louisa tapped the box lid with her free hand and squinted at her sister. "Well, he kept his emptiness locked up his whole life, didn't he?"

"Christ." Earl gave a snorting laugh. "You two are making symbols out of thin air. Maybe it's just a box he made and he liked it." He got up and scrubbed the soaking cast iron pan in the sink. "Maybe he did the best he could."

Cody pulled the box toward her and slid it back into the bag.

"I think he did," she said.

MARGARET KINZLER

JOSIAH, I HAVE TO TELL YOU SOMETHING—I talk to you more than you'd guess, all these years later, maybe more than I did when you were alive even—and it's a confession, I suppose, but also just news I've been wanting to share. I have fallen in love with someone. His name is Jerry and he is a sweet and silly man who makes me laugh until I am helpless and then he dances me around the room. I can hardly stand up with how embarrassed I get. I'm sure you can picture it.

I have fallen in love with a man who is nothing like you, Josiah. He is a pediatrician and he hums while he makes coffee in the morning and I hear him talking in the kitchen when he's alone. He talks to his food: *Hello, delicious!* he'll say to his dry toast. He sings the worst songs from musicals in the shower, the ones I hate! I can't see any damage in him, not hidden, not waiting to rear. He's a person who got a gift, got to be easy in his skin. In living with him I grasp how quiet our marriage was, Josiah, how heavy with all we held back from each other. Out of shame or temperament, I guess, both of us at fault, but neither one to blame.

I wished, after you were gone, that I had loved you differently. Better, I suppose. I wish I could have thrown myself into your arms because I knew you would catch me and waltz me around in front of our girls. I wish we had shown them some cavorting. I wish I had teased you more. Me and Michael and Dorie—my Lord, did we use to tease. You didn't have enough laughter of your own inside you and instead of hushing mine I should have shared it with you. I wish I had not let you move so quietly away, alone. There was Freddy, by then, and no matter what else, I was glad of that. You thought that was what you needed, I know, I know. That's what I thought, too.

We never fought, did we? Rarely. A simmer from time to time, but sometimes I longed for a fists-out brawl and after you were gone, I raged at you, I did. I punched walls and threw glass and let out all the recklessness hidden in me that I never let you see. Sometimes I thought you couldn't handle it. Or was it that I never trusted you to?

Now I've fallen for Jerry Winkleman—Wink, I call him, really, even his name with a lightness that makes you smile. I surprised everyone marrying him, the girls most of all, and moving to Portland. A city! Can you believe it? The years in Missoula after you died were up and down, so difficult to dig out from, and then I met Jerry—he was a docent at the art museum, like me—and before I knew it, we were lovers, though if you'd asked me that likelihood, I would have said I'd as soon jump off the Higgins Street Bridge. I'd have thought it would be hard to start up with another man. I'd only ever been with you—never with Doyle, not once—and by the end of our marriage, our old intimacy sporadic and charged, when it happened at all a bit fumbling. With Wink it was easier than I thought it would be. How strange, at first, him touching places no one had seen besides you. You take my breath away, Wink said.

After the first time I didn't think of you at all. A new body made it new.

But some things don't go out of a mind because others enter. I still think, every so often, of how we met and fit each other, how no part of my ordered world had prepared me for you. Now I have this other kind of love, a free and unruly love so unlike our quiet one, and despite how safe I feel and how known, how lucky I am to have found Jerry and this version of me so late in the game, there's this loss alongside of it: I wish I could share her with you.

REVISITING (2006)

"MOM," SAID CODY on the first morning of her visit, "are you eating enough?" Cody poured hot water from the kettle into a teapot and set the timer on her watch. Spring drizzle speckled the windows and the kitchen filled with steam.

At the table, Margaret laughed out loud. "Flesh of my flesh or not," she said, "I have never set a watch for tea."

Cody stayed with Margaret when she came to the city every few months to restock a gallery that carried her and Jess's work. It was still hard to believe, that they made a living now from wood. And that this was Margaret's life—a light-filled second-story apartment, a job at the library, a haircut that skimmed her shoulders. A husband who was not Josiah, long enough now that Cody had grown used to him, fond even. This spring weekend, Jerry visiting his own kids in Washington, Margaret and Cody were alone for the first time in many months.

"Did you hear me, Mom? You look too skinny."

"I'm not withering away, dear," Margaret said, deflecting worry, sharp. "I eat plenty."

Cody poured two cups of the brewed tea. Margaret and Cody shared a reserve that meant they had never talked easily—both would admit this—and so were used to the silences that grew up around the two of them alone. Louisa filled spaces with effortless chat, full of questions and offhand news—oh, Mom, guess who I saw—or reports about the twins, who'd done what hilarious or terrifying thing. When Cody and Margaret were together, a shared task eased them toward intimacy—a sink full of dishes or canning tomatoes or working in the garden. They were both lightened by movement.

When Cody was younger, she wondered if it was possible to feel awkward with your mother for your entire life. She remembered when she got her first period—not the time she bled at twelve, with no breasts, a child still, and Margaret wrung out of her that she'd walked the split fence and fallen on her crotch, which must have broken her hymen. Her mother spelled the word out for her, and Cody always associated it with the word *hymnal,* which was embossed in gold on the front of the songbook at Grandma Blanchard's church, and not once after would she open the songbook without thinking of that bloody pain. But later, when her first real bleeding came in a clenching hot rush that stuffed Cody's breath in her throat, she was too ashamed to tell Margaret about it. After school Louisa helped her place a sticky pad in her flowered underwear, but Cody didn't tell her mother until the following month, ashamed all along of being ashamed. What was so hard about telling her mother the most girlish, bonding news? She still didn't know.

The last several visits, Cody had heard welcome glimmers in Margaret of an unusual openness, below the decorous conversation something more ragged and confessional, which occasionally crept out and took Cody by surprise, as it did now when, sitting in the breakfast nook overlooking the city street, drinking tea from a dainty china cup, Margaret said, "The quilt was here last weekend."

Cody waited, unsure of the coming position.

"I went to see it. Michael's wasn't there, of course, I didn't expect he would be. But it was something. So big, it's amazing, isn't it, that's only a small part?"

"Yeah," said Cody. Bigger every year. A thing that got sadder the more it grew.

"While I was there, I saw these two men, close to my age. The way they leaned into each other with such love—no hugging or kissing, but a closeness, like no one could see them, no one else mattered. It reminded me of your father, how we were at our best. I don't think I've seen two people who reminded me so much of us. Their way."

Margaret rarely spoke of Josiah anymore. Cody reeled her mind back to think of the last time, what they'd talked about, when. Margaret meant to highlight what flowed between the men, a lovingness, and not the men themselves, but mention of the quilt freed Cody, and finally, she said to Margaret the words she'd never been able to bring herself to, the thing she'd worried at for years, held on to, naggy, always waiting until the next time. There it was, spoken:

"Mom, I know Pop was gay." She couldn't remember when the thought had first occurred to her and even now, the word "know" surprised her. She'd guessed. She'd wondered. Had she known? But once out of her mouth, the words changed from the heavy rock in her gut into a butterfly, a brilliance that darted around the room, out of her control.

Margaret looked out the window for a bit before she answered. "Was he? I suppose. I don't know what he was, what he'd say. He loved a man, I do know that."

"Freddy?" She already knew, the response more to keep her mother talking.

"Yes, Freddy, how could you not love Freddy?" Margaret laughed and sipped her tea. How indeed. For months, a year, Cody had shadowed Freddy closely, learning her father's craft alongside him. She could still picture Freddy from behind, the way his legs bowed slightly, a gap between the knees, and how he swung his arms when he walked, tapping the side of his thigh with his open palm, as if keeping a beat.

Margaret went on. "But Josiah loved me too, until the day he died. I know it. And I don't know if loving one man made him gay. I've hesitated to say so. I do know he struggled with something big. 'I'm queer, Margie,' he used to say to me. It didn't mean that to him, what it means now, I don't think. He meant he didn't fit. He never felt he fit."

"I found a letter, years ago." Cody began to encapsulate it for her mother, but once she started, she knew it by heart, like an old poem memorized in high school, and so she recited it to Margaret, her voice dropping into the low, soft register she associated with her father's speech.

"I love you both," she closed. Margaret listened, unmoving, and when Cody finished, she said, "That's true, he did not want children. The first time wasn't planned, the baby that didn't make it." She opened her eyes and looked at Cody. "He always thought that his anxiety about having a child must have made that one leave. I told him it didn't work that way, but maybe it does. Maybe it does."

"You had us anyway."

"A while after we lost that little one, he said we should try again if I wanted. He was very serious, he still worried, about—about the wounds in his family, he said, passing them on, but together we decided, well, I wanted to try. And he would do it for me. He was a wonderful father." She waved her hand. "You know."

"When did you guess he was gay? When did he? When he moved?" Cody used the word again—*gay*—not to push, but because once it was out, it honored him more than shying away would have.

"I don't have any idea how long he knew, but no, the cabin—now that was because of his depression. He had such a black time that year. The light, the work in the woods, usually summer was an easier time for him. When he was so flat even in June, we knew it was big. The winter was worse—you remember."

"Why did he move, then? Wouldn't he be worse, alone?"

"No, no—for Josiah, it was other people, the world, how he couldn't relax into it, that's what exhausted him. Alone, with his own limits, he could bear up better. It's hard to explain. I say it now like I understand, but it took years, Cody, to see it clear. For him, too. The cabin was an experiment. He didn't want to leave you girls, check into some hospital, which looking back, might have helped. But he did get better. His own place, the wood. You girls, and me, coming and going. The money was hard, but that spring he was good, and much better, for quite a few years."

Margaret looked out the window. In her mind she had said almost all of it, and to Wink a good deal, but to her daughter, laid out like this, all the pieces and the fitting, it became something it had never yet been. Not a story. Not quite that.

"And Freddy—he lived with Pop in the cabin, didn't he?" Two placemats on the table, not one for Josiah alone, not three for her and Louisa. Books stacked by the woodstove, paperback spy novels she could not imagine her father reading. All the times she came to the cabin and Freddy was there, drinking a beer on the porch, or involved at the workbench, not like a visitor at all. Your pop will be right back, Cody, he'd say. Pat the bench—come sit. And she'd stay, talking to Freddy until Josiah returned.

"He never lived there really, he always had his own place in town. But they had a life together. That I know."

"Did Pop tell you?"

"He did. He was brave that way. He came up to the house once, when Louisa was getting ready to leave for college. He wanted me to know that I might see Freddy around more. To learn woodcraft, an apprentice, of a sort, but also—I want to be discreet, Josiah said, but I want to be clear. Is it all right? he asked me. That old-fashioned way he had, chivalrous with me, delicate. He knew I'd guessed for a long while. Maybe because of Michael, I was differently tuned, I had a frame for what some clues might mean. I didn't want to put that on him, though. I never assumed."

Cody's tea had gone cold as lake water. She drank it anyway. Margaret kept talking, and though Cody was in some way enthralled and contained in the moment between them, she also hovered above, watching it unfold.

"Did Mr. Doyle know?" She used the childhood nickname without thinking, as if they had stepped into the past.

"I think so. We never talked about it directly, but after your father was killed, it was a hard . . . We talked it through, and he knew what was behind it, my questions."

"What do you mean?" Cody sensed an edge to the acres they were walking in, a fence nearby. They could trail along it for hours, hand on the top rail, not leaving, not entering, walking close. How odd it was, the way the landscape on two sides of a fence was nearly identical, yet one side was yours and one was not. A fence line could run between two trees so close together there wasn't room to squeeze between. Once, Josiah was bucking a spruce and found barbed wire grown into the heart of it, his saw kicking back and the chain instantly dulled. "I guess this one's only half mine," he said.

"After your father died, the life insurance man came." Margaret pushed open a gate. No cattle guard, no warning. A place in the fence swung open, and Cody hesitated, almost interrupted, wary to pass through.

"They always investigate, especially because your father died young, quite tragically, and his family history—depression, his mother. So, when the man called, and came out, I was not surprised."

"Where was I?"

"I don't know. I didn't think much of it, it was routine, until the man said he'd had the truck looked over—it had rolled, and your father's side was smashed, you know this, why the casket was closed. Blood and hair on the bumper from the elk. But they found a brake line cut. That's what the insurance man told me. Cut. Not worn, not a tear, severed. No accident, the mechanic said. It was a garage in Kalispell, so no one knew Josiah's truck, which I am glad of, considering the questions it raised. To cut a brake line, you'd have to mean harm. To someone else, or yourself."

"What did you tell him?"

"I knew that Josiah had thought about—he told me the time he came close, the letter you found. But later? He had Freddy. Money was better. He seemed settled, to me. Of course, if he'd killed himself, we wouldn't have had the insurance. That pushed me in how I saw it, I'm sure. I told the man I could think of one—one person who might have done him harm, and I'd look into it. That's when I went to Doyle. We talked about it, the possibilities, who was where that night. Doyle was gracious, considering what I suggested to him. He was an old friend. He loved me, and he knew I was grieving. And Doyle said to me before I left, Does Freddy know? Did Freddy know what I suspected, he meant. And why would he say that? That told me a lot. Doyle was protecting his own, but he was protecting mine, too. He loved your father. They were brothers, in a way.

"Clint. You mean Clint? You think he cut the line?" Tea rose up in her throat like a fish, a thrashing tail, scales.

"Ah, I used to. I don't know anymore. He had no reason, really, just drunkenness, but—he was tough, always was. Doyle saw that too, it's why he didn't run me out for asking what I did. But I don't think that's enough. In most people it isn't, anyway."

Cody lurched around the room like a calf in a pen. She felt like hollering, a pressure building up in her, the closest she'd ever come to what people called a blinding rage.

"How could you never have told me this? It's been years! I think of my father every single day, not a day goes by I don't miss him. Why have we never talked about any of his?" Her face hurt. She stormed the perimeter of the living room and as she thought her mother wouldn't answer, Margaret's voice came, slow and measured.

"I didn't know how much of it was yours to take on. It's not always better, honey, knowing. I didn't want to burden your life with what wasn't yours."

"Burden? Pop *is* mine." The last words came out strangled and she bit her teeth together so hard her jaw hurt. Margaret sat looking at her lap. One finger rubbed an unraveling seam.

Cody put her hands to her hips and squared to her mother. "What happened with the insurance guy? Obviously, we got the money and Clint's not in jail." Finances soothed her, the possibility of questions with exact answers.

"That was a gift. I told the man I knew two things. That my husband was depressed, I did not think suicidal, but I couldn't be sure. And that there was an old grudge, an unstable family friend, and I doubted we could get to the bottom of it short of a courtroom, and that I'd prefer not to have to try. I told him that if he ruled it a suicide, we'd survive, but our days would be harder. He listened to me and he said, 'I'll call it an accident.' I'm not sure, maybe he fudged the paperwork, maybe the garage wasn't on record with the brakes. I never asked. All I know is one person, a bureaucrat you could call him, looked at a messy situation and decided to read it in one way, when he could have chosen the opposite. I've always been very grateful to him."

"Mom, I—" Again, tears in her throat flooded Cody's words and her anger morphed to shame faster than she could turn away. She fled the kitchen.

Margaret had always been relieved when her children cried. Comforting them was easy to do, holding them close, the hugs, the patted back, a swaying hush. Cody was not a child who let herself be held, but when she was sad, sometimes her resistance softened and she'd allow her mother to comfort her. Margaret could count the times Cody trembled in her lap, a part of her kept rigid even while Margaret soothed, It's okay, sweetie, cry it out, it's okay. When Cody eventually went to her room, her sobs through the closed door punctured Margaret. Only alone would Cody collapse, and nothing Margaret did could assuage that.

Now, Margaret knew that her daughter was right. Cody and Josiah's bond—Margaret had never been able to approximate it. To call her jealous was too much. She watched it though, their luxury together. She saw how her withholding desecrated what Cody and her father had made.

In the guest bedroom, Cody flayed her duffel bag open and jammed her unpacked clothes inside. The task calmed her. On the way to the bathroom for her toothbrush and soap, she passed her mother's room across the hall, the bedspread tight as a trampoline. Margaret's bed never went unmade unless she was sleeping. Cody had planned to stay until the next day but now she wanted to go to the gallery, then drive home. Ten hours, maybe twelve. She loved driving at night. When she went back into the kitchen, Margaret had not moved.

She didn't look up. "I'm sorry, Cody," Margaret leaned back in her chair. Cody watched her mother's face and saw its aging. Not the lines so much, though there were those, but a certain veil, a gauzy patina that softened features and made Cody think of time—how much passed, or left.

"I loved him more than I can tell anyone about." Margaret whispered, and it drew Cody close, the way her kindergarten teacher would talk softly so the noisy class quieted to hear her.

"I wish everyone in their lives could love someone that way." Margaret put her forehead to her hands, pressed into a sturdy cup to hold her face in.

She looked up. "He was mine, too, Cody." Such ordinary words to say about a husband, yet once out, not entirely true. Yes, Josiah had loved his wife, and yes, his daughter loved him. But he was no one's. Maybe not even his own. That was a point that both of them knew.

Margaret widened her eyes to dry them and wiped the tablecloth in a broad sweep with her arm, though there were no crumbs or spills. "Cody, I'm sorry. Please believe, every day, I tried my best."

Cody sat down across from Margaret. She had never imagined what her mother had carried. "I believe you, Mama."

Cody reached out and closed her hand around her mother's thin wrist, the kind of bone you would say is birdlike, which had always bugged Cody because birdlike could mean "eagle" as much as "wren." *If you were a bird,* Cody thought, *Mama, if you were a bird, you would have complicated feathers. They'd look one way in the light and another in the darkness, a bird whose stillness wakes you after the night is over, silence the disturbance. If you were a bird, you'd build me a nest with a song.*

ON THE DRIVE HOME, the weather cleared and the sun strengthened the farther east she drove until, crossing Fourth of July Pass, the car was warm, a hurtling cocoon. Cody thought of her father, scene after scene unrolling, in the woods, the shop, the times he was distant and she didn't know why, the times they laughed together, his quiet chuckle that got louder the longer he went, like he forgot to hush himself. She thought back over all the hints, when she had asked about Freddy and he bit off his words, or waited too long to answer. Clues she might have picked up on. But she had never thought of him as someone to investigate.

Now, Cody tried to insert herself into her father's possible lives. So many men he was, or could have been. First come the clichés, the easy scenes—a modern apartment, a bright kitchen, Cody bringing a bottle of wine up a narrow flight of stairs. A man raises a toast—he wants to be Freddy, but she can't recall him well enough, and so he's the gay roommate from a sitcom with a pressed shirt and neat haircut—and he kisses Josiah on the mouth, this less surprising to her than the way her father's always-steeled back and shoulders relax into those arms. Then, in a bathroom, he's preparing for bed. Josiah removes his glasses and sets them on the counter, and from the bedroom a man calls, Will you bring a glass of water? The room is wet with steam.

After the movie images pass, she imagines Josiah alone, reading in his cabin at night, the dim aura of the lamp with the glass-paneled shade refracted through the colored panes. He turns the pages of a magazine with a licked fingertip, as he always did. A car's tires rumble the gravel, and he looks up from the page. Last, Cody sits across from Josiah on a train, a subway riding into a city, where she watches him give up his seat for a pregnant woman. They trade a comment about the newspaper she's reading and then Josiah grips the arm strap and turns so Cody can see his face reflected in the window. He wears clean dark Wranglers, his town boots peeking out at the hems. His face is shaven and he's going somewhere. For what? To whom?

As she dropped down the east side of the pass and the gnarled alpine trees thickened into forest, the realization hit Cody like a shove: she had loved him, and she had never known him. She had always imagined Josiah as her own, a father, and later, a friend, though one with his own distances built in. She had never imagined him a stranger to her. Now she tried. The loneliest thing she had ever done.

JESS MCCAFFERTY

LATELY I'LL LOOK ACROSS at Cody over dinner, her same face that I can honestly say I have seen in a new light almost every day since I met her when we were kids, and now, she's the woman I know best one minute and then in another, like someone I might have made up to suit me. Everyone does this, I'd guess. But it's confusing.

I remember her buoyancy, first a little scrapper, and then when we met again, she was so serious, but she had this liveliness about her, it made you want to follow her close, as if she had something planned. That's not gone. But it's buried further. She doesn't rise to the surface as easily as she did. Maybe the surface has changed.

When we first broke apart after Josiah died, I thought that was the end. But I waited—what else would I do?—and she came back to me. I know that matters. Since then, we've had easy times and almost-fucked times, the latter a ways behind us. Still, between us, lately it's like a stick-framed house before the siding's on, a hollow empty space full of angles and air. She's far away again. Has it been years building on something we haven't said? Her or me, I don't know who should speak first. If we start at the same time maybe the actual words won't matter, just the saying.

That summer on the fire crew, the first day, when I saw it was her, all this stuff came back in a flood, more than I would have said I'd known: How Louisa talked about her with a fondness I couldn't imagine my older brother felt toward me. Cody on that horse, in a truck, grubbier and wilder than any other teenaged girl I knew. And this way she'd smile, on the edge of a group or a conversation, like she knew what was next and we did not. It made you want to ask her about it. To this day, I always want to know what she's thinking.

In the mornings, when the eastern sky gets light, the first thing I'm aware of is Cody beside me, still deeply asleep. She breathes loud, not quite a snore, but an open-mouthed huff. She sleeps like a child, with heavy limbs and a sweaty forehead, as if she is escaping herself. Sometimes I lean on my elbow and watch her. I can see in her face all the versions: the kid I knew, the little sister of my first crush, the girl who followed her father everywhere. Then the one I met on the fire crew, the heat between us so fierce I believed people could see the air buckle when we stood side by side. Now there's a woman I know, layered, as scrappy, as sexy, as much of a puzzle as she ever was. My love, she's that. Even distant, I can't help it.

I tend toward compassion, I always have. My mother said it when I was six and I cried when I watched the older boys at a campground catching bullfrogs and beating them to death, the mud banks slick with blood and skin. I take things to heart. Still, it surprises me, when I watch Cody's sleeping face, how easily I can let go of the resentments and worries. They float out of my hand like a foil balloon. I let her be complete, a perfect thing. Imagine if she did the same for me. Maybe she already does. How would I even know?

I touch her cheek—so often smudged with ash or mud or rust or stain. Her father is gone and I can't replace him. Someday she might trust me with the parts she conceals. She will sidle up to the old stories, the ones she has never yet made new for me, and I hope I am paying attention enough to listen.

I think I know her best when she's asleep—nothing hidden, face open, at ease. She doesn't wake until she wants to.

IN THE BALANCE (2007)

WHEN CODY BANGED ON CLINT'S DOOR, a ratty screen that didn't close on the front of a travel trailer up on blocks, she thought how ironic it was, how similar to her father—trade Josiah's tidiness for Clint's squalor—a guy sequestered on a corner of his family's property, secrets stacked around him liked junked cars. Clint was back from Lander and Cody came out as soon as she'd heard he was home. When had she last seen him? Her mind blanked. All the memories were old ones.

He took forever to answer, long enough that Cody considered leaving. Then the door opened and Clint squinted at her through the screen.

"Cody? What brings you?"

It was maybe the kindest tone he'd ever used with her. But Clint looked rough, his face gaunt and baggy at the same time, dark pillows under the eyes, his chapped lips chewed. Exactly like you'd picture an addict, down on his luck, fuzzily hung over. It was obvious to Cody why she had chosen morning for her visit, picking a time she knew he'd be off-guard.

"I want to know what happened with my dad."

"What?" Clint said. His gaze shifted behind her shoulder so dramatically that she actually turned to look.

"I want to know what happened with my dad's truck. The brake line. The accident?" She'd sensed going into this that full-bore was her only choice.

"Jesus, Cody, that was years ago."

"Nine."

Clint disappeared into the trailer and for a moment she thought he had fled and she'd have to run to catch him hightailing it out the back door, though of course, most trailers only had one. Eventually he emerged with a beer, cracked it open.

"I'd offer you one, but you don't strike me as the before-noon type and I'd ask you in, but—" he shrugged and tipped one hand at the porch. Rotting, dirty, scattered with beer cans and half-done this and that. Boots without laces, a soaked pair of jeans pinned under a fallen section of gutter. Also, at the edge of the porch, a pot flooded with vibrant yellow pansies. Cody wondered where they'd come from. Clint settled on the edge of a truck bench seat propped up under the window and left Cody to stand on the steps. He picked at a rip in the vinyl with his thumb.

"I knew you'd come. Honestly, I thought it'd be sooner."

"Cut the bullshit, Clint. This isn't some movie."

Clint rested his forehead in his hands. His face looked so much like the kid she'd known her whole life, she had to remind herself they were long grown. Cody wished for Louisa, suddenly. She needed an army, but she was alone.

She'd expected him to start with the truck, the brake, a denial or evasion, and she'd prepared her cross-examinations: what about, prove that, then how? But Clint went his own way.

"Your dad. Josiah Kinzler. All my dad talked about was him,

you know. How smart he was, what a good rider, a good sawyer, your beautiful mother. If your own father thinks you aren't good enough, it's pretty easy to want someone else's."

Cody felt a flare of sympathy she hadn't prepared for. She forced herself to fix him in her mind: a brute, an idiot.

"Don't tell me about my dad. I'm asking about the truck."

"You be careful what you want to know, Cody." His voice was blunt and hot as welded pipe and like a swung weapon, it stalled her.

"Always the bully, right, Clint. Still work for you?"

Clint breathed in through his nose, a long inhale that pinched his nostrils. "It never really worked, Cody." He twisted the can in his hand and fiddled the pull tab until it sheared off. He flicked it into the patchy grass alongside the porch.

"I walked in on him and Freddy, in his shop, once." Clint offered what she had never even thought to ask. "You want me to tell it, Cody, you have to hear it all." Clint held up his hand as if she were interrupting him, though she hadn't said a word.

"That summer I worked for your dad—he wasn't hard on me, not like everyone else. So, I came over for years, any excuse."

"I remember. You showed up all the time."

"One time, near the end of high school, I went to the shop. I heard his voice from the back room, then—other sounds," he paused and forced air out his mouth like a fighter at a heavy bag. "First, I thought it was animals, some hurt critter he had laid up in back. But then—when I—I went further in. Your mother—I wanted to see. But it was Freddy and him."

Clint went on as if he were talking to himself, and Cody wasn't there at all. He'd run out, they didn't hear him leave. Later he'd confronted Josiah, who did not deny it, and asked only that Clint not tell Doyle, not tell his girls. Margaret knew, Josiah said. He'd like to keep the rest private. That put Clint on his heels. He'd expected denial, anger, maybe a fight, but not a request, a simple request made by one man of another.

Cody could picture her father the way Clint described it, measured, not pleading. Josiah had always taken a person's word seriously, both the giving and also the asking. *You have my word*. She'd heard him say it many times.

Clint went there to accuse and left having promised to keep Josiah's secret.

"I never saw Freddy after that. In a store maybe, the bar, but not close," Clint said. But knowing and not saying made him angrier, as if he were tainted by it. I almost told Nate, he said. But it made him sick inside, the words he'd have to say. So, he didn't.

"I've never said it out loud until now," Clint told Cody. She thought he was finished, but when she began another question, he plowed through her.

"I never came over again. For years I didn't see him, maybe out somewhere, with your family, whatever. But not alone. Then out of the blue," said Clint, "Josiah rode up to our place and told me he needed to ask me a favor. Nate lived in town by then. My dad wasn't home. I was the only one there. I was the only one he trusted," Clint said, "that's what he told me. Why, I have no idea. I hadn't talked to him in years. He wanted me to cut the brake line of his truck. Don't tell me when, he said, and I won't tell you why. It's an experiment, and it needs to be unexpected. I didn't think it through, didn't think about it at all really."

"I said, whatever, Josiah. I wanted him to go away." Clint swigged from his can.

Since they were kids, Clint could always talk. He would go on and on, not stopping when others would, blind to listeners turning away. The way Clint talked now turned Cody's stomach. She almost told him to shut up, but what was coming out of him seemed more important than how.

"First I blew him off. But a month or two later, the night he—I was at the bar and I saw your dad's truck. We were drunk, dicking around, letting the air out of tires. Okay, I know this guy, I said, let's fuck with him. I lay down on the gravel, slid under, and I cut the line. I could feel the rubber, easy to find even in the dark. One pull, with my Buck knife. It was through. Do you know what your dad said to me once? That an old knife had history in it, like an old tree. I thought of that later. Not then." Clint put his head in his hands again and scratched at his hair and a torrent of white flecks drifted from his scalp and on to the legs of his jeans. He pressed his palms against his head in a fierce cradle. Cody waited.

"Anyway, the other guys were flirting with a waitress having her smoke. Maybe one of them saw me, I don't know, but we were wasted, I doubt they knew who was who. Even drunk as I was, right then, when it was cut through, I thought *fuck*, and I almost went in and told him, offered him a ride home. There was music, that country swing band. Cash for Junkers. You could hear it in the parking lot." Clint took a long swig and swished it in his mouth before swallowing.

"I didn't go in. I partied some more, passed out. I don't think I even went home that night. Didn't find out until the next afternoon when my dad told me." Clint lifted the beer to his face again but stopped short of drinking, set it on the stairs.

Cody guessed that Clint had never been inclined to imagine the insides of other people. Did he do it now? For a moment, in his face, Cody could see he was somewhere he didn't usually go. She could imagine they were on the same boat, the same little boat floating out in the middle of a rough lake, the water too dark to call blue.

Clint looked right at her then and Cody wondered if, when he saw her, he thought of the child her, the way she saw the child him. Wiry and smart and bruised, full of magnetic danger, like ice or flame.

"Here's the thing, Cody. I am sorrier about that than anything I've done in my life. By far, by *miles*. And I've done some shit. Talk about regrets." He put the can to his mouth and this time drank long, his Adam's apple moving like a tiny piston. He wiped his lips as he said the rest.

"But he *asked* me, Cody. He *thanked* me. A fucking note. In the glove box of my old car that I was working on and I didn't find it until months, probably two months, later. Hold on." He went back inside.

Cody thought she might be sick. In the growing heat, the area around the porch reeked of old beer and urine. She tested the soil of the pansies with her finger and found it damp. Clint had a fresh can when he returned, and a piece of thin yellowish paper, which he handed to her. *Thank you for your help, Clint,* it said. *I am sorry I had to ask. My best, Josiah.*

Cody's mind went first to the insurance man her mother told her about and she had the urge to rip the paper—proof—into pieces, though absent the context, the note meant nothing, and anyway, the claim was long closed. The note seemed a too-tidy end, like a prop from the crime novels Jess read. But there was Josiah's distinct handwriting. She'd mimicked it for years, to make hers look like his. She could tell those letters anywhere, the neat scrawl.

Clint cleared his throat and spit. "He left that note before—he *knew* I'd do it. What a fucking coward."

He glanced at her, then away. "I'd have done anything he asked me to."

Cody looked up at him, standing on the porch, her still at the bottom of the stairs—no part of her wanted to approach him closer—and when she saw his face from that angle, his eyes were flooded, spooky, his features gone soft as if his face had begun to melt. She had never imagined this, never in all those years, though she knew that bullies were the weakest ones: Clint crying.

"You should be in jail."

"Fucking *look* at me, Cody. I'm not going anywhere." He held out his arms, turned in a slow circle, the beer can held plumb from his fingertips so as not to spill. Arms out, his sleeves rolled up, tracks stitched the pale undersides of both arms like a ripped and mended seam. He'd been in rehab for heroin and meth, was supposedly clean, but HIV positive, Doyle had mentioned. He had no symptoms, maybe never would. He was lucky to be born later, after research and prescriptions, but he didn't look lucky. His Wranglers hung on him, not in the trim manner of a cowboy, belted and dusty, but ill-fitting, pouched at the front and loose with grime.

As she steeled herself to hate him for good—no more of the seesaw she'd been on since childhood—Clint surprised her. "You know, I've always admired you, Cody."

All the mocking came back, the mean words, how easily he could shrink her. "Yeah, right."

"You've always been your own world. Enough on your own. Most people wouldn't have come here, to see me." He waved his hand widely, as if to outline the scope of what was his. "And here you are. Brave little fucker."

He shifted his feet and Cody saw how Clint was kept off-kilter by his cravings—for oxy, for trouble, for love—which shoved him from behind as firm as two strong hands on his shoulders. He'd been trying to balance all along.

This world is full of wrecked men, Cody thought, and though she was broken, too, her mother, her sister, all of them really, right then, these men were by far the saddest to her: her busted-up father, and Clint, who he took down with him. Any lines she'd imagined, the closure she'd planned for herself, maybe even a phone call to the police—why had she thought that stuff would mean anything?

"I'm taking this," she told Clint, folding the note and putting it in her pocket. "It isn't yours."

Cody walked to the truck and backed out the short driveway, watching the shoulders in the mirrors. Keep it between the ditches, her father used to say. Later, she'd heard the line in bars from drinkers hoping to make it home without a DUI, but Josiah had said it when he taught her to drive and to her, it connoted a sense of possibility within parameters, a gamble on safe passage. If you kept it between the ditches, you had a chance to make it home.

In her rear view, she saw Clint on the porch, his head back and his hands out wide near his hips, beer can dangling. Cody knew then she'd been wrong, she'd been totally wrong. Of course the note belonged to Clint. She shouldn't have taken it. Who else had ever thanked him for anything?

Kinship flooded her, against her will—this deflated boy, her almost-cousin. His words were a flash in her brain—*on your own, on your own*—and it was so obvious, suddenly: how holding herself apart was a comfort that threatened to take her down. Her own special brand of loneliness, a compulsion as thick as Clint's hungers. She checked her mirror to cut the turn, and when she backed onto the road and straightened the wheels to pull away, she saw Clint crouched at the flowerpot, pulling dried petals and cupping them in his palm.

JOSIAH KINZLER

DARK NIGHT, SPLIT MOON, half of it in some other sky. Josiah closes the door of the bar behind him and night enfolds his body like water he's jumped into. The air is clear, soft as Western Montana can be in spring, suggesting early summer's ease before the heat rises and scalds.

Josiah puts the truck in gear and when he makes the turn onto the road from the parking lot and feels the empty brake pedal push to the floor, he knows what he's up against. It was months since he'd asked and he cringes with the shock of it, that what he'd been coward enough to request, Clint had been brave enough to do. Right then he could have pulled over. He almost does. The blackness has passed again, as is usual—so bleak mid-grip and then when it's over, like a feverish dream. This is not a night he would have chosen, flush with music and spring air, Freddy heading home by a different route. Tomorrow, a Sunday ride with Margaret. The shop full of orders, a wardrobe for Bob Mitchell, half-done. He almost pulls over.

But he can't evade the old draw, that familiar tug toward oblivion, and up surge all the plans and wishes, the almost times—rope coiled, pistol loaded, never in hand but near enough to bank on. Edge of the quarry, the drop mimicking the hole he felt in himself, bottomless and unknowable. No matter how deft his evasions, Josiah has always wondered what's at the end, what place there might be where the weight is less, the steps simpler. He drives slowly, now, thinking it through. Rounding corners, floating through stop signs, driving the careful way you would if you knew you could not stop. On Main Street, at an empty traffic light, he downshifts, the engine leaping between second and first gear like a bucking horse and Josiah tightens his thighs instinctively, as if to hold on.

Dark night, split moon, half of it shining on another place, a place where there is no one to love, no one to worry over. No one to let down. Josiah leaves the intersection, speeding up at the edge of town where the limit goes to 65, but he drives much slower than that, testing, not yet abandoning himself to an outcome. He could drive all the way home like this, no brakes, gearing down, coasting to a rest beside Freddy's car. Fix the brake line in the morning. He'd go to Clint and apologize for the burden he had placed. A chance looked at, head-on, and turned away from. A relief.

Freddy loved live music and he sought it out, but Josiah didn't often join. Crowds made him uneasy and he didn't like to be around drunks. He'd always avoided bars, scarred by the musty booths where he'd huddled, waiting for his soused father to drag him home in a belligerent scuffle. But that night, with Freddy, the bar had been loud and a neighborly sort of crowded, full of people he knew and a few of them, even trusted. Friends sharing drinks jostled each other, the dance floor packed, passed glasses overhead. Hands rested on shoulders, an ease of arms and legs, the usual spaces between people entangled. In the dark parking lot on the way to the door, Freddy had kissed the back of Josiah's neck. Later amid the pressing crowd, Josiah touched Freddy's hip with his open palm, then slipped one finger beneath the waistband of his Levi's where the skin was warm. He left it to rest there longer than he ever did outside of home, and the thrill of that filled him so full he almost cried.

He's west of the old Thorpe barn when Josiah sees the bull elk in the road. The barn has been rotting since he was a kid, and the skeleton has stood all those years above a drop sharp to the creek below. At first, he thinks he's imagined the elk, a totem he's brought up from his mind to teach him a lesson, though he's always been skeptical of making animals into symbols when it's their own survival they're bent on. Anyway, that kind of magic belongs only to those who watch the world for purposes beyond their own, he knows, though the ski resort cowboys grasp for it. But another bull follows the first out onto the asphalt, and another, gathered up in numbers rare outside October's rut. They are as real, as fleshed, as he is, and why would he need three symbols, four, five, all their legs, antlers, their measured stomping panic under the high beams? Whatever that might teach him—that the land is full, that even a herd can't save you—he already knows.

Josiah glances at the dash, 40 mph, 45, and as he weighs his options a second too long, he's on them, brown and tan hides scattered, the truck fishtailing. Instinct sends his brake foot to the floor though his mind knows it's useless. There is no thud, no breaking glass. The animals part before him and he thinks, oddly, of Moses opening a passage in the sea.

As the wheels hit the shoulder, Josiah sees what it took, all the steps toward this turn. Not just a family and its blighted blood in his veins, not just a cheap knife in the hands of an angry boy, not even himself deciding to drive on, but the unexpected elk, too. A largeness agreeing to conspire.

When the gravel gives way to the steep slope and the truck leans,

leans, tips toward the creek, so slow he thinks it might actually stop, he says their names, aloud: *Margaret, Louisa, Cody, Freddy, forgive me. Clint, please forgive me.* Then the truck rolls, and Josiah seizes a moment to look, to see the needles of the forest out the upturned window—Doug fir, larch, lodgepole—their bristles nudging sky. A thought surprises him: *My god, I will miss the trees.*

ENOUGH (2009)

THE WINDOWS ABOVE the main workbench faced southeast, where Josiah had placed them to maximize the morning light. Cody sat on a stool, elbows on the bench in front of her, drinking a cup of black tea and waiting for the sun to crown the line of trees. Dry birch snapped in the woodstove, the room's only heat. In October, 9:00 am passed before the first direct rays. The expanse between the shop and the trees was only a few acres, arid meadow dotted with old red-barked ponderosas, easy enough to see past, and her eyes found the open middle ground, resting blankly until movement caught them—a woodpecker hopping up a trunk or the quick dart of a vole in the white grass.

This morning, a larger disturbance—a man, walking the path to the shop from the driveway. She could see at fifty yards it wasn't Jess, a night owl who rarely made his way down from the house before ten. This difference in their makeup was a gift. Mornings alone insulated Cody against too much togetherness, sharing as they did the business and the shop and all the ordinary details of a life. After a morning apart, she was glad when Jess arrived, bearing a hot drink or news of the world. But it wasn't him.

The man approaching was tall and slender, in a green down vest. She could see, as he got closer, his rectangular glasses, a city haircut. He walked carefully as if to keep his feet dry, though the meadow hadn't been wet in months. He carried something under one crooked arm, the other swinging loose at his side. At first, she thought he'd taken a wrong turn and came to seek help, but the man's alertness suggested a mission, some purpose beyond wandering: he was coming to her. Cody traced a line along the row of glass jars holding hardware (finish nails, rivets, tacks, turnbuckles, wood screws) and waited to rise until the footsteps on the front porch, and a rap, not aggressive, not timid, just a statement: Hey, I'm here.

Cody opened the door expecting a client, someone Jess had spoken to about a piece ready to be claimed. A little early to be usual, but not exactly rude. The man's face opened into an easy smile, his teeth white and even, bringing to mind the way a fox can look friendly. Curious, but wary. With the door open and the screen between them it took her a few seconds to recognize him.

"Cody," he said.

"Freddy." Spoken alone like that, no other words surrounding, their names sounded related, two syllables each, the Y at the end, gentling any tension. She had not seen Freddy in years. It must have been the day or so before her father died. There was no specific memory, a last time. He was around, and then, after the accident, he wasn't. She hadn't missed him until later, the first weeks her father's absence enough on its own, but after, Freddy gone was another fissure up the center of her old ground. She had spoken about him with her mother and Jess, and to Clint, but she hadn't heard word of Freddy since he'd left.

Cody opened the screen and Freddy held out his hands in front of him, waist-high, facing slightly up, as if for her to take them. She laid her palms across his and he squeezed firmly.

"I'm sorry to be here so early," Freddy said. "I've been awake for ages, waiting in my hotel. I couldn't watch any more TV."

"Yeah, yeah, come in. The fire's getting hot. Want some tea?"

Freddy nodded and took in the room, changed from when Josiah worked there—brighter, with the log walls sanded, the whitewash Cody needed to be able to work indoors all winter—and also, much the same. The workbenches under windows, the cradled sawhorses, the same pulleys and hooks on the ceiling beams for lifting logs too heavy to move alone.

Cody took the kettle from the woodstove and poured water into mugs. As the tea steeped Freddy wandered around the room. He didn't nose, exactly, staying a bit distant, not touching, but he took his time. He didn't talk, as if he'd forgotten she was in the room. Cody liked his quiet; the unsure clutch inside her gave way to a welcoming.

When the tea was ready, she picked up the mug and spoke. "What brings you here, Freddy? Where are you coming from?"

He turned and removed his glasses. She couldn't picture him in glasses from before, and though he looked ageless, tan and fit and clean, he was probably in his forties, as Josiah was when he died. Had it been more than ten years? Her mind swam.

"You've made this place your own, Cody. Such beautiful work. Your pop would be awfully proud." He used the name she'd called her father by, and it made her wonder what Freddy had called Josiah—what private nickname, an endearment for the person he had loved.

The back of the room was full, organized by style—furniture, Jess's specialty, the glowing wood reminiscent of Josiah's pieces, but the joints more modern, the whorls and wain of trees less visible. The bowls, aspen, cottonwood, some birch with a thin strip of bark left at the rim. The boxes they were both known for, stacked in corners, with wooden slats and varied colors, like pallets polished to shine. And Cody's found animals, the recent sculptural stuff for the gallery in Portland, pieces carved from odd-shaped limbs and hunks of wood in which she saw the neck of a swan or the whisk of a marten's tail.

"Thanks." Cody handed him the mug and went to the stove. She opened it and pried at the logs with the iron poker Jess made her out of a straightened horseshoe. Her "fuckwith," he called it.

"Do you work in wood anymore?" she asked. She kept her back to him. Freddy's presence in the room whittled the gap of her father, a trick of negative space so acute and shifty, she had to blink.

"Not really. I'm a teacher. A lot of work. Not so much with my hands." He shrugged, looked at her almost sheepishly, as if she might think those years with Josiah were a phase, a lark, instead of a turning point.

"I hope it's all right, dropping in like this. I would have called to tell you I was coming, but somehow that step, ah—I doubt I would have come." He'd always had a clarity of speech, saying what he meant, but not apologetic. Never trying to make himself less in the face of what was expected. Cody pondered, for the first time, what it was like for him to hide. Not just for any man, but for Freddy, so at ease with himself. What it must have cost him.

Freddy raised his hand to gesture at one piece, a large unusual bowl built in horizontal strips around a thick pedestal base, and his ring finger glinted, the early sun against a gold band on his left hand. As Cody noticed it, he dropped his hand into the other palm and twisted the ring.

"My partner's from Northern California. We're legal there now. Or, we were." He smiled and lifted his eyebrows. "We live outside San Francisco, on the Headlands. He had a conference in Missoula, so here I am."

Cody nodded. She recognized his test: how much did she know? No answer meant she knew enough. Not everything, but enough. She had followed the news with interest the last few years as states passed laws, then rescinded them, as people began to identify their partners without avoiding pronouns or looking away. She bought a bumper sticker at a coffee shop in Whitefish a year ago that said, *Marriage Is for Anyone Who Loves*. It bookmarked the Gazetteer atlas she kept behind the seat of her truck. Brave, and then not.

"Me and Jess got married," Cody said. "Maybe you knew that. My mom's in Portland. She remarried. Louisa's in Missoula. Husband, and twins." My dad's here, she almost but did not say.

Freddy walked closer to her so they stood a few feet apart, the woodstove between them. The fire gave a loud pop, the bluish flames cranking out heat to radiate against her legs. The stack thermometer needled into the red, 550 degrees, and she closed the flue a half-turn.

Freddy said, "I should have come to the funeral. I didn't think there was a place for me. I was a fucking mess and I didn't want to make anyone uncomfortable, so I left. But I should have stayed." He looked right at her. "I'm so sorry."

Cody put her hands up over her face, a tendency of hers since she was a little girl when a strong feeling came over her, as if she could hide. This only made her grief more evident, but she couldn't help it. Her face felt full of water and light and sand.

Freddy edged around the stove. Had he tried to hug her, Cody would have steeled herself rigid, or wheeled away, but he only stood beside her and, with his hand on her far shoulder, pulled her toward him so they leaned against each other. She wanted to run, to leave the cabin altogether, but his arm was solid and undemanding, and for a moment, standing there in the sun, it was as if someone had finally seen into a deep part of her, a little box up on a shelf in a tiny closet in the back of a room in the structure she built around a fragile thing. She stood beside Freddy, shoulder to shoulder, hands over her face, and Freddy stayed.

THE SHOP WARMED and the morning frost retreated to the edges of the windowpanes in icy waves. Cody added another log to the stove, and they walked through the work, talking about wood. They finished their tea. Freddy wanted to see the old cabin, so they walked there. Cody waited on the porch while he went inside, giving him the space she would have wanted. The cabin hadn't changed much since Josiah died. After the year she'd lived there, it sat mostly empty. She or Jess might spend a night when one or the other needed quiet; the occasional guest stopped over. The sheets were different, the blankets new. But most details—the fold-down table, the sun-faded chair by the stove—were exactly the same. Even Freddy's paperbacks still sat on the shelves between bird guides and the yellowing paper manuals of tools.

After ten minutes Freddy came out and gave a hesitant smile, like a simple gift he wasn't sure would suit her. That did me good, he said. Another cross of paths seemed unlikely, but they said goodbyes, see you again. Walking by the porch of the shop on his way out, Freddy said, "Ah, I almost forgot." He bent to the log bench and picked up a blanket, folded, what he had carried under his arm as she saw him approach. He must have set it down before he knocked. He handed it to her—Josiah's saddle blanket. The last time she'd seen it was tucked in around her saddle, under the tree the night she was lost. How old was she? Eleven? Twelve? That ride came back to her as strong as if it had been last week, how brave and grown she felt that day, until the dark. Daisy. Uncle Michael. Brindle. The first time she sensed the world's bigness, bigger than her, by a long shot.

She looked at Freddy and tilted her head.

"Your dad was going to give you this for your birthday. Before the accident."

"Where did he get it? It was lost for years."

"Yeah, it was filthy, all chewed. You can still see the holes." Freddy grabbed an edge and pinched at it, poking his finger through a threadbare corner. "Josiah washed it and he was so excited to give it to you. It was in my car, folded in the back. He hid it where you wouldn't look. I found it weeks after I left, under my stuff. I kept it all this time. Sorry if there's dog hair. It's been in the trunk of three, four cars. "

"I lost this when I was a kid," Cody said. "Pop thought a badger took it, a fox or something, for a den."

Freddy nodded. She could tell he hadn't heard the details. The story belonged to Josiah and her. She took the blanket and shook it out. In a corner his initials were sewn in red thread: *JHK*.

"It was his, you know. My dad's. When he was a kid. His mother embroidered that."

"Yeah, he said it was old. I think one of the Lindsay boys found it."

At the mention of them, Cody realized what Freddy didn't know, the same way she hadn't for years. Josiah's depression, yes, in the years they spent together, Freddy knew about that. But not Clint, the brakes. All Freddy knew about the crash was some elk and flipped truck and *what a tragedy*. It was possible he sensed more, but he left so quickly afterward, and not living edged up to the half answers, far from a town's muttering, it's possible he'd never known. For a moment, Cody considered telling Freddy the possibilities—suicide, accident, murder, all her guesswork, the figuring, her mother's confessions, the note she took from Clint and then mailed back to him. But there was no answer they'd ever know for sure. And she knew her aim would not be kind. No generous urge. It was only momentary company she wanted, his realization alongside hers: you weren't enough, either.

"Happy birthday, Cody," Freddy said, and his easy grin, it made Cody smile. There was no reason to further wound this man.

"Thank you," she said.

CODY WATCHED FROM THE PORCH as Freddy walked down the drive to his car. It had been years since he'd been on the property, but she saw in his movements the same man she'd known, the one who strode alongside her father, a touch taller, darker hair, glancing toward Josiah as they talked. His slightly pigeon-toed stride, a certain rolling looseness in his hips but his torso held straight, as if he were marching.

Freddy waved as he pulled away. The brake lights blinked when he negotiated the potholed gravel and the washboard ruts. Not everyone took the time to come and say a difficult thing. He would feel relief, leaving. To have found Cody, given her the blanket. To have seen a place that he left before he wanted to. To have said *I'm sorry*. Perhaps one sentence finally spoken, if it released you from regret, could be a highlight.

Early morning gave way to day and Cody felt the press of hours like a person too close. She let the blanket fall open from her arms and held it wide in front of her so the hem touched the ground. It had been so *large* once, big enough to fold a few times, or roll into a slim log behind her saddle. Now she could easily pull each corner taut between her stretched arms, like a curtain. Even in the golden fall sun which burnished everything, the blanket looked small and worn, the holes unraveling. Daisy had died only a few years ago, put down when her teeth got too bad to fix. Almost thirty years old.

Cody folded the blue wool to her nose and inhaled. No familiar scent of animal or juniper, not even dust. It smelled like someone else's car. She shook the blanket and wrapped it around her shoulders like she used to, pretending to be Chief Joseph, the man her father had admired. The blanket had swaddled her smaller self so tight it was hard to run. Now it stopped short at her armpits, and she had to clasp the hem in her fists to keep it from slipping.

Cody walked the edge of the clearing and looked back at the cabin and the shop as she made her way around. The porch overhung the house like a big hat, the green gutters its brim. The dog bed was empty but for the depression of a body left behind. Maggie and Sara were long dead, Lear run off to be wild again, but Finn was loyal; he wouldn't leave the house until Jess did, and then he'd stay curled on the workshop bed until he followed Jess back home. The stovepipe stood shiny and streaked with ash, the off-kilter cap blown from plumb by the fall winds. When Cody turned to complete the circle, she looked out to the treed ridge beyond the Lindsay place and the pale blue ridge beyond that, clear to the large peaks in the park that stayed snow-covered all summer, though less so every year. At the far edge of the ridge, the Washburn lookout perched empty and prominent. Nobody watched her, but she could look up and there it was, like a constellation. Orienting.

ALL AFTERNOON, Cody paced the shop. She couldn't keep at what she started. Hours passed with no progress on a piece and no sense of what else she'd done. Seeing Freddy, so familiar, was welcome, a balm she had never known to wish for. Yet, she was unsettled. Details of the accident came back, snippets that hadn't haunted her in years, and Freddy's *I'm sorry* put Clint in her mind, what she might owe him. Winding between it all, a drifty agitation. She found herself standing with a hammer in her hand or the cord of a sander—no idea why. When she went to the stove to add a log she found the flame out, a casualty of her distraction. Not even a coal left to blow on, though the stove was still warm, so she rekindled it and the pile lit fast. She closed the door. Then, as if her body were a house she'd stepped outside of, she watched herself: strike another match, flick it away into the room, a tiny flaming rocket. The air put it out and it landed a few feet away, a thin trail of smoke dissipating from the tip.

Cody struck another and then kneeled and dropped the match in the saw chips beneath the workbench and watched the tinder go ashy red in gray-edged curls. She looked around the room and inventoried the flammable: Jess's finished pieces and her half-finished ones. Wooden tool handles. The scrap pile, the lumber racked along the ceiling, piled to the rafters. The pack rat's midden beneath the building, and whatever burnable debris the packrat had saved. A fire in here would be huge, a massive column in the sky. If the Lindsays were home, they'd see the heat.

As if thought to life was how it began: a tiny cinder caught the spiraled shavings from a hand plane, one quick spark to the next, coaxed by resin stain and oily chips, and within seconds, on the floor of the building her father had made, a fire. Cody lurched to her feet and stomped at the edges of the flame. It looked small enough to grind out, but the sole of her shoe went hot and she stepped back. Fuck, she said. Two seconds more, the blaze was the size of a small campfire gobbling air, a sudden enemy in place of a test. Cody spun, almost frantic, her water bottle near empty, the ash bucket by the door, too far away. She pulled the blanket from the table saw with stretched out fingers and spread it so it dropped loose over the fire. She pressed the edges with her feet. The blanket settled like a parachute over the heat and lay flat. Instantly the room smelled of new smoke. The fire smothered as quickly as it started.

What had worried at her mind all day emerged as if she'd unwrapped it. Cody had never put an exact name to the grief that mapped her last decade. For years, she thought the tragedy was her father's death—too early, too sudden, unfair—and her own loss, all of him she hadn't known. But now, having seen Freddy alive and whole, thriving and making his amends, the bigger tragedy was the rift in her father's life: to be loved, but never feel fully known. Her chest hurt like a twisted ankle, an ache she couldn't weight without collapsing.

Cody picked up the blanket. In the middle was a burn hole the size of her palm but the edges were intact, the fringe unscathed. Dust and ash billowed in the air and she kicked the smoking debris apart with her feet. No ember, no coals. The fire hadn't burned long enough for lasting heat. Cody noted all the unburnable things: glassed bubbles in her father's wooden levels. The tin bucket, the iron fire tools, the stove. Hammer heads, pliers, glass jars of fasteners. A chunk of basalt she used for a doorstop. A horseshoe that hung on the wall above the entry, the moose antler made into a door handle. Sand, metal, bone, stone.

Cody swept up the mess in a dustpan and emptied it into the ashbin by the door. She folded the blanket and set it back on the table saw. A deep breath, a door swung shut. Burning was the opposite of building, what she'd always been good at. A flame inside her laid down.

LATE EVENING, Jess rang the bell for dinner and Cody went up to the house. She couldn't make herself say Freddy's name out loud. Had she ever told Jess about the blanket? She didn't think so. That ride, that night, it was locked up, like so much else. No one could see it. Where would you even look?

Inside, the rooms felt close, Jess trying to catch her attention and Cody evading, a game of tag that brought neither any pleasure. What's up, he asked her with a bump to the shoulder, but she shook her head and he knew to leave her be.

After she lingered over the dishes and watched her reflection in the kitchen window, Cody went into the living room where Jess sat reading by the woodstove. The dim light shadowed his face into planes and whorls, almost a disguise. She meant to say good-night and retreat upstairs but instead she crouched on the rug a few feet away and the words made their way out as if by their own volition.

"Freddy came by today."

Jess looked up and closed his book around his finger. "Really? Freddy Coughlin?" He said the full name, the way you would with a childhood friend or a teacher, someone who left an impression. Cody described Freddy's visit—his ring, the partner, his undiminished kindness—and then as Jess listened without interrupting, the book set aside and his face canted toward her, she told him about the blanket and the lost saddle, that night sleeping out with Daisy and trying to stay warm. The story coursed out like a fast-moving stream with side currents and a rapid momentum floating her above the actual words she chose. The details were as clear as if she had just returned to the neighbors' kitchen, where Mrs. Lindsay stood warming cocoa on the stove. She told about the sore on Daisy's withers and the hunch of her shoulders against the cold and the jagged stars. How she'd imagined Uncle Michael on the saddle in front of her. Brindle nosing her hand.

"You were so little," Jess said. "Were you scared?" She shrugged.

Jess asked to see the blanket so Cody had to admit to the fire, which was the reason she'd begun talking in the first place—to confess, her experiment gone almost tragically wrong. As she described the sudden flare and her panic at its potential, she saw as she never had until that moment Jess' ownership. Her father, yes, but the rest left behind belonged to both of them, a shared stake whose value to Jess she had never properly accounted. As she watched Jess imagine for a minute his own loss, she wondered how much else she had failed to consider.

"I can't believe I did that, a *fire*." Cody said. "So stupid."

"A near miss?" said Jess. Cody smiled despite herself. "A close fucking call."

They pulled on coats and hats and walked down to the shop in the dark. Too early for stars, a quarter moon low on the horizon: *light on the right, increasing in might*. The hills sat in their solid arc. Jess was quiet beside her, company that bordered but did not crowd.

The dark was a cloak. "I guess I was scared," Cody said. Even as she said so, that didn't quite capture it. A word came to her she didn't have the name for back then: shame.

"I lost my way. And I wasn't brave enough, I wasn't tall enough to reach, wasn't strong enough to lift the saddle by myself." Jess turned to look at her. She glanced away, retreating to her instinctive curl.

"I wasn't enough." The sentence she'd been chipping around, holding at arm's length for her entire life, it seemed. It felt so bold and so stark to have said it out loud that she nearly looked around to see if anyone else had heard.

There was no one else. Only her and Jess, who stopped in front of her so suddenly she stepped on the heel of his shoe. He held her by the forearm.

"Stop," he said. She looked at him, quizzical.

"It's night, we're lost. We're late for dinner, your parents are worried." His voice not quite a whisper but a staged voice, for her:

revising the story. Cody reached to tuck an errant strand of hair near his temple, catching the top of his ear in her fingers. Jess didn't look up.

"Cody, the saddle—it's too high." He crouched before her and interlaced his hands as if to lift. Jess knew her stubbornness. He knelt, waiting.

Daisy's nicker. Her small, tired body, the saddle's weight in her arms. The pointed stars. Cody looked at the horizon, the eastern sky cleared to its purest blue dark. She laid her hands on Jess's shoulders and set one foot in his clasped palms. She breathed the chill in as deep as she could take it and then eased the air out, warmer, to join the night. She let herself be raised.

ACKNOWLEDGMENTS

A few weeks before finishing the final draft of this book, I came across a quote from *Moby-Dick*. In Chapter 32, Herman Melville's narrator lists the essential elements required to complete a formidable project: "Oh, Time, Strength, Cash, and Patience!" Call me sympathetic.

Lookout was a long haul and a slow burn. About a short story written in 1997 that would much later become the first chapter, the iconic writer and teacher Bill Kittredge told me, "This is a novel." Oh, Time! I thank him for seeing the possibility long before I did. Janet Silver read early drafts and her perspective helped me to clarify my intentions. Elizabeth Bradfield, Angela Small, and Carlene Bauer gave not only hours to the novel but also the full force of their minds and hearts. I thank them, each and all.

Oh, Strength! I credit and thank the following for helping me carry the book to the end:

Kate Garrick, my stellar agent, who welcomed these characters with warmth and lobbied for them with persistence, even during the unsettling first months of the pandemic.

Jill Meyers, my exceptional editor at A Strange Object/Deep Vellum, whose astute eyes helped me see the book anew and whose love for this story buoyed me in innumerable ways.

Will Evans, publisher at Deep Vellum, for his enthusiasm, support, and commitment to literary culture; and everyone at ASO/DV who helped with book production, promotion, and sales. This team makes me proud to be part of the independent press community.

My large and loving family, both born and chosen: siblings, parents, in-laws, extended family, and friends near, dear, far or gone.

The American West, my formative place, its history and terrain both gorgeous and brutal, and particularly northwestern Montana, a land worthy of many kinds of stories.

For financial and logistical support (Oh, Cash!) I am grateful to the Rasmuson Foundation; Peggy Shumaker and the Alaska Literary Award; and Margot Knight and the Djerassi Resident Artists Program.

Finally, Patience. My last and lasting thanks belong to Gabe Travis, first reader, best reader, companion through all the years since the first words, and the partner with whom I build everything that matters.

NOTES

1. Although all of the characters in this novel are imagined, many of the places are real and I have tried to honor the geographic, natural, and cultural details of those that I named to the best of my ability. Northwestern Montana is the ancestral and current home of Niitsitapi (Blackfeet), Sqelix-Ktunaxa (Flathead/Salish-Kootenai) and many other Indigenous people who have been its residents, stewards and defenders since time immemorial.

2. In the chapter "Family Dinner," Cody speaks of her visit to the AIDS quilt. This project's official title is the NAMES Project AIDS Memorial Quilt. Its inception is credited to AIDS activist Cleve Jones, in 1985. Still growing, it is, as of the time of this writing, the largest community folk art project in the world. Although the quilt's presence in Spokane in 1991 is fictional, many of the names and quotes on the quilt in that scene are real. They are

cataloged in the book *The Quilt: Stories from the Names Project*, by Cindy Ruskin (Pocket Books, 1988).

3. Some of Josiah's thoughts and philosophies on trees, tools and woodcraft were informed by the books *A Reverence for Wood* by Eric Sloane and *Toolchest* by Jan Adkins.

ABOUT THE AUTHOR

Christine Byl is the author of *Dirt Work: An Education in the Woods* (Beacon Press, 2013), a book about trail crews, tools, wildness, and labor; it was shortlisted for the 2014 Willa Award in nonfiction.

Her prose has appeared in *Glimmer Train Stories*, *The Sun*, *Crazyhorse*, and *Brevity*, among other journals and anthologies. A grant recipient from the Rasmuson Foundation and the Alaska State Council on the Arts, and winner of the Alaska Literary Award in 2015, Byl has been a fellow at Bread Loaf Writers' Conference and writer-in-residence for Fishtrap's Writer-in-the-Schools program.

Christine has worked as a professional trail-builder for more than twenty-five years; she lives with her family in Interior Alaska on the homelands of the Dene.

ABOUT A STRANGE OBJECT

Founded in 2012 in Austin, Texas, A Strange Object champions debuts, daring writing, and striking design across all platforms. The press became part of Deep Vellum in 2019, where it carries on its editorial vision via its eponymous imprint. A Strange Object's titles are distributed by Consortium.

Thank you all
for your support.
We do this for you,
and could not do
it without you.

DEEP VELLUM

Support for this publication has been provided in part by grants from the National Endowment for the Arts, the Texas Commission on the Arts, the City of Dallas Office of Arts and Culture's ArtsActivate program, and the Moody Fund for the Arts:

NATIONAL ENDOWMENT for the ARTS
arts.gov

Texas Commission on the Arts

City of Dallas | Office of Arts & Culture

MOODY FUND FOR THE ARTS

PARTNERS

FIRST EDITION MEMBERSHIP

Anonymous (9)

Donna Wilhelm

TRANSLATOR'S CIRCLE

Ben & Sharon Fountain

Meriwether Evans

PRINTER'S PRESS MEMBERSHIP

Allred Capital Management

Charles Dee Mitchell

Cullen Schaar

David Tomlinson & Kathryn Berry

Jeff Leuschel

Judy Pollock

Loretta Siciliano

Lori Feathers

Mary Ann Thompson-Frenk & Joshua Frenk

Matthew Rittmayer

Nick Storch

Pixel and Texel

Robert Appel

Social Venture Partners Dallas

Stephen Bullock

AUTHOR'S LEAGUE

Christie Tull

Farley Houston

Jacob Seifring

Lissa Dunlay

Steven Kornajcik

Thomas DiPiero

PUBLISHER'S LEAGUE

Adam Rekerdres

Justin Childress

Kay Cattarulla

KMGMT

Olga Kislova

EDITOR'S LEAGUE

Amrit Dhir

Brandon Kennedy

Dallas Sonnier

Garth Hallberg

Greg McConeghy

Linda Nell Evans

Mary Moore Grimaldi

Mike Kaminsky

Patricia Storace

Ryan Todd

Steven Harding

Suejean Kim

Symphonic Source

Wendy Belcher

READER'S LEAGUE

Caitlin Baker

Caroline Casey

Carolyn Mulligan

Chilton Thomson

Cody Cosmic & Jeremy Hays

Jeff Waxman

Joseph Milazzo

Kayla Finstein

Kelly Britson

Kelly & Corby Baxter

Marian Schwartz & Reid Minot

Marlo D. Cruz Pagan

Maryam Baig

Peggy Carr

Susan Ernst

ADDITIONAL DONORS

Alan Shockley

Amanda & Bjorn Beer

Andrew Yorke

Anonymous (10)

Ashley Milne Shadoin

Bob & Katherine Penn

Brandon Childress

Charley Mitcherson

Charley Rejsek

Cheryl Thompson

Chloe Pak

Cone Johnson

CS Maynard

Daniel J. Hale

Daniela Hurezanu

Danielle Dubrow

Denae Richards

Dori Boone-Costantino

Ed Nawotka

Elizabeth Gillette

Elizabeth Van Vleck

Erin Kubatzky

Ester & Matt Harrison

Grace Kenney

Hillary Richards

JJ Italiano

Jeremy Hughes

John Darnielle

Jonathan Legg

Julie Janicke Muhsmann

Walmart

pixel texel

ALLRED CAPITAL MANAGEMENT of RAYMOND JAMES®

LIFE IN DEEP ELLUM

EMBREY FAMILY FOUNDATION

COMMON DESK COWORKING

ADDITIONAL DONORS, CONT'D

Kelly Falconer
Kevin Richardson
Laura Thomson
Lea Courington
Lee Haber
Leigh Ann Pike
Lowell Frye
Maaza Mengiste
Mark Haber
Mary Cline
Max Richie
Maynard Thomson
Michael Reklis
Mike Soto
Mokhtar Ramadan
Nikki & Dennis Gibson
Patrick Kukucka
Patrick Kutcher
Rev. Elizabeth & Neil Moseley
Richard Meyer
Sam Simon
Sherry Perry
Skander Halim
Sydneyann Binion
Stephen Harding
Stephen Williamson
Susan Carp
Theater Jones
Tim Perttula
Tony Thomson

SUBSCRIBERS

Andrea Pritcher
Anthony Brown
Aviya Kushner
Ben Fountain
Brian Matthew Kim
Caroline West
Caitlin Jans
Courtney Sheedy
Elena Rush
Elif Ağanoğlu
Erin Kubatzky
Eugenie Cha
Gina Rios
Ian Robinson
Joseph Rebella
Kasia Bartoszynska
Kenneth McClain
Lance Salins
Margaret Terwey
Matthew Eatough
Michael Lighty
Michael Schneiderman
Ned Russin
Ryan Todd
Shelby Vincent
Stephen Fuller

AVAILABLE NOW FROM DEEP VELLUM

MARIA GABRIELA LLANSOL · *The Geography of Rebels Trilogy: The Book of Communities · The Remaining Life · In the House of July & August* · translated by Audrey Young · PORTUGAL

PABLO MARTÍN SÁNCHEZ · *The Anarchist Who Shared My Name* · translated by Jeff Diteman · SPAIN

DOROTA MASŁOWSKA · *Honey, I Killed the Cats* · translated by Benjamin Paloff · POLAND

BRICE MATTHIEUSSENT· *Revenge of the Translator* · translated by Emma Ramadan · FRANCE

LINA MERUANE · *Seeing Red* · translated by Megan McDowell · CHILE

VALÉRIE MRÉJEN · *Black Forest* · translated by Katie Shireen Assef · FRANCE

FISTON MWANZA MUJILA · *Tram 83 · The River in the Belly: Selected Poems* · translated by Bret Maney DEMOCRATIC REPUBLIC OF CONGO

GORAN PETROVI΄C · *At the Lucky Hand, aka The Sixty-Nine Drawers* · translated by Peter Agnone · SERBIA

LUDMILLA PETRUSHEVSKAYA · *The New Adventures of Helen: Magical Tales* · translated by Jane Bugaeva · RUSSIA

ILJA LEONARD PFEIJFFER · *La Superba* · translated by Michele Hutchison · NETHERLANDS

RICARDO PIGLIA · *Target in the Night* · translated by Sergio Waisman · ARGENTINA

SERGIO PITOL · *The Art of Flight · The Journey · The Magician of Vienna · Mephisto's Waltz: Selected Short Stories · The Love Parade* · translated by George Henson · MEXICO

JULIE POOLE · *Bright Specimen: Poems from the Texas Herbarium* · USA

EDUARDO RABASA · *A Zero-Sum Game* · translated by Christina MacSweeney · MEXICO

ZAHIA RAHMANI · *"Muslim": A Novel* · translated by Matthew Reeck · FRANCE/ALGERIA

MANON STEFAN ROS · *The Blue Book of Nebo* · WALES

JUAN RULFO · *The Golden Cockerel & Other Writings* · translated by Douglas J. Weatherford · MEXICO

ETHAN RUTHERFORD · *Farthest South & Other Stories* · USA

TATIANA RYCKMAN · *Ancestry of Objects* · USA

JIM SCHUTZE · *The Accommodation* · USA

OLEG SENTSOV · *Life Went On Anyway* · translated by Uilleam Blacker · UKRAINE

MIKHAIL SHISHKIN · *Calligraphy Lesson: The Collected Stories* · translated by Marian Schwartz, Leo Shtutin, Mariya Bashkatova, Sylvia Maizell · RUSSIA

ÓFEIGUR SIGURÐSSON · *Öræfi: The Wasteland* · translated by Lytton Smith · ICELAND

DANIEL SIMON, ED. · *Dispatches from the Republic of Letters* · USA

MUSTAFA STITOU · *Two Half Faces* · translated by David Colmer · NETHERLANDS

SOPHIA TERAZAWA · *Winter Phoenix: Testimonies in Verse* · POLAND

MÄRTA TIKKANEN · *The Love Story of the Century* · translated by Stina Katchadourian · SWEDEN

BOB TRAMMELL · *Jack Ruby & the Origins of the Avant-Garde in Dallas & Other Stories* · USA

BENJAMIN VILLEGAS · *ELPASO: A Punk Story* · translated by Jay Noden · MEXICO

SERHIY ZHADAN · *Voroshilovgrad* · translated by Reilly Costigan-Humes & Isaac Wheeler · UKRAINE

FORTHCOMING FROM DEEP VELLUM

MARIO BELLATIN · *Etchapare* · translated by Shook · MEXICO

CAYLIN CARPA-THOMAS · *Iguana Iguana* · USA

MIRCEA CĂRTĂRESCU · *Solenoid* · translated by Sean Cotter · ROMANIA

TIM COURSEY · *Driving Lessons* · USA

ANANDA DEVI · *When the Night Agrees to Speak to Me* · translated by Kazim Ali · MAURITIUS

DHUMKETU · *The Shehnai Virtuoso* · translated by Jenny Bhatt · INDIA

LEYLÂ ERBIL · *A Strange Woman* ·
translated by Nermin Menemencioğlu & Amy Marie Spangler· TURKEY

ALLA GORBUNOVA · *It's the End of the World, My Love* · translated by Elina Alter · RUSSIA

NIVEN GOVINDEN · *Diary of a Film* · GREAT BRITAIN

GYULA JENEI · *Always Different* · translated by Diana Senechal · HUNGARY

DIA JUBAILI · *No Windmills in Basra* · translated by Chip Rosetti · IRAQ

ELENI KEFALA · *Time Stitches* · translated by Peter Constantine · CYPRUS

UZMA ASLAM KHAN · *The Miraculous True History of Nomi Ali* · PAKISTAN

ANDREY KURKOV · *Grey Bees* · translated by Boris Drayluk · UKRAINE

JORGE ENRIQUE LAGE · *Freeway La Movie* · translated by Lourdes Molina · CUBA

TEDI LÓPEZ MILLS · *The Book of Explanations* · translated by Robin Myers · MEXICO

ANTONIO MORESCO · *Clandestinity* · translated by Richard Dixon · ITALY

FISTON MWANZA MUJILA · *The Villain's Dance* ·
translated by Roland Glasser · DEMOCRATIC REPUBLIC OF CONGO

N. PRABHAKARAN · *Diary of a Malayali Madman* · translated by Jayasree Kalathil · INDIA

THOMAS ROSS · *Miss Abracadabra* · USA

IGNACIO RUIZ-PÉREZ · *Isles of Firm Ground* · translated by Mike Soto · MEXICO

LUDMILLA PETRUSHEVSKAYA · *Kidnapped: A Crime Story,* translated by Marian Schwartz · RUSSIA

NOAH SIMBLIST, ed. · *Tania Bruguera: The Francis Effect* · CUBA

S. YARBERRY · *A Boy in the City* · USA